ROGUE IN PORCELAIN

ROGUE IN PORCELAIN

Anthea Fraser

Severn House Large Print
London & New York

This first large print edition published in Great Britain 2007 by
SEVERN HOUSE LARGE PRINT BOOKS LTD of
9-15 High Street, Sutton, Surrey, SM1 1DF.
First world regular print edition published 2007 by
Severn House Publishers, London and New York.
This first large print edition published in the USA 2007 by
SEVERN HOUSE PUBLISHERS INC., of
595 Madison Avenue, New York, NY 10022.

British Library Cataloguing in Publication Data

Fraser, Anthea
    Rogue in porcelain. - Large print ed.
    1. Parish, Rona (Fictitious character) - Fiction 2. Women
    authors - England - Fiction 3. Murder - Investigation -
    Fiction 4. Detective and mystery stories 5. Large type
    books
    I. Title
    823.9'14[F]

    ISBN-13: 978-0-7278-7629-4

Printed and bound in Great Britain by
MPG Books Ltd, Bodmin, Cornwall.

CURZON FAMILY TREE

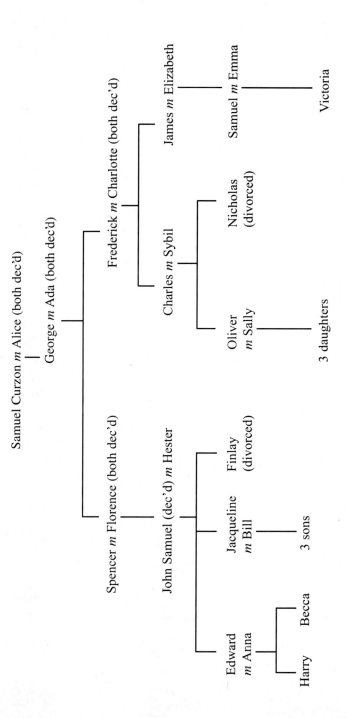

One

Tom Parish looked round the small, cramped dining table with satisfaction. Though he'd been renting the flat for nearly four months, this was the first time he'd managed to have all the family here. All except – obviously – his wife. Odd, he reflected, not for the first time, that despite Catherine's central role in his life, Avril was not yet his ex, the decree absolute being two long years away. Their own decision, of course; it could have been rushed through, but at their age such haste struck him as unseemly, as would Catherine and himself living openly together before they were married. Which no doubt made him a hypocrite, since they enjoyed all the benefits of married life, despite sleeping under different roofs.

This evening, Lindsey's presence was a particular pleasure; his twin daughters had been equally upset by the split, but it had taken until now for Lindsey – who'd sided firmly with her mother – to bring herself to accept Catherine's place in his life.

Rona, his other daughter, traced a finger

round the rim of her side plate. 'I see the best china's been brought out for the occasion!' she said. 'This isn't from home, though, is it? I've not seen it before.'

'Actually, it's mine,' Catherine said quietly. 'The crockery provided is fine for everyday, but Tom felt this evening warranted something special.'

'And special it certainly is,' Lindsey commented. 'Curzon, no less. Hugh's parents have a dinner service in it, and they treat it like the Crown jewels.'

There was a brief silence. These casual references to her ex-husband were becoming increasingly frequent; proof, Tom deduced worriedly, that they were meeting fairly regularly.

'As it happens, I saw Charles Curzon last week,' he remarked, to break the silence.

'I didn't realize you knew the family.' Max, Rona's husband, nodded acceptance as Tom held up the wine bottle.

'It started professionally – they bank at the National – but Avril and I have been to several of their parties. I'd not seen Charles since I retired, and as he was in town, he rang to invite me to lunch.' He paused. 'Actually, I'm slightly concerned about him. He didn't look too well.'

'He must be getting on a bit,' Rona said. 'Surely he's not still involved in the business?'

'Not actively, no, but he was telling me it's the firm's hundred and fiftieth anniversary this year, and they're bringing out some new line, which is cloaked in secrecy. I had the impression he's finding the build-up rather a strain, added to which, he and his wife are about to move house.'

'A hundred and fifty years?' Max glanced at his wife. 'That qualifies them for your brief, darling.'

Rona, a freelance journalist on the monthly magazine *Chiltern Life*, was engaged in an intermittent series detailing the history of long-established local firms and businesses.

'So it does,' she agreed. 'I'll add them to my list.'

'I'd slot them in sooner rather than later,' Tom suggested. 'They'll be extra newsworthy with this anniversary coming up. I can give you a letter of introduction, if you think it'd help.'

'Thanks, Pops, I'm sure it would. I'm coming to the end of the piece I'm working on, so I could try them next.' She sipped her wine reflectively. 'Such a long time span might need a couple of articles, rather than cramming it into one. It's not only the firms that I research, but the lives of those who've contributed to them.'

Tom laughed. 'In that case, it could take four or five. They're a large and diverse family. I still haven't worked out the exact relationship between the younger ones.'

'The business didn't just pass from father to son, then?' Catherine asked.

'Well, yes, but way back there were two sons, each of whom had sons of his own, and so on,

9

so now there's a clutch of cousins and second-cousins. Charles has two sons himself, but one has three little girls, while the other's divorced with no children. From the way he was speaking, I think he's worried his branch might peter out.'

'Girls don't count then?' Rona asked quizzically.

'Not in running the business, no, they never have; but since they get their fair share of the proceeds, they don't miss out.'

'Unless,' Lindsey put in, 'they happen to have a flair for business and would give their eye teeth to be involved. So much for women's lib!'

Tom held up his hands. 'All right, all right, I didn't make the rules! I have to say, though, that in all the years I've dealt with the Curzons, I've never heard of there being any resentment.'

'Well, you wouldn't, would you? They're not likely to come into the bank and say, "We had an almighty row with our daughter last night, because she wants to join the firm."'

'All this,' Catherine put in humorously, 'because of my poor china!'

The discussion ended in laughter and the conversation turned to other matters.

'That was a lovely meal, Pops,' Lindsey said as they were about to leave. 'I bet Catherine had a hand in it!' And she turned to her with a smile.

Tom's heart lifted. 'You're right; the casserole was down to me – albeit after tuition – but Catherine takes full credit for that creamy concoction. I don't even know what it's called!'

As the door closed behind them, Catherine observed, 'To the best of my knowledge, that's the first smile I've ever had from Lindsey.'

'I knew she'd come round eventually. Thanks, love, for all your help. I think we can consider the evening a success. May it be the first of many.'

Catherine began to stack the dishes. 'You know, I once mistook Lindsey for Rona, but when you see them together they're not identical, are they?'

Tom laughed. 'Near enough to have caused mayhem in their schooldays. But yes, it's possible to tell them apart. Lindsey's not quite as tall, for one thing, and for the moment at least her hair's longer. The main differences, though, are below the surface. It amazes me how close the two of them are, when their characters are poles apart.'

'Perhaps they complement each other?' Catherine suggested. 'Two sides of the same coin?'

Tom grinned. 'That's too deep for me at this time of night! Let's get the dishwasher loaded, then we can have a nightcap before I take you home.'

'It went well, didn't it?' Rona observed to Max as they drove off. 'I think Pops was a bit apprehensive, bless him, but Linz being there meant a lot to him.'

'It's taken her long enough,' Max returned.

'Well, she couldn't bury her head in the sand for ever, and seeing Mum more settled helps.'

'How are the alterations going?'

When Tom moved out, Avril had decided to turn the box room into an en suite bathroom and refurbish the guest room, with the intention of taking in paying guests.

'Very slowly, I gather. There've been the usual hold-ups – workmen not turning up when they said they would, then ordering the wrong thing.'

'Well, there's no panic, is there? It's not as though she needs the cash.'

'But she hates living alone. Between you and me, I think she's a bit nervous.'

'Advise her to vet applicants very thoroughly. We don't want any undesirables moving in.'

'Don't worry,' Rona told him. 'Whoever it is will have to pass muster with all of us.'

'So you dined with the Scarlet Woman?' drawled Jonathan Hurst. 'So much for your principles!'

Lindsey flushed. 'As you well know, principles are a luxury I can't afford. Still, she's making Pops happy, I'll say that for her, and Mum seems to be doing fine without him.'

'What's she like then, this woman who's been bugging you so much?'

'She seems quite pleasant, but nothing out of the ordinary. She's an ex-head, though, so she might have hidden depths. Come to think of it, it must have been quite an ordeal for her, having us all together for the first time. To give her her due, she handled it very well.'

'So she's won you over.' Jonathan removed his arm from her shoulders to look at his watch. 'Time to make a move, sadly. I've an appointment at two thirty.'

Lindsey lay back and watched him as he padded, naked, to her bathroom. She and Jonathan were partners in a firm of Marsborough solicitors, and these snatched lunchtime sessions, confined to the days when she worked from home, were often all they could manage. For Jonathan had an unsuspecting wife and children, a fact Lindsey preferred not to dwell on.

And then, she thought despairingly, there was Hugh. He'd arranged to be transferred back to Marsborough, confident they would get together again, and been both hurt and furious when she'd refused to have him back. Which didn't mean they weren't still strongly attracted to each other. There was no denying she needed a man in her life, but at the moment her association with Jonathan filled the bill, exciting her with its aura of secrecy and wrongdoing, and giving her the strength to keep Hugh at arm's length. Playing with fire, Rona called it, and she could be right.

Reluctantly Lindsey climbed out of bed and reached for her dressing gown.

* * *

13

'They're taking bets on the new product at school,' Harry Curzon remarked at breakfast the next morning. 'And they won't believe I don't know what it is. I feel like a real jerk.'

'Would you tell them, if you did know?' his sister asked through a mouthful of cornflakes.

'Of course not, idiot!'

'There you are, then,' she said enigmatically.

Their parents exchanged a glance. 'You'd better hurry,' Anna said. 'The bus will be here in five minutes.'

'Dad?' Harry persisted. 'Surely all the family should be in on it?'

'Very definitely not,' Edward said firmly. 'The more people who know, the more chance there is of it getting out. Though you wouldn't disclose it intentionally, there are experienced people out there hell-bent on worming it out of us ahead of time, and they get up to all sorts of tricks. You're much better off not knowing, believe me. Your mother doesn't, nor either of your aunts. Sometimes I wish I didn't myself!'

Becca pushed back her chair. 'I left my French book upstairs. Have I time to get it?'

'If you run,' her mother said. 'And Harry –' as her son opened his mouth to argue further – 'enough! You'll miss the bus.'

With bad grace, he stood up, stuffed the last piece of toast in his mouth, and bent to retrieve his satchel.

'See you,' he muttered indistinctly, and as Becca came clattering down the stairs, they left

14

the house together, the front door slamming behind them.

'And now,' Edward said, 'perhaps I can have my second cup of coffee in peace.'

Anna poured it. 'I have to say, I'll be glad when the announcement can be made,' she said. 'All this cloak and dagger stuff's becoming quite a strain.'

'Only another six months, and all will be revealed.'

'Was that true, about underhand tricks being employed?'

'Only too true; believe me, industrial espionage is alive and well.' Edward drained his cup. 'By the way, there's a board meeting after work, so I'll be late back. You eat with the kids and leave me something in the oven. I've a business lunch, so I shan't want much.'

She nodded, lifted her face for his kiss, and, as he too left the house, stood up and began to clear the table. What would be the reaction, she wondered, when the news did break? Edward had hinted at a revolutionary product that could turn the industry on its head. In which case, by no means everyone would welcome it.

The sound of the back door reached her, followed by the inevitable 'Cooee!'

Anna picked up the tray and carried it into the kitchen. 'Morning, Betty,' she said.

'Morning, Mrs Curzon.' Her cleaner was tying an apron round her ample waist. 'Anything special you want doing today?'

15

'The silver could do with a polish, if you've time.'

'Righto. Oh, and I meant to tell you, we're getting low on floor polish.'

'I'll put it on my list.'

The woman flashed her a glance. 'My sister-in-law – the one that lives in Chilswood – says there's a lot of guessing going on about what they're up to at the pottery. People have even been going through the dustbins.'

Thank God for shredders, Anna thought. 'Really?' she said evenly. 'I don't know what the panic is; they'll know soon enough.'

'That's what I told her,' Betty answered righteously, and, standing her bucket in the sink, she turned on the taps.

Anna, on her way upstairs, wondered if Edward knew of the dustbin-raiders. He hadn't mentioned it. Perhaps it was all part and parcel of the industrial espionage campaign. The thought left an unpleasant feeling, and she was glad she was meeting Sally and Emma, fellow Curzon wives, for lunch. Unlike the men, who of necessity saw each other every day, the women of the family met only occasionally, each otherwise engaged in her own pursuits. Today was to be one of those times. It would be interesting, Anna thought, to hear what Sally had to say; she lived and worked in Chilswood, so her ear was correspondingly closer to the ground.

* * *

Rona had just left the post office when her mobile rang, and she juggled dog lead and handbag in an effort to retrieve it.

'Pops? Hi; could you speak up – I'm on Guild Street and there's a lot of traffic.'

'Just a brief message, sweetie. I phoned Charles Curzon to ask whom you should approach with your idea.'

'Oh, thanks. And who did he suggest?'

'Finlay Curzon. It seems he's their Sales and Marketing Director.'

'Where does he fit in the family hierarchy?'

'Charles referred to him as his nephew, but that's not strictly accurate. I happen to know Finlay's father was Charles's cousin, which would make Finlay his first cousin once removed.'

'I'll settle for nephew! So what happens next?' A bus lumbered past, obliterating her father's voice. 'Sorry, could you say that again?'

'He suggests you write to Finlay at the pottery – they're out at Chilswood, of course – outlining what you have in mind and asking for an appointment. You don't need anything from me – Charles will explain who you are. He doesn't foresee any difficulty; on the contrary, he thinks it would help build public interest in the lead-up to the anniversary.'

'That's great. Thanks, Pops.'

'Where are you off to at the moment?'

'The Bacchus, to meet Linz for lunch.'

17

'Well, enjoy yourselves, and give her my love.'

Lindsey was already seated in one of the booths, and bent to pat the dog as he padded past her and settled under the table.

'Pops sends his love,' Rona told her. 'He's just rung with the name of a contact at Curzon.'

'You're not letting the grass grow, are you?'

'Well, as he said, with this anniversary coming up, it's the ideal time to go for it.' She glanced at the menu in her sister's hand. 'Have you decided what you're having?'

Lindsey passed it across. 'I'm torn between hot chicken salad and moules marinière.'

'I'll go for deep-fried mushrooms with garlic mayo. And a bottle of Chablis?'

'Fine. And I'll settle for the salad.'

They gave their order, asked for the wine to be brought straight away, and looked across at each other.

'So,' Rona began. 'How are things? Talk was pretty general the other evening.'

'Probably just as well!'

'Love life still complicated?'

'As ever.'

'Pops registered your remark about the Curzon dinner service.'

'Yes, I realized that. Well, he knows Hugh and I still see each other.'

'Is that all you do?'

'Pretty much, though he's invited me to go to Lucy's with him next weekend.'

Lucy Partridge was Hugh's sister, who lived in Guildford.

'Will you go?'

Lindsey shrugged. 'Might as well, I suppose. Jonathan plays Happy Families at weekends.'

'Don't you think you're being unfair to Hugh, keeping him dangling?'

Lindsey raised her eyebrows. 'Am I hearing right? *You* championing *Hugh*?'

'We mightn't see eye to eye, but I still think you treat him badly.'

They paused while the waiter opened a bottle of wine and poured some into their glasses.

As he moved away, Lindsey said, 'He keeps coming back for more. And, to be realistic, he *is* the safer bet, long-term. Nothing's ever going to come of the thing with Jonathan – we both know that.'

'That's a pretty cold-blooded assessment.'

'But true.' Lindsey sipped her wine.

'You do realize that if you go to Lucy's, Hugh will expect you to sleep with him?'

'Of course.'

Rona stared at her for a moment and, meeting her eyes, Lindsey laughed.

'You despair of me, don't you, but once in a while is fine. The perfect arrangement was when he worked in Guildford and only came up at weekends. The point is, I don't want him around day in, day out – or even night in, night out. That's when we start to grate on each other. Also, I've got used to having my own space.'

19

She looked consideringly at her sister. 'You've got it just about right, I reckon, with Max sleeping at Farthings three nights a week. That, I could cope with.'

'But it's because of our work schedules, not because we don't want to be together.'

'I know that, but the result's the same. Half the week you can do your own thing – change into your nightie at seven o'clock if you feel like it, and have supper on a tray in front of the telly. Or not eat till ten, then read in bed till you fall asleep with the light on.'

'All of which you can do, too.'

'At the moment, yes, that's my point. A part-time lover suits me fine.'

'Or husband?'

'Part-time husbands are harder to find.'

Their food arrived, and for a while they ate in silence. Beneath the table, the golden retriever shifted position, resting his heavy head on Rona's foot.

'Have you seen Mum this week?' she asked.

'No, but I phoned on Wednesday, to tell her we were going to Pops's. I thought it might somehow get back to her.'

'Was she OK about it?'

'Yes, fine. In fact, she seemed more interested in the problems she's having with the plumbers.'

'What now?'

'Oh, just more of the same; they never come when they say they will, and she spends all morning hanging round waiting for them, when she should be at the library.' Lindsey refilled their glasses. 'Did she mention that she's decided not to have a couple as PGs?'

'No? Why, exactly?'

'Partly my doing; I told her she'd be unlikely to find one. With a double income, they'd be much more likely to rent till they could afford to buy. Also, if, God forbid, there should be any falling out, she'd be better having to deal with just one person.'

'It's strange, to think of someone else living in the house,' Rona said reflectively.

Lindsey shrugged. 'It's not as if either of us is likely to go back. And if we *did* want to spend the odd night there, our rooms are still available. Incidentally, when we spoke, Mum said she's going to ask us round for supper, probably on one of Max's class nights, so there'd just be the three of us.'

'All girls together?' Rona asked with a raised eyebrow.

'Nothing wrong with that,' Lindsey said briskly. She toyed for a moment with the stem of her wine glass, then looked up, meeting her sister's eyes. 'Can you keep a secret?'

'Don't I always?'

'I've met someone who's rather intriguing.'

Rona put down her fork. 'So that's why you're so blasé about the Jonathan affair being short-lived.'

'I didn't say short-lived, I said not long-term.

They're not the same.'

'I hope this one's not married?'

'I've no idea. No, really –' in response to Rona's grunt of disbelief – 'I've not even spoken to him.'

'Then you can't say you've met him, can you, let alone know if he's intriguing or not.'

'I just do. I have an instinct for these things.'

'Don't tell me: it was the "across a crowded room" syndrome.'

'You can scoff. All I'm saying at this stage is, watch this space.'

'You're incorrigible,' Rona said resignedly.

Finlay Curzon glanced at his watch, stretched, and switched off his computer, more than ready for his lunch break. It was very wearing, having continually to fend off questions on Genesis, when all his marketing instincts balked at the prevarication. This was the anniversary *year*, after all; why wait till the actual date to launch it?

He made his way to the lift and went down two floors to the directors' dining room. Though it retained its name, it was in fact where all the senior staff met for lunch, providing a valuable opportunity to discuss views and hammer out problems.

Finlay joined his three cousins at one end of the table, feeling some of his tensions ease.

'Steak and kidney pie today,' Sam commented. 'That'll temper the March winds!'

Oliver said, 'Did that bloke ring back, Finn? About the tour?'

Finlay started to reply, breaking off in surprise as Charles Curzon came into the room. Well into his retirement, he seldom visited the pottery.

'Dad!' Nick exclaimed. 'What brings you here? I didn't see your name on the lunch list.'

'It was a snap decision,' the older man replied, pulling out a chair. 'I wanted a word with Finn here, and it seemed easier to talk in person. Besides, apart from you and Oliver, I've not seen anyone for a while.'

He glanced down the table. 'Edward not in today?'

'He was earlier, but he's lunching at Pembrokes',' Finlay told him. 'They're hoping to open up a new outlet.' He poured water into their glasses; wine didn't appear at lunchtime unless guests were present.

'So,' he continued, 'what can I do for you, Uncle?'

The courtesy title, traditionally used by all the Curzons, was one he felt comfortable with. Despite his progressive ideas, he couldn't imagine calling his older relatives by their first names, and it was surely only in the novels of Jane Austen that people addressed each other as 'Cousin'.

'I had a call this morning from Tom Parish,' Charles replied.

'The bank manager?'

'The *retired* bank manager, yes. His daughter writes sporadically for *Chiltern Life*, and is working at the moment on a series about family businesses. She'd like to do one on us, and I told him you were the person to speak to.'

Finlay said resignedly, 'Someone else I'll have to fob off, when she starts probing about Genesis.'

'I've been thinking about that,' Charles said slowly, leaning to one side for the waitress to place a bowl of soup in front of him. 'Since she'll be aiming to publish about the time we make the announcement, I suggest we let her in on the secret a little ahead of time. Then it can be incorporated into the article.'

There was a sudden startled silence, and Charles glanced down the table. 'I shall, of course, consult everyone before reaching any firm decision, but remember she'll be starting with old Samuel and the founding of the business. She won't get down to the present for some time, so we'd only be jumping the gun by a few weeks. Still, you don't need to worry about that now, Finn. I told Tom she should write to you, outlining what she has in mind and asking for an appointment.

'So –' he looked round their still-apprehensive faces – 'what's the news from the coalface?'

Taking it as a signal that the subject was, for the moment, closed, the atmosphere lightened and, as Sam began to talk of production figures, the rest of them picked up their soup spoons and began their meal.

On the way home from lunch, Rona called in to the offices of *Chiltern Life*, handing Gus's lead to the willing receptionist before she went upstairs. The dog was already wagging his tail in anticipation. 'Only one biscuit, Polly,' Rona warned smilingly. 'We have to watch his figure!'

Barnie Trent, the features editor, was bent over his desk when, after his terse 'Enter!', Rona pushed open his door. However, he smiled at the sight of her and leant back in his chair.

'There's a sight for sore eyes!' he said.

'You're looking fraught, Barnie. Having problems?'

'Just the usual – getting the copy in on time. Got something for me?'

'Not this time, no; it's a social call.'

'I'm honoured!'

'Max and I were wondering how you, and particularly Dinah, are feeling, now the nest's empty again? It must seem very quiet, after having Mel and the family for so long.'

The Trents' daughter, who lived in the States, had been staying with her parents while her husband was on a six-month assignment in the Gulf.

'Dinah is a bit depressed,' Barnie admitted, 'but it's early days yet. She'll soon settle down.'

'How about coming over for supper? Would that cheer her up?'

'No better way.'

'I'll give her a ring, then.' She hesitated. 'You weren't expecting the article, were you? Surely it's not due yet?'

'No, that's one thing I'll say for you, you're always in good time.'

'I added another name to the list this week: Curzon, the porcelain firm.'

'Good one, yes. They're in the news a lot at the moment – an important anniversary coming up. Have you made contact?'

'Not yet; Pops knows one of the older directors, and he's given me the name of the person I'm to contact. I'll get the letter off this afternoon. Could we manage to slot it in around the time of the anniversary?'

'If you get it to me soon enough, as I have no doubt you will.'

'You're an angel, Barnie.' She reached for her shopping bag. 'I won't hold you up any longer, but tell Dinah I'll phone when Max and I have compared diaries.'

'We'll look forward to it,' he said, and had returned to his papers before the door closed behind her.

Sam Curzon, who had been reading his daughter a bedtime story, paused in the doorway of the sitting room to look at his wife. She was sitting cross-legged on the floor, a frown of concentration on her face, her dark head bent over *The Times* crossword, and he felt a lurch of love for her.

Aware of his presence, she looked up. 'All settled?'

'Yes; she wanted another chapter, but my voice was giving out.'

He walked across and seated himself in the armchair she was leaning against, running his hand over her sleek hair. He loved the way she wore it, in thick, well-defined layers down the back of her head, leaving her nape exposed and somehow vulnerable.

Feeling his caress, she tilted her head back and he gave her an upside-down kiss.

'God, I'm lucky,' he said.

'Why in particular?'

'Having you and Victoria, my two girls. When I think of Finn and Nick going home to empty houses, it puts the fear of God into me.'

Emma patted his hand. 'It's a high divorce rate, certainly, two out of the five of you. I wonder what went wrong.'

'Well, we know the catalyst in Nick's case.'

'But things couldn't have been right before that.'

'Who knows?' Sam reached for his whisky glass. 'He certainly hadn't seen it coming, and was pretty cut up when she went, though how much was hurt pride, I don't know. At any rate, he lost no time selling the house and moving into that luxury apartment of his, and has had a string of girlfriends ever since.' He sipped his drink. 'Finn, though, is a different matter; seldom seen on the social circuit, and still living in the house he shared with Ginnie. Perhaps he's hoping she'll come back.'

'Unlikely, I'd say, after three years,' Emma replied. 'Maybe we should try some discreet matchmaking; invite him to dinner with a few attractive divorcees.'

'Do we know any?'

'I'll ask Sally to go through her clients.'

Sally Curzon owned a day spa in Chilswood, offering more beauty treatments than Emma had ever heard of to a clientele of glamorous women.

'Pity I didn't think of it earlier,' she added. 'I met her and Anna for lunch today. Anna's a bit worried about all the gossip on the new line.'

'Surely it's a good thing, whetting everyone's appetite?'

'Is it true the factory dustbins have been raided?'

Sam laughed. 'Beloved, the factory dustbins are raided on a regular basis. It's a way of life.'

'They can't find anything important, can they?'

'Not a chance.'

'Nevertheless, I'll be glad when all this secrecy's over.'

'And so say all of us. On which subject, Uncle Charles put in an appearance at lunch today. It seems some journalist is wanting to write us up, and Uncle stunned us all by suggesting she should be told of Project Genesis ahead of the announcement.'

Emma swivelled to stare up into his face. 'You're not serious!'

'*He* seemed to be. So that it can be incorporated into her article, due out about the same time.'

'But how can he be sure she'll keep quiet? You know what journalists are.'

'Well, in her defence, she's not a tabloid one; she works for *Chiltern Life*.'

'All the same,' Emma said dubiously.

'Exactly. All the same ... However, there's no point in worrying about it. Uncle did promise to discuss it with everyone before he makes a decision.'

'Perhaps, after consideration, he'll decide against it. Has he spoken to your father?'

Sam shrugged. 'He didn't say so. I'll give Pa a buzz later and see if he's heard anything.'

Emma got to her feet. 'And in the meantime, since there's been no sound from upstairs, I'll take in the dinner.'

Two

Avril Parish came out of the library and stood for a minute on the steps, looking about her and breathing in the sharp spring air. The trees along the pavements were already greening, and in the library forecourt a tub of daffodils was in full bloom. This morning she'd managed to track down an elusive reference book for a grateful customer. A minor achievement, no doubt, but satisfying nonetheless, and a reminder of how much she enjoyed working at the library, which – another advantage – was within walking distance of home. This afternoon she'd a game of bridge to look forward to, and this evening she must phone her daughters to arrange for them to come to supper.

Furthermore, the plumbers had actually arrived before she'd had to leave for work, and it seemed, after endless delays, that the shower room would soon be completed. The guest-room, on the other hand, should be finished today, and the curtains she'd ordered were promised by midweek. Everything was at last falling into place, and she felt an unaccustomed surge of well-being. Life, she thought in mild surprise, was, after all, good.

She went slowly down the steps, still revelling in this unfamiliar *joie de vivre*. Once everything was straight again, she could start looking for a paying guest, she told herself, as she set off along the pavement. It would be wonderful when she'd no longer be the only one in the house, when she could expect someone home in the evenings. Even during those painful last weeks with Tom, she'd at least had someone to cook for, someone in the house with her. It was some small consolation that he too now lived alone, and hadn't moved in with his lady-love. Avril doubted this had been for her benefit, but she was grateful nonetheless.

Her thoughts returned to the proposed lodger; Lindsey had advised against trying for a couple, and Avril saw the sense in her reasoning. She'd therefore reverted to her original idea of a school teacher, for whom, situated as she was not far from Belmont Primary, she was ideally placed. She could only hope some new teachers were expected at the start of the summer term, and would be looking for accommodation. In which case, she thought suddenly, she'd be well advised to start advertising now, rather than wait till the house was in order. She'd draft the wording over lunch, then phone the *Gazette* before she went out. And it would do no harm to put notices in the post office and on the library board as well.

Full of plans, Avril turned into Maple Drive,

noting with relief the two vans still parked at her gate. The worst was behind her, she told herself on a wave of optimism. Though Tom's leaving had left her shattered, it had also been a wake-up call. In the last few months she'd changed radically, in both appearance – at Lindsey's instigation – and in attitude. The world was now her oyster, and she determined to make the most of it.

Finlay Curzon leant back in his chair and reread the letter from the journalist. After a brief résumé of previous work, it set out how, with his permission, she hoped to research the history of the firm. It was clear, concise, and businesslike, and the signature, in bold black ink, had been written with a flourish: *Rona Parish.*

Thinking back, Finn remembered meeting her parents at a party at his uncle's, a year or so ago. They'd seemed an agreeable couple. Well, he was all for extra publicity, and if it was decreed she be made privy to Genesis, so be it. She could probably be trusted to keep it to herself.

He pressed the buzzer for his secretary and, when she came in, handed her the letter.

'Phone Miss Parish, would you, Meg, and make an appointment for later in the week. How's Wednesday looking?'

'So far, the morning's clear.'

'Fine, let's make it then. She'll be coming from Marsborough, so allow her a little time.

Around ten o'clock.'

'Right; I'll get on to it straight away.'

'Has my brother anyone with him at the moment?'

'I can check for you.'

'If he's free, put me through, would you?'

A minute later the phone rang on his desk, and he lifted it to hear Edward's voice.

'It just struck me,' Finlay said, 'that you weren't at lunch on Friday, and we haven't been in touch since.'

'So?' Edward asked drily. 'Did you all go down with food poisoning?'

'Seriously, have you spoken to anyone? About the lunch?'

'Now you *are* making me curious. No, I haven't.'

'The point is that Uncle Charles joined us, with the information that a journalist wants to do a write-up on us.'

'Nothing world-shattering there, is there?'

'He suggested she should be told about Genesis ahead of the announcement.'

There was silence, followed by a low whistle. 'Did he indeed?'

'How do you feel about it? It's your baby rather than mine.'

'You say "suggested"; nothing definite, then?'

'He promised a full consultation before reaching a decision. Has he actually got the last word on this, if, for instance, the rest of us were against it?'

'I suppose so. He *is* Managing Director, after all. The point's never arisen before; in important matters, there's always been a consensus of opinion. Perhaps, when we've weighed the pros and cons, there will be this time.'

'Admittedly there's no question of *publication* ahead of time; it's her *knowing* that's the crux of it, so it can be incorporated at the end of her article.'

'How long do we have to think about this?'

'Oh, several weeks, I'd say; it'll take her a while to work her way down to the present. In fact, she says in her letter it might spread over more than one issue. She writes for *Chiltern Life,* by the way.'

After a moment's thought, Edward asked, 'How did the others react?'

'I don't think any of us reacted at all; we were too stunned, and Uncle swiftly changed the subject. With its being the weekend, I've not spoken to them since, but I wanted to put you in the picture, in case it comes up at lunch.'

'Well, thanks for that. I'll mull it over. By the way, Anna was wondering if you'd care to join us for Harry's birthday on Friday, in your guise as godfather?'

'What form are the celebrations taking?'

Edward laughed. 'Cautious as ever! You won't be required to play football or anything. He's having a thrash with his friends on Saturday, but Friday's his actual birthday, and we're taking him out to the Deer Park for dinner.

Mother's coming, of course, and you'd be very welcome to join us.'

'That's good of you, Edward. And Anna.'

'You'll come, then?'

'I'd be delighted. Thank you.'

'Great; I'll let you know the times later. Are you going down for lunch now?'

'In a couple of minutes, yes.'

'See you there, then.'

Finlay replaced his phone and sat for a moment, drumming his fingers on the desk. God only knew what sixteen-year-old boys wanted for their birthday. A cheque would probably be the best bet. He'd need to buy a card, though; he'd ask Meg ... No, damn it! The boy was his godson, after all. He'd leave a little early, and choose one himself.

He pushed back his chair and went down to lunch.

'Rona?'

'Hello, Mum; how are things?'

'Fine, thank you. I was wondering if you're free for supper on Thursday? I'm asking Lindsey, too.'

'That'd be lovely; I've not seen you for a while.' Despite her New Year's resolution, Rona thought guiltily.

'How's work going?'

'OK, I think. I'm still on the local businesses series. I finished the one on Mycroft's this morning.'

35

'My goodness, yes! I remember going there with my parents as a child, and it was old-fashioned even then! They seemed to stock everything conceivable in the ironmongery line. My father used to say, "If we can't get it at Mycroft's, we won't get it anywhere."'

'It's still much the same.'

'Any thoughts on another biography? You did so well with the others, it seems a shame to confine yourself to ephemera.'

'Pretty long-lasting ephemera; there was a gratifying response to our binder offer, so people are obviously collecting the articles.'

'Even so, you can stretch yourself further than that.'

Rona sighed. 'The trouble is, Mum, bios take so long to do, and if they go wrong an awful lot of both work and time has been wasted.'

Her last fledgling bio had certainly 'gone wrong', Rona reflected ruefully. She hadn't allowed for stumbling over dead bodies when she'd embarked on it. Come to that, she'd been metaphorically stumbling over them ever since.

She said quickly, 'I hear work on the house is almost finished?'

'Yes; with luck, you'll see the end result on Thursday.'

Although her mother had visited her since Christmas, and they'd met a couple of times at Lindsey's, Rona hadn't been to the family home. Only now did she acknowledge she'd been subconsciously avoiding it. In the house

36

where she'd grown up, permeated as it was with her father's presence, the realization that he was no longer a part of it would, she feared, be altogether too painful.

'Rona?'

'I'm still here.' Her voice wasn't quite steady.

'It'll be all right, you know,' Avril said gently. And at her mother's unexpected understanding, Rona's eyes filled with tears.

'I know it will, Mum,' she said.

The phone rang on Sally Curzon's desk, and she caught it up with an exclamation of annoyance. She'd asked Lavender to deflect her calls.

'Yes? I thought I—'

'I'm sorry, Sally,' the receptionist broke in, 'but your brother-in-law's on the line, wanting to know if we can fit him in for a haircut at twelve thirty. He asked for you, but you'd said not to put calls through.'

'With reason. At this rate, I'm never going to get through this.' She glanced despairingly at the papers and folders on her desk. 'And he's *always* doing it, isn't he – ringing up at the last minute and expecting us to accommodate him. *Is* anyone free?'

'Unfortunately not; Sharon will be on her lunch break, and the others are fully booked.'

'You'd better put him through,' Sally said resignedly.

'Will do.'

She replaced the phone, lifting it again as it

rang a minute later.

'Hello, gorgeous!' said Nick's voice in her ear. 'You're not going to turn me away, are you?'

'Why can't you make proper appointments, like everyone else?'

'Family perk?'

'None of the others try it on.'

'Oh, come on, Sal. I'm taking Saskia to a formal dinner this evening, and it's struck me I look a bit shaggy.'

'Saskia now, is it? How long will this one last?'

'Variety's the spice of life! Please, Sally. Look, how about I take you to lunch afterwards?'

'I can't spare the time, Nick. I've a mound of paperwork to get through.'

'Then you'll need some sustenance to keep you going.'

She smiled reluctantly. 'All right; since it'll be my lunch break anyway, you're on. But this is the last time you'll get away with it. As it is, there's not a slot free, so I'll have to do you myself.'

'Couldn't be better,' said the unrepentant Nick. 'See you in an hour, then.' And he rang off.

Her concentration broken, Sally picked up one of the new brochures that had arrived that morning. At the head of the sheet was the logo she'd spent so many sleepless nights over, an ornate hand mirror reflecting a stylized woman's face, and underneath it, in bold gothic script, the name of the business – *Image Day Spa* – followed by the words 'Proprietor: Sally Curzon' and a string of letters denoting her qualifications. Listed below were the treatments on offer, which went, as Oliver had remarked, from A to W, starting with aromatherapy and ending with waxing, by way of facials, massage, manicures, pedicures, reflexology and a range of hairdressing procedures.

The phone rang again. Lavender, even more apologetic. 'I'm really sorry, Sally, but Mrs Seacombe is insisting on speaking to you about her tint.'

Sally sighed. 'All right; I'll come down.'

She stood up and, as always before leaving her office, glanced in the full-length mirror to check her appearance. It was a matter of principle that she should always look well-groomed. Then, on impulse, she moved forward to study her reflection more critically. Oval face, perfectly made-up, grey-blue eyes; dark blonde shoulder-length hair, discreetly highlighted. She didn't look forty, she noted with satisfaction, partly thanks to her profession, but also to a certain amount of self-discipline. Her slim figure gave no hint that she'd given birth to three children, whereas Anna, she thought suddenly, was undeniably putting on weight. She'd noticed it over lunch on Friday. Impossible to mention it, of course, though if asked, she'd be happy to help her reverse the trend.

With a last tug at her skirt, Sally went down to reassure her client.

Wednesday morning, and at ten to nine Rona and Gus walked round the corner into Charlton Road, to the lock-up garage where she kept her car. The only disadvantage of living in an avenue of Georgian houses was that none of them possessed its own garage, but in Rona's case the inconvenience was minimal, since she seldom used the car.

As always, Gus gave a hopeful tug on his lead as they passed the slipway leading to the park, but she shook her head.

'Sorry, boy, not today. I'm taking you round to Max.'

Farthings, the cottage where Max had his studio and spent three nights a week, was in Dean Street North, a ten-minute walk away. Being the rush hour, it took Rona almost as long by car. Max was an artist, who divided his time between private commissions, taking classes at Farthings, and teaching one day a week at Marsborough School of Art.

'Thanks for taking him,' Rona said, as she handed over the dog. 'I don't know when I'll be back; will you have time to walk him at lunch-time?'

On Wednesdays, Max had two afternoon classes, but was then free to come home.

'I'll try, but if not, he'll have the run of the

garden, such as it is. Don't worry, he'll be quite happy on the living room rug.' The studio was upstairs, and, as at home, Gus wasn't allowed above the ground floor.

'See you both this evening, then.'

It was only a forty-minute drive to Chilswood and her appointment wasn't till ten, but rush-hour traffic could be unpredictable, and Rona had no intention of being late for her first meeting with the Curzons. In her briefcase on the seat beside her were her recorder and a new digital camera, which she hoped to be allowed to use. Pictorial aides-memoires would be useful when she came to write up her notes, though illustrations in the article would be the province of a *Chiltern Life* photographer.

Having negotiated the traffic in central Marsborough, Rona settled down for a more leisurely drive, letting her mind drift back over what she'd gleaned of Curzon from the web. She'd been surprised to learn the pottery covered quite a few acres, and apart from factory and office buildings, incorporated a museum, visitor centre, restaurant and a couple of shops. Maps were provided, showing its location in relation to motorways and major roads, and factory tours were on offer, which should prove useful.

All in all, she'd been taken aback by the wealth of information available, and it had come as a relief to find, when she reached the history heading, that attention was focused almost exclusively on the development of ceramics and glazes, and the innovations introduced. The only personal note she could find was that Samuel Curzon founded the pottery in 1856 and his descendants had carried on the business to the present day.

It seemed to Rona, therefore, that her first instinct had been right, and she should concentrate on bringing to life those early pioneers, detailing their marriages, and how inter-relationships had developed and continued, presumably amicably, down to the present. In short, she would write about the people behind the porcelain, and her first step must be to familiarize herself with that complicated family tree her father had warned her about.

Her musings had brought her to the outskirts of Chilswood, and in front of her on the left she could see a tourist sign pointing the way to the pottery. She slowed down and turned into the road indicated, following one or two other cars headed in the same direction. She'd been advised to park in the public car park, make her way to the Visitor Centre, and tell a member of staff that she had an appointment. Finlay Curzon's secretary would then come to collect her and escort her to his office.

Accordingly, ten minutes later Rona found herself walking across the gravel to a tall building behind the Visitor Centre, accompanied by a pleasant, middle-aged woman who had introduced herself as Meg Fairclough.

'Are you by any chance the Rona Parish who wrote the Conan Doyle biography?' she asked, as they entered the building and waited for the lift.

'The latest one, yes,' Rona admitted.

'I enjoyed it very much. What other lives have you done?'

'Sarah Siddons and William Pitt the Elder. My family wants me to write another, but they involve quite a commitment and at the moment I keep finding interesting, short-term projects to write about.'

'Like potteries?' queried Meg Fairclough with a smile.

'Like family businesses,' Rona amended.

'Well, Curzon is certainly that.'

The lift arrived and took them up to the second floor. Meg led the way down a carpeted corridor, knocked at a door, opened it, and announced, 'Rona Parish to see you, Finlay.'

Then she stepped aside and as Rona went into the room, closed the door behind her.

Finlay Curzon rose from his desk and came to meet her with his hand held out.

'You found us all right, then. Come and sit down.'

He steered her to a couple of easy chairs near the window. As Rona seated herself, she took surreptitious stock of him, liking the directness of his dark blue eyes and reflecting that his smile must stand him in good stead in tricky business deals.

'I've ordered coffee,' he said. 'I hope that's all right?'

'I'd love a cup; thank you.'

'So.' He studied her in his turn. 'What exactly do you want to know? We have quite an extensive range of literature—'

'But it only gives *facts*,' she broke in. 'In the series I'm doing, I look behind my subjects' well-documented achievements, to the people they actually *were*: their characters, who married whom, how their children reacted to a career more or less ordained for them, and so on. For instance, did any of the sons refuse to go into the business?'

'Not that I'm aware of,' Finlay said slowly.

A knock at the door heralded the arrival of Meg Fairclough bearing a tray of coffee and biscuits. She set it down on the table between them, gave them each a smile, and went out again.

'How far back can you remember your relatives?' Rona asked. 'Grandfather? Great-grandfather?'

'Not that far, I'm afraid. I barely knew my grandfather, old Spencer. He died when I was very young.'

Rona leant forward and picked up her coffee cup. 'What do you remember about him?'

'That he wore a watch and chain. I was fascinated by it, particularly by the fact that when you pressed a button, it would chime. He used to let us play with it.'

'"Us"?'

'My brother Edward and me.'

'Are there just the two of you?'

Finlay passed her the plate of biscuits. 'No, we have a sister, Jacqueline.'

'But, of course, she doesn't count,' Rona said without thinking.

'I beg your pardon?'

She looked up quickly, meeting his puzzled eyes, and felt herself flush. 'I'm sorry; I mean she's not connected with the business. Aren't only male family members acceptable?'

He made a rueful face. 'It's never been put so bluntly, but yes, that *has* been the practice; underlined by the fact that although my father and uncles all had sisters, they're not shown on the standard family tree. You'll have to check the full version in the museum if you want to trace them.' He smiled. 'All the same, don't let Jackie hear you say she doesn't count. She's quite a forceful lady, my sister.'

'I'm sure,' Rona said placatingly. 'You mentioned the family tree; I was going to ask about that. It might help me to see where you all slot in.'

Finlay gestured behind her. 'Take a look for yourself.'

Rona turned, and saw on the wall a framed record of the Curzon lineage.

'Perfect!' she exclaimed, laying down her cup and walking over to it. Finlay followed her.

'Samuel Curzon founded the business,' he

said, pointing to the name at the top of the tree. 'He had a son, George, and an anonymous daughter.' She heard the smile in his voice. 'As I explained, since she didn't count, she's not recorded.'

'I'm not going to live that down, am I?'

'The truth of the matter is that we're quite a large family, and whoever designed the tree must have reckoned there'd be more room if he kept to the direct male line.'

'Which, I can see, divided quite early on.'

'Yes, because George had two sons: Spencer, my grandfather whom I've just mentioned, and Frederick. In due course, Spencer and Grandma Florence produced a couple of daughters and, of course, my father, John Samuel – universally known as JS – who died a couple of years ago. There's a Samuel in every generation, by the way; my brother's boy has it as his second name.'

His finger moved to the other side of the chart. 'Meanwhile old Frederick here, like his father, had two sons, complicating things still further, and so in turn did one of *his* sons, my Uncle Charles – or my cousin, to be quite accurate. Are you still with me?'

'Just about.'

'I know it's complicated.'

'Are there any copies I could take away with me?'

'I'm sure we could rustle one up somewhere. In fact, I think it's printed in one of the brochures. I'll ask Meg to look it out for you.'

He turned away, but Rona still lingered in front of the tree. 'So there are five of you in your generation?'

'That's right: Edward and myself, and our cousins: Oliver and Nick, who are Uncle Charles's sons, and Sam, who's Uncle James's. As you can see, that's as far as the chart goes, but there's another generation coming on apace. Trouble is, of us all, only Edward so far has produced an heir. I'm going to his birthday dinner on Friday.'

'And the rest are girls. What would happen if one of them wanted to join?'

'Thankfully, we won't have to worry about that for a while; the eldest is only nine.'

Finlay had re-seated himself, and after a minute, Rona did the same.

He eyed her appraisingly. 'So: how else can I help you?'

'Have you any archives I could look at? Family documents – marriage certificates, or even better, letters or diaries?'

'We do have archives yes, but they're held in Buckford Museum. They can be seen by appointment for research purposes, but I have to warn you that they mostly consist of moulds and designs. The only personal things, apart from a few birth, marriage and death certificates, are Samuel's journals, and again, they're chiefly concerned with the growth of the factory. You'd probably do better here; there are

47

some personal items in the museum.'

'Thanks. Well, in the meantime, I'll just walk round and familiarize myself with the layout.'

'You'd do better taking a factory tour.' Finlay glanced at his watch. 'Actually, there's one on today. If you hurry, you should just be able to catch it; it starts from the Visitor Centre at eleven.'

'That would be perfect.' She quickly gathered together her recorder and camera, neither of which she'd asked permission to use. 'And thanks for sparing me your time, Mr Curzon. I'm very grateful.'

Finlay had also risen. 'Ask Meg on your way out about a copy of the tree,' he said. 'And if there's anything else we can help with, just let us know.'

'Thank you.'

He walked her to the door and opened it. She had started back along the corridor when his voice halted her.

'It's just occurred to me that the tour ends about twelve thirty. I could give you lunch in the directors' dining room, if you'd care to join us? It would be a chance to meet the other members of the family.'

'That would be great. Thanks very much.'

'Come back to this building, then, and we'll take it from there.'

Finlay went back into his office and closed the door thoughtfully. He'd surprised himself with that impulsive invitation, but he'd been unaccountably reluctant to let Rona Parish walk out of his life so soon. She was an attractive young woman, with an air of independence and self-confidence that he found appealing. He wondered what the others would make of her – and of his inviting her to lunch. Nick, of course, would try to monopolize her, notwithstanding the wedding ring on her finger. Finlay smiled to himself. He reckoned Rona Parish would be more than capable of dealing with Nick and his advances.

He sat down at his desk and rang for his secretary.

Three

Lindsey laid some papers on Jonathan's desk. 'Shall I be seeing you later?'

He looked up. 'Sorry, sweetie; we've a parents' evening and I have to be a dutiful father.'

He pushed back his chair and came round the desk, putting his hands on her shoulders. 'Pity it's not one of your days for working at home.' He bent his head and kissed her, slowly and thoroughly.

She said plaintively, 'It's been almost a week...'

'Makes it all the sweeter when we do manage it.' He slid his fingers inside her blouse, feeling her quiver in response. 'We could drive out to the Watermill for lunch,' he suggested, 'and maybe park somewhere on the way back? Or we could do without lunch altogether, and—'

There was a token tap on the door, giving them just time to leap apart before the door opened and Jonathan's wife stood looking at them, her expectant smile fading.

'Oh – I'm so sorry. Am I interrupting something? Stephanie said there was no one with you.'

Lindsey half-turned away, trying inconspicuously to fasten her top button and wondering in panic if Jonathan's mouth bore any incriminating lipstick.

'Nothing important,' he was saying.

'It's just that since I was in town, I thought perhaps we could have lunch. I'm really sorry to burst in like that – I thought you were alone.'

'No harm done,' Jonathan assured her. 'You've met Lindsey Parish, haven't you?'

Carol Hurst smiled. 'Only *en passant*. But I did meet your sister at a party, and mistook her for you.'

'That often happens,' Lindsey murmured. Damn and double damn! So much for their planned escape. *Am I interrupting something?* Carol had asked. If only she knew! 'I won't hold you up,' she added brightly, turning to Jonathan, 'but if you could let me have those papers back by mid-afternoon, it would be helpful.'

'I'll read them when I get back from lunch.' He wasn't meeting her eyes, and, because she'd no option, Lindsey smiled at his wife and quickly left the room.

'Avril!'

She turned swiftly. 'Oh – hello, Tom.'

He eyed the carrier bags she was holding. 'Stocking up on groceries?'

'Yes, I – I've got the girls coming to supper tomorrow.'

'That'll be good.' He paused. 'Have you had lunch?'

'No, I thought I'd—'

'Nor have I. Shall we have it together?'

Avril stared at him, nonplussed. 'We – can't, can we?'

'I fail to see why not.'

'But – wouldn't Catherine mind?'

He relieved her of the carrier bags and started walking her along the pavement. 'Of course not. Didn't we resolve, on Christmas Day, that we'd be friends from now on?'

'Well, yes, but—'

'No buts. In any case, I want to hear about the alterations to the house. Have you had any applications for lodgers yet?'

'I only started advertising this week. Lindsey said couples would be hard to find, so I've reverted to a single school teacher.'

'Very wise. The Gallery all right for you?'

'Of course.' They started up the wrought-iron staircase leading to the walkway where the café was situated. 'Suppose we meet someone we know?' she asked nervously.

'Avril, *we're not doing anything wrong*. OK?'

'OK,' she repeated, and her spirits suddenly rose. She was going to spend the next hour or so with an attractive man whom she'd thought lost to her for ever, and even though, in all ways that counted, he was no longer her husband, she was going to enjoy the experience.

* * *

52

Finlay Curzon was waiting in the office block foyer, and came forward with a smile.

'Well, what's the verdict on the tour?'

'Very enjoyable,' Rona said, 'though I seemed to be the oldest person on it!'

He laughed. 'We have a lot of school visits during term time. I hope you've worked up an appetite; it's a set menu, by the way, but the food's good.'

He led her down a short corridor to a set of double oak doors and pushed one of them open, gesturing her ahead of him. The room in which she found herself was quite large and would have comfortably held more tables than the single long one that stood in the centre. She was, Rona realized, the only woman present – which, given the Curzon ethos, should not have surprised her. The men already seated rose as one and stood as Finlay introduced them. They'd plainly been forewarned of her attendance.

She nodded to each one as Finlay introduced him, trying to keep track of names and relationships. Not all of them were Curzons; several senior managers were present and were also eying her with interest. She wondered what they'd been told about her. Then – Edward, was it? – pulled out a chair for her, and they all sat down. She was, she saw, firmly entrenched in the Curzon enclave, with Finlay opposite her and Nick on her right.

'So what gave you the idea of writing us up?'

Oliver enquired from the end of the table.

'Believe it or not, dining off your china. It led to my father saying he'd met Mr Charles Curzon recently, and that you had an anniversary coming up.'

'Hadn't you heard about it before?' Finlay, as Sales and Marketing Director, cut in. 'The anniversary, I mean?'

'If I had, I'm afraid it hadn't registered.'

'Room for improvement, Finn,' Edward said jovially. He turned to Rona. 'You home in on anniversaries, then?'

'Not especially; I'm doing a series on the history of family businesses, for *Chiltern Life*. It's really centred on Marsborough, but I made an exception in your case, since you're Buckfordshire-based, and so well known.'

The first course arrived – chicken pâté and Melba toast – and to Rona's relief the spotlight turned off her as they began their meal. At the other end of the table the senior managers were engaged in their own conversation, and during the brief lull in what she suspected would be a minor inquisition, she had time to sort out her first impressions of the cousins. In appearance, there was only a faint resemblance between them, no stronger in the two sets of brothers than in the group as a whole. If anything, Finlay and Sam most resembled each other, being fairer than the others, though Sam's hair was a lighter shade than Finlay's gold-brown.

'You live in Marsborough, then?' Nick enquired.

'That's right.'

'Lucky you; it's one of my favourite towns, with all that Georgian elegance.'

'Do you live here in Chilswood?'

'No, in Nettleton – several of us do. It has the advantage of being convenient for work, without being on the doorstep. You need some distance between home and the daily grind – helps you to switch off.'

'I wouldn't know,' Rona said. 'I work from home. And don't,' she added as his mouth opened, 'say it's different for a woman!'

Nick laughed. 'Touché. So how do you wind down? By preparing elaborate dishes for your husband? I've heard that's good therapy.'

'Not in my case. I loathe cooking and do as little as possible. My husband's the cook in our household – when he's at home, that is.'

Nick raised an eyebrow. 'He's away a lot?'

Rona bit her lip; she'd not meant to get involved in this. 'Three nights a week,' she said reluctantly. 'He's an artist who gives evening classes, and it's easier if he stays at the studio on those nights.'

'So you're a *class* widow?'

She smiled. 'You could say that. Fortunately there's an excellent Italian restaurant close by, and several good take-aways.'

Sam leaned forward. 'You're serious? You don't cook at all?'

'Only under duress.'

'Ms Parish, I'm sure, believes cooking is as much men's work as women's,' Finlay said unexpectedly. 'She doesn't believe in stereotypes; I warn you, we'd better be nice to her, or she'll report us to the Equal Opportunities Board!'

Edward looked surprised. 'Why? What have we done?'

'Kept female members of the family out of the business.'

'I wasn't aware they'd been clamouring to get in.'

Rona lifted a hand in self-defence. 'Look, I didn't mean to criticize. It just seems strange, in this day and age, not to have any women on the board.'

'She has a point, you know,' Oliver conceded. 'In family firms, sisters if not wives are often involved. In ours, though, it so happens that the women are otherwise engaged. Cousin Jackie's an accountant, and as for the wives, mine runs a health-cum-beauty spa, Sam's is an interior designer and Edward's is a magistrate. With the possible exception of Sally, I'm sure you agree their jobs are unisex, and they're not chained to the kitchen sink.'

Rona said humorously, 'Should I go out, and come in again?'

Everyone laughed, and as their plates were removed and the main course laid before them, she again felt a sense of reprieve. She must be careful, though; the last thing she wanted was to antagonize them. Embarking on Thai fishcakes

56

and stir-fried vegetables, it struck her that the tally of wives hadn't attached one to either Finlay or Nick. Hard to believe that arguably the two most attractive members of the family had no significant other. She'd check later on her copy of the family tree.

Feeling it would be wise to toss the ball into their court, she asked brightly, 'Are you planning anything special to celebrate the anniversary?'

There was sudden, total silence, and she looked round in bewilderment. *'Now* what have I said?'

'Nothing, really,' Edward assured her quickly. 'It's just a subject we're a little sensitive on. But to answer your question, various displays and exhibitions are planned...' His voice tailed away, and it was Oliver who continued.

'But the main event will be the launch of a totally new product we've been working on for some time. Naturally we want to keep it under wraps till the announcement, but concerted efforts are being made to gain access to it. We've had attempted break-ins and even a fire a couple of months ago, though fortunately it was put out before any damage was done. Still, it's led to considerable stress all round.'

'But that's awful!' Rona exclaimed. 'Have you any idea who's behind it?'

'Nothing concrete, and certainly nothing that could be proved.'

'Are the police working on it?'

'Not so that you'd notice,' Sam said. 'Which is why we've doubled our security staff for the next few months. The trouble is that when week after week goes by with nothing happening, they tend to lower their guard.'

'Do you think whoever it is just wants to uncover the product, or are they out to sabotage it?'

'That,' said Edward, 'is the sixty-four thousand dollar question. Admittedly our competitors mightn't be too happy with what we've come up with, but at this stage they've no way of knowing that. Nor can I believe any of them would stoop to these kinds of tactics. But enough of our problems: how else can we help you? Are there any particular papers you'd like to see?'

Rona glanced at Finlay. 'We were discussing that earlier. Letters or diaries would be invaluable, and I believe there are birth, marriage and death certificates in the museum. Unfortunately, I was too late for that part of the tour.'

'It's only small, you know,' Nick told her; 'not like those of the larger factories, but yes, it has a few personal items, and there are facsimiles of some of them for sale in the factory shop.'

'Those would be fine. Also, of course, I'd be very interested in personal memories any of you might have about your relatives, past or present. I'm hoping to see you individually at some stage, to discuss that aspect.'

Dessert was served, followed by coffee, and the meal came to an end.

'Have you everything you need for the moment?' Nick asked, as they all left the dining room.

'Enough to be going on with, thanks. As I said, I missed the museum, but it'll be closed now, so that'll have to wait till my next visit. I just want a look at the gift shop before I go.' She turned to Finlay. 'Thanks so much for lunch. It was good to meet you all.'

'If there's anything else I can help with, please let me know.'

It had been an interesting and informative visit, Rona thought fifteen minutes later, as, slipping her purchase into her bag, she left the shop and made her way to the car park. As she'd intimated, she'd like at some stage to interview each of the Curzons separately, to tap their recollections of earlier generations and family folklore. In the meantime, she'd plenty to sort out before she made a return visit.

Emerging onto the main road, she set off for home.

The telephone was ringing as she opened the front door, and she caught it up, pushing the door to with her foot.

'Ro?' It was Lindsey's voice, taut and trembling.

'Linz! Is something wrong?'

'Is Max home yet?'

'No, he won't be for a couple of hours.'

'Can I come round, then? Straight away?'

'Of course, but what's the matter? What's happened?'

'Tell you when I see you,' Lindsey said rapidly, and rang off.

Rona frowned, shrugged off her car coat and hung it on the hall stand. She'd intended making a cup of tea, but now she'd wait for Lindsey. She'd sounded upset, Rona thought worriedly, as she took her briefcase up to the study. Dropping it on a chair, she extracted the brochures and leaflets she'd collected and laid them on the desk, ready to be gone through in the morning. She did, however, unfold the family tree Meg Fairclough had given her. Beneath both Finlay and Nick's names was printed the stark word 'Divorced'.

She was still looking at it when the door bell sounded through the house and she ran downstairs to admit her sister.

'Lindsey, what—'

Lindsey pushed past her into the house and promptly burst into tears. Thoroughly alarmed now, Rona put an arm round her.

'It's not Mum or Pops, is it?'

Lindsey shook her head and Rona, breathing a tremulous sigh of relief, led her down the basement stairs to the kitchen, where she collapsed onto a chair. Rona put the kettle on and leaned back against the Aga.

'Now, what is it?'

Lindsey fumbled in her bag for a handker-chief and blew her nose. 'Carol Hurst called at the office this morning,' she said.

'And?'

'And Jonathan and I were – together.'

Rona frowned. *'How* together?'

'Kissing, that's all,' Lindsey said impatiently, 'but my blouse was undone. God, Rona –' she pressed both fists against her temples – 'I *hate* myself for what I've done to that woman! Let-ting myself be hoodwinked by all that "what the eye doesn't see" spiel. Of *course* we're hurting her, cheapening her marriage, if nothing else.'

Rona cut sharply into the tirade. 'Are you saying she caught you?'

'No, but only just not.'

'So why the drama? You've known all along what you were doing.'

Lindsey's eyes fell. 'It was the first time I've seen them together,' she said in a low voice. 'I'd convinced myself it wasn't a happy mar-riage, and just – blotted out her and the child-ren. But it's obvious she thinks the world of him, and she was so *trusting*, Ro. She even asked if she was interrupting anything.'

The kettle shrilled and Rona turned to pour the tea. Behind her, Lindsey went on speaking.

'At first, I was just relieved we'd managed to get away with it, but I couldn't get her out of my mind. I've been thinking of her all after-noon.'

Rona put two mugs on the table and sat down

opposite her. 'Go on.'

'After lunch I went to Jonathan's office to collect some files, and he was so bloody *cool* about it. He even put an arm round me and said, "To continue where we left off ...". And I realized I'd been burying my head in the sand, aiding and abetting him in his sordid little affair, while all the time he'd been playing the perfect husband.'

'Did you tell him any of this?'

'I tried to, but he wasn't having any. He said I'd had a fright, that was all, and I'd soon recover my balance, and Carol didn't suspect a thing. As though that would make me feel better! Then he actually said, "It adds a bit of spice to it, don't you think? Like that time your mother came to your flat while we were in bed." She flashed a glance at Rona. 'I told you about that. I just couldn't *believe* how unfeeling he was.'

She took a sip of the scalding tea. 'What's wrong with me, Ro? Why can't I find someone like Max and settle down, instead of lurching from man to man like this?'

'Because you're a poor judge of men; I've always said so. But you told me Jonathan would not last much longer, so why the histrionics? Here's the ideal chance to cut your losses. Anyway, I thought you'd found someone else?'

'Wrong on both counts: What I *said* was that the thing with Jonathan wasn't long-*lasting*, but I certainly didn't expect it to end this soon. And

I haven't *found* someone, I've *seen* him, that's all. Nothing may come of it.'

'You seemed pretty confident last time we spoke.'

'Only because I usually get my way,' Lindsey said bitterly.

There was a brief silence. 'Do I gather Jonathan doesn't want to end it?' Rona hazarded.

'Oh no, he's perfectly happy with his bit on the side. He's convinced I'll get over my pangs of conscience.'

'Well, mind you don't. Think how you'd feel if she *had* caught you, and you were responsible for the break-up of her marriage. Heaven knows, I never thought I'd say this, but why don't you just stick to Hugh? At least he has no other commitments.' She paused. '*Are* you going to Guildford with him this weekend?'

'I might as well, mightn't I? It could help me sort myself out. I might even take your advice, though both parents would have a stroke if Hugh and I got back together.'

'Well, there were plenty of pieces to pick up last time.'

'You won't tell Max about this, will you? I don't want to lower his opinion of me still further.'

'Secrets of the confessional. That's what twins are for.'

'So.' Lindsey blew her nose again. 'Enough about me; what have you been up to?'

Rona smiled. 'Today, I had lunch with two

attractive, unattached men.'

Lindsey gave a brief laugh. 'Some people have all the luck,' she said.

Rona didn't mention her sister's visit when Max and Gus returned shortly after Lindsey'd left. It would have been impossible to do so without giving some reason for it, and she'd plenty to tell him about her trip to Chilswood.

'So what are they like, *en famille*?' Max asked, pouring them both a drink.

'They seemed very pleasant, even if they have antediluvian ideas about women.'

Max grinned. *'Kinde, kurche, küche*?'

'Pretty much, but they didn't like me commenting on it. Would you believe, no women members of the family have ever had any part in the firm?'

'Perhaps they didn't want to,' Max suggested mildly, passing her a glass.

'That's what they tried to tell me. Anyway, I went on a factory tour, which was interesting; it began with a twenty-minute film on the firm's history, and should have ended with a visit to the museum, but I had to skip that because we were running late and I was meeting the directors for lunch. So I've earmarked it for my next visit.'

She sipped her vodka. 'They're pretty freaked out about this new product they're launching. It seems they're beset on all sides by people trying to break in and discover what it is.'

'Par for the course, I'd say. If you announce you've got a secret, you're inviting trouble. They should have kept quiet about it.'

The telephone rang, and he reached behind to retrieve it. 'Yes – hang on a minute. Who shall I say is speaking?'

He raised his eyebrows and handed Rona the phone. 'For you. Reigate police.'

She stared at him in bewilderment. *'Who?'* Then, as he merely shrugged, she said into the mouthpiece, 'Hello?'

'Rona Parish?' It was a woman's voice.

'Yes, speaking.'

'It's Reigate police station, ma'am, phoning to say we've found your handbag.'

'My handbag?' Rona repeated blankly.

'It was handed in this afternoon. No money in it, I'm afraid, only—'

'But – I haven't lost a handbag,' Rona protested.

There was an uncertain pause. 'Perhaps I should have said shoulder-bag? Brown leather, with a broken strap? Of course, it mightn't have *been* broken when—'

'I haven't lost *any* kind of bag!' Rona interrupted. 'And Reigate, did you say? I've never been there in my life!' She frowned. 'How did you get my name?'

'It was inside the bag, on a slip of paper. *Rona Parish, 19 Lightbourne Avenue, Marsborough*, and the phone number I've just rung.'

'But that's – weird,' Rona said slowly. 'Where

was it found?'

'In some bushes by the side of the road. Thrown there, I should say, after everything of value had been taken. There's no purse or wallet, not even a diary or keys; just toiletry things – lipstick, comb and so on.'

'And no one has reported losing it?'

'Not so far. You seemed our best lead.'

'Who handed it in?' Rona asked after a moment.

'The wife of a local vicar.' Another pause, then: 'Have you any friends in the area, who might have jotted down your address?'

'No, I don't even know anyone in Surrey. So what happens now?'

'We'll keep the bag in Lost Property, and if no one claims it within a certain time, it'll be disposed of. It's not as though there's anything of value.'

The policewoman waited, and when Rona made no comment, continued, 'I'm sorry to have troubled you, Ms Parish, but if you remember anything that might identify the owner, perhaps you'd let us know.' She gave a phone number and reference, which Rona wrote down, and rang off.

'What the hell was that all about?' Max demanded.

'You heard most of it. A handbag was found in Reigate with a piece of paper in it, giving my name, address and phone number.'

'It could have been supplied by *Chiltern Life*.'

66

Rona shook her head emphatically. 'They never give out private details. It's weird, Max. We *don't* know anyone living in or near Reigate, do we?'

'Not that I recall, no, but I suppose someone could have been passing through.'

'And why didn't she – and it has to be a she – report losing the bag? It must have contained credit cards, not to mention house and car keys, and quite likely a mobile as well.'

'The point is, *how* did she lose it?' Max mused. 'It could have been snatched by a mugger, or pinched during a break-in, or simply taken from under her chair in a restaurant.'

'Whichever way, you'd report it, wouldn't you?'

'Not, perhaps, if it was in an incriminating place.'

'*Incriminating?*'

'Somewhere the owner had no reason to be.'

Rona shook her head dismissively. 'It was *found* in some bushes; there'd be no way of telling where it had been taken from.'

'Then there might have been something in it she didn't want to be linked with – drugs, say. For all she knows, they, or traces of them, could still be in the bag.'

Rona picked up her glass and drank from it. 'We can speculate all night, but the fact remains that an unknown person has been walking round with my name and address in her handbag. Not a very comfortable thought.'

'I admit it's odd, but there has to be a logical explanation.'

'I'd certainly like to hear it.'

'Well, there's no point in worrying, so sit down and relax while I make a start on the meal.'

After a moment Rona shrugged, and pulled out a chair. 'The Curzons were amazed when I said you did the cooking. Not in their scheme of things at all.'

'Let's face it, it's not in most people's. Generally speaking, it's the women who do the cooking, whether or not they go out to work. I hope you realize how lucky you are.'

'Oh, I do. Talking of cooking, I told Barnie we'd fix a date for them to come to supper. Dinah's feeling rather down, now Mel and the family have left.'

'Fine by me. This week's out, of course, with the visit to Tynecastle, but next Wednesday or Friday would be OK, if they're free. Now, how about making yourself useful, and peeling some potatoes?'

Four

Lindsey, who lived out of town, had offered to collect Rona on her way to supper with their mother, to avoid taking two cars. On the drive out to Belmont, the suburb where Avril lived, Rona told her about the mysterious handbag.

'Creepy!' was Lindsey's less than reassuring comment.

'Don't mention it to Mum,' Rona warned her. 'She'd only panic that there's a stalker after me, or something.'

'Perhaps there is,' Lindsey rejoined.

'Well, at least it's a female one. Max says there must be an explanation, but I can't think of one. I've never been near Reigate in my life.' She flicked a sideways glance at her sister. 'Did you see Jonathan today?'

'Of course I saw him,' Lindsey said testily. 'We work together, don't we?'

'You know what I mean.'

Her sister sighed. 'There wasn't a chance to talk privately, but frankly, I didn't want one.'

'You haven't changed your mind?'

'About finishing with him? Not really.'

'What do you mean, not really? You're not

69

having second thoughts, are you?'

'Oh God, I don't know, Ro. He has a point, though, hasn't he? Provided Carol doesn't find out, we're not hurting anyone.'

'I just don't *believe* you!' Rona said flatly.

'I'm not sure I believe myself. Anyway, we'll see what transpires with Hugh this weekend.'

Perhaps fortunately, the conversation was cut short by their arrival at Maple Drive, and Rona braced herself for this first visit to the house since her parents' separation.

Avril opened the door to them, trim and attractive in plum velvet. An appetizing smell of garlic pricked at their nostrils as they hung their jackets on the hall stand, now bereft of their father's overcoat. Otherwise, Rona thought, relief mingling with indignation, the house looked surprisingly the same.

As though to negate the impression, Avril said eagerly, 'Shall I show you the alterations before we sit down?' and at their assent led the way upstairs and into her bedroom. On the right-hand wall, where Tom's wardrobe had always stood, a doorway now led into an en suite, converted from the old box room next door.

'It's lovely, Mum,' Lindsey exclaimed, taking in the ivory fitments and pale blue tiling.

'You wouldn't believe the problems I had!' Avril told them. 'First there was a delay in delivery, then when the units did arrive, they were the wrong size and I couldn't close the door, so we had to start all over again. The guest

70

room was just as bad; the decorator had barely stripped the walls when he went down with flu, and was off for two weeks.'

'Let's see the finished result, then,' Rona prompted, and they crossed the landing to the other front room, where their grandmother, now dead, had stayed on her infrequent visits. Re-decorated and with new curtains and bed cover, the ambience was altogether fresher than Rona remembered, and though the familiar furniture remained, including the button-back chair that had been Grandma's, a drop-leaf table now stood in the window, and a small television in one corner.

'You've done wonders with it,' Lindsey said warmly.

'The curtains only arrived yesterday. I was on tenterhooks in case they wouldn't be up in time for you to see them.'

'It all looks lovely, Mum,' Rona told her. 'Now all you need is an occupant.'

'I may have some news on that front, too,' Avril said happily. 'Come downstairs and I'll tell you about it over a drink.'

'You've surely not had a reply already?' Lindsey asked, when they'd all seated themselves.

'Not to the ads, no. But it turned out that Mary Price, who works at the library, has a friend at the school, and when she happened to mention I was looking for a lodger, this woman said she knew of someone who might be interested. A new teacher is due to start after Easter, and so far she's not found anywhere to live. Mary passed on my name, and I'm waiting to hear from her. It would certainly be a bonus if it could be settled so quickly.'

'Oh – I almost forgot.' Rona leaned over to retrieve her bag from the floor. 'I've a present for you.'

'But you brought some wine; that's more than—'

'This is a little extra,' Rona told her, handing over a small package and watching with a smile as she unwrapped it. Inside was a china marmalade pot and spoon, and as Avril exclaimed with pleasure, Rona added, 'It's to mark your venture into B&B.'

'Oh darling, it's lovely!' Avril jumped up and went to kiss Rona's cheek. 'It's Curzon, isn't it?'

'Yes; I was at the pottery on Wednesday – I'm going to feature them in the series. I had a wander round the shop, and when I saw that, I couldn't resist it. I'm assured it's in this year's design – scenes from the Chilterns. I think that one's the Bridgewater Monument.'

Seeing her mother's delight in the gift, Rona marvelled again at the change in her. For several years she'd let herself go, not bothering with make-up, wearing the same dreary clothes and, even worse, continually criticizing her husband and daughters. Ironically, it had taken the end of her marriage to shake her into a realization of what she had become. Now, with

72

an attractive new haircut, her recovered sense of style, and an interesting job to stimulate her, she seemed a different woman. Too bad it had come too late to save her marriage.

Half an hour later, it was apparent that Avril's cooking too had transformed itself. She'd always been a good plain cook, happiest with roasts and casseroles, but this was nothing like the 'stew' Rona remembered from childhood. Beef, mushrooms, peppers and garlic blended to form a delicious combination, served with a bowl of fragrant Thai rice. It was almost, Rona thought, up to Max's standard.

Dessert was pavlova, also an innovation, and as she served it, Avril glanced from one daughter to the other. 'Have either of you spoken to your father today?'

They both shook their heads.

'Then you won't know that we had lunch together.'

There was a startled silence. Lindsey was the first to find her voice. 'Really? How did that come about?'

'We bumped into each other yesterday, in Guild Street, and as it was nearly one o'clock and neither of us had eaten, he suggested we join up. It was – very pleasant.'

'Well, that's – great,' Rona said lamely.

Avril gave her a brittle smile. 'Don't worry, I'm not under any illusions that we'll get back together. Too much water under the bridge for that, on both sides. But it's nice that we're able to meet on friendly terms again. And I really have you and Max to thank for that, for more or less insisting we all spent Christmas together.'

And a traumatic day it had been, Rona recalled, though not due to her parents.

Impulsively, she laid a hand on her mother's. 'I'm really glad, Mum,' she said.

Charles Curzon glanced at his wife, half-hidden behind the evening paper. 'Oliver tells me the journalist turned up yesterday, and had lunch with them.'

Sybil lowered the paper. 'How did she seem?'

'They were quite impressed with her, Finn particularly. They think she'll do a good job.'

'And publication will be over the anniversary?'

'That's the idea.'

'What about that suggestion of yours, to make her privy to Genesis?'

Charles pushed out his lower lip. 'Time enough to consider that; I'll need to meet her myself and form my own opinion. At the moment, though, I'm far more concerned with this move of ours. I must say, I'll be glad when it's over.'

'So shall I.' Sybil looked about her. 'I thought I'd be upset to leave, having lived here for so long, but actually I'm quite looking forward to it. There are so many rooms we no longer use, and since all the family's nearby, there's no call for them to come and stay. We'll be much cosier and more compact at Coppins.'

Coppins was a large manor house on the edge of town, recently converted into luxury apartments.

'My only regret is having to get rid of so much,' Charles replied.

'Well, the boys have taken a fair bit, but you have to admit neither of them has room for those large pieces, especially Nicholas in his bachelor pad.'

'Some of them have been in the family for generations,' Charles said gloomily.

'Then offer them to the museum. They'd be glad to have them – old Frederick's desk, for example. Then you needn't feel you're parting with them.'

Charles's face brightened. 'Sybil, you're a marvel! That's a splendid idea. Once we start enlarging the museum, there'll be plenty of space, and in the meantime they can be stored in the back room.'

'Talking of the move, James and Elizabeth have invited us for supper on the day, to save us the bother of cooking. Elizabeth sounded quite envious; I shouldn't be surprised if in a year or two they follow us to Coppins.'

'There mightn't be anything available,' Charles reminded her. 'We were lucky to get in on the ground floor, in both senses of the term.' He smiled sheepishly. 'And I'm not sure I'd like my brother and sister-in-law literally on our doorstep, however fond I am of them. Our living in the same town has been an advantage in many ways, but the same building is another matter.'

'Well, I shouldn't worry about it, it was only an impression. They might feel the same about living close to us!'

'Indeed. Only another week to go. Did I tell you the boys have volunteered their services for unpacking the crates?' He glanced out of the uncurtained window to where lawns and flowerbeds spread away into the darkness. 'It will be good this summer to have all the pleasure of a garden, with none of the responsibility.' He straightened. 'Yes, my love; it took us a long time to reach this decision, but I think we've done the right thing.'

'I'm sure of it,' Sybil said equably, and, with a fond smile at her husband, she returned to her paper.

On Fridays, Max's only commitment was to his own work. At the moment, this consisted of a commissioned calendar of local views – which he'd almost finished – and an eighteenth birthday portrait of the Lord Lieutenant's daughter. Today, he'd elected to work on the latter.

After a quick breakfast, therefore, he went up to the studio, slotted a CD into the machine and, as the room filled with music, sat down at his easel. The girl had given him a couple of sittings, and he'd a sheaf of photographs and sketches from which to work, but as he picked up his brush, his thoughts were elsewhere.

That evening, he and Rona were flying up to Tynecastle to spend the weekend with his sister Cynthia and her family. The main object, though, was to see his father, who'd not been well. In fact the state of his health had necessitated a flying visit last December – the first time Max had seen him in over a year, which, though the fact had not previously concerned him, had since become a source of guilt. On that occasion Rona hadn't accompanied him, as the old man would then have refused to discuss his ailments and Max needed his undivided attention. But both father and sister had requested her company on his next visit, which he'd promised would not be too far distant. In the event it was now three months, longer than he'd intended, but regular phone calls had reassured him that the old man's health was slightly improved. He'd even started to paint again, a sure sign that Roland Allerdyce, Royal Academician, was on the mend.

Max smiled to himself. In their teens, Cynthia's sons had irreverently christened their grandfather RA, RA, which had soon degenerated into Rah-Rah. The old man had accepted the soubriquet with equanimity, even pride, which, as Max well knew, would not have been the case had he and Cyn bestowed it on him in *their* youth. Age, it appeared, mellowed everyone, even his father.

His eyes refocused on the unformed face on

his easel, and, pushing aside his musings, he began to paint.

Avril was preparing lunch when the phone rang.

'Mrs Parish? This is Sarah Lacey. Your name was given to me by Mrs Haydock at Belmont Primary.'

'Oh yes; you're the one looking for accommodation?'

'That's right. I was wondering if I could come and see the room?'

'Of course. When were you thinking of?'

'Would tomorrow morning be convenient? I live in Stokely, but I could be with you any time after ten.'

Avril worked at the library on alternate Saturdays, but this was her free weekend. 'That would be fine,' she said, 'though it'd suit me better if you made it nearer to eleven.' She liked to get her weekend shopping done before the crowds descended.

'No problem,' Sarah assured her.

'Then if you've a pen handy, I'll give you directions. I'm quite close to the school, so you shouldn't have any difficulty.'

After all the delays, things were moving swiftly, Avril thought with satisfaction as she replaced the phone. Belatedly, she hoped that she and her proposed lodger would like each other.

The Deer Park Hotel and Country Club was a

ten-minute drive from the outskirts of Nettleton, and the car park looked ominously full as
Finlay drove into it. Eventually he found a
space at the far end, and, since it was raining,
was fairly wet by the time he reached the foyer.
His family, he saw, was awaiting him in the bar,
and, smoothing down his damp hair, he went to
join them.

'Happy birthday, Harry,' he said, holding out
his hand, which the boy took.

'Cheers,' Harry replied, unaware of his grandmother's wince. 'And thanks a lot for the
cheque, Uncle. It's very welcome.'

'My pleasure.' Finn bent to kiss first his
mother, then Anna and Becca.

'What are you drinking?' Edward asked him.
'We're all on champagne cocktails, if that ap-
peals?'

'All except us,' corrected Becca, eying her
soft drink with resignation.

Finn flashed her a sympathetic smile. 'Sounds
wonderful, thanks.' He sat down next to his
mother. 'You're looking glamorous, Mama.'

'Thank you, my dear.'

He spoke no more than the truth. Before her
marriage, Hester Curzon had been an opera
singer, and the lessons she'd learned in make-
up and deportment had stood her in good stead
for the rest of her life. Her pale gold hair was
only faintly touched with silver, and her skin,
nurtured over the years and meticulously pro-
tected from the sun, had remarkably few lines

for a woman of her age. In the two years of her widowhood, Finn reflected with pride, there had been no shortage of escorts.

Edward returned with his drink, and they all toasted Harry, who flushed, looked away, and muttered something inaudible in acknowledgment.

'Too bad Jackie couldn't make it,' Edward commented. 'Bill has a weekend conference in Edinburgh, and she's gone up with him. She sent her best, Finn.'

Finlay turned to Hester. 'She never showed any interest in joining the firm, did she, Mother?'

Hester looked at him in surprise. 'Jacqueline? Not that I remember. What put that thought in your head?'

Edward laughed. 'Not "what", but "who". It was our chronicler, wasn't it, Finn?'

'Your *what*? Oh – that girl you mentioned, who's writing the article. Has she met Jacqueline?'

'Not yet,' Finlay replied, 'but she will; she wants to see everyone. It's the family that interests her.'

Hester raised her eyebrows. 'Even if we're not in the firm?'

'Yes; that was the point of my question. She was surprised no female members of the family had joined. It hadn't struck me before, but it does seem a bit odd, particularly these days.'

'We've all done our own thing,' Hester said

complacently.

'That's what I told her.'

'Didn't you say, Edward, that her name's Parish? She's not the biographer, by any chance?'

Edward looked surprised. 'I've no idea, but I shouldn't think so. She writes for *Chiltern Life*.'

'It's not mutually exclusive,' Hester pointed out. 'If she interviews me, I shall make a point of asking her.'

A waiter appeared at Edward's elbow to inform him their table was ready. They finished their drinks and followed him through to the restaurant, where they were shown to a window table. In daylight, the windows that made up this entire wall overlooked the golf course. Now, on a wet March evening, heavy curtains closed off the view.

The congestion in the car park was explained; every table was either occupied or reserved, and the room was filled with the hum of voices. Finlay was studying the menu when Anna suddenly touched his sleeve.

'Look who's just come in!' she said in a low voice.

He glanced up to see a man and woman being shown to a table not far from their own.

'Well, well,' he said softly.

Edward turned to look behind him, by which time the couple had seated themselves.

'Who was it?'

'Nigel de Salis and his wife.'

Hester gave an exclamation of annoyance.

'Who's Nigel de Salis?' Becca asked curiously.

'The man who broke up your uncle Nicholas's marriage,' her grandmother answered tightly.

'But not, apparently, his own,' Anna remarked.

'No; she took him back, more fool her. No pride, some women.'

'Perhaps she still loves him,' Becca said innocently, and Hester, nonplussed, changed the subject.

Finlay did not immediately join in. Mention of the breakdown of his cousin's marriage necessarily reminded him of his own. Its ending had been considerably less dramatic than Nick's: no passionate accusations, no lovers fleeing their respective marital homes. He and Ginnie had simply, over the years, grown apart, and the fact still hurt him. He'd had no news of her since the divorce, and wondered now if she'd remarried.

'Finn?'

Anna was smiling at him, and he saw she understood his momentary withdrawal.

'Sorry,' he said, 'I was miles away.'

'We were wondering if you've chosen your starter?'

He glanced back at the card in his hand. 'I'll go for the whitebait, please,' he said.

* * *

It was also raining in Tynecastle, and Cynthia's raincoat was glistening with moisture as she hugged them.

'Rona! It's been ages since we saw you! You're looking great!' She turned to Max. 'You too, you old reprobate! The car's in short-term parking; I'm afraid it'll mean a dash through the rain.'

'We won't melt,' Max assured her. 'How's the old man?'

'Looking forward to your visit. You'll see an improvement since you were last here; he's eating better, according to Mrs Pemberton, though he still has that cough. Paul's picking him up on his way home from work.'

They emerged from the airport building, opened their umbrellas, and hurried after Cynthia's small, round figure. The rain slanted down in the beams from the overhead lights and the ground was treacherous with puddles. The sanctuary of Cynthia's roomy car was more than welcome.

'The boys will be in for dinner,' she told them, as she slowed at the exit to slot money into the machine. 'Did I tell you Michael's bought a new car? It's his pride and joy, and I rather think, Max, he's hoping to persuade you to do a painting of it.'

'What kind is it?' Max asked guardedly.

'A red MG. He's taken photographs of it from every angle, for you to take back with you if

83

you agree.'

'I don't see why not,' Max said. 'It'll make a change from views of Buckfordshire and pretty debutantes.'

Cynthia laughed. 'Don't tell him I forewarned you.'

Paul's car was in the driveway when they arrived at the house, and Roland Allerdyce came into the hall to greet them. Despite Cynthia's optimistic assessment, Rona was shocked at the change in him. Though still tall and straight-backed, his features stood out prominently from his sunken cheeks and his clothes seemed to hang on him. But his grip was as strong as ever as he pulled her towards him for a fierce hug.

'Too long since I've seen you, my girl,' he said gruffly, before turning to take Max's hand.

Paul also came to welcome them, but his sons had not yet returned from work. 'Come in and get warm,' he said. 'It's a wild evening out there.'

Roland resumed his place on the sofa, and tapped the cushion beside him. 'Sit next to me, Rona,' he instructed, and, as she did so, enquired, 'That boy of mine looking after you all right?'

'We look after each other,' she answered, and he gave a bark of laughter.

'You modern young women! Independent as always. Mind you, it's no bad thing; I couldn't be doing with those shrinking violets, who took to their beds with smelling salts.'

'Really, Father!' Cynthia protested. 'What century were you living in?'

'All I'm saying is that on the whole I applaud the change, though it can be disconcerting when they decline to take your seat in a bus, or to allow you to open the door for them. Throwing out the baby with the bath water, I call it.'

'You can open the door for me any time,' Rona told him, patting his hand.

Catherine put the tray of coffee on the table and joined Tom on the sofa.

'I was just thinking,' she began.

'Uh-oh! What have you come up with now?'

'Nothing controversial, I hope. It's just that it's my birthday in a few weeks—'

'And you'd like the Kohinoor diamond?'

'Will you please let me finish! It occurred to me that now we've broken the ice with your family, it might be time for our respective clans to meet.' She glanced sideways at him as she poured the coffee. 'What do you think?'

'Might it be a bit soon? Lindsey's only just coming round.'

'For heaven's sake, Tom! At this rate, they'll meet for the first time at our wedding! Surely it's the ideal opportunity, and if we leave it much longer, Jenny mightn't feel up to making the effort. She'll be seven months by my birthday, as it is.'

Tom took the cup and saucer she handed him.

'Were you thinking of dinner here?'

'Either that, or out somewhere. If we met halfway, no one would have to travel too far.'

'There's not much of interest between here and Cricklehurst,' Tom pointed out. 'We'd do better going all the way, to the Golden Feather. You're sure of a good meal there, and Jenny'd have no travelling at all.'

'But it's a good hour's drive for the rest of us, which would make it late getting home.'

'How about lunch, then? That might suit her better anyway.'

Catherine brightened. 'Now that *is* a good idea. The only drawback to eating out is that it's Easter weekend, and the Feather might well be booked up. We ought to phone straight away and see if they can take us, before we start issuing invitations.'

'No sooner said than done.' Tom reached for the phone. 'What date are we talking about?'

'Preferably Saturday the fifteenth; otherwise, any date they're available.'

'Leave it to Jeeves,' Tom said.

Five

Eleven o'clock the next morning found Sarah Lacey on Avril's doorstep. Well-built without being overweight, she was wearing a denim jacket with matching skirt, and suede boots. Her mid-brown hair was drawn back in a low ponytail, accentuating the length of her face, and her eyes, meeting Avril's in frank appraisal, were a clear grey.

A very self-possessed young lady, Avril thought, registering her firm handshake.

'Do come in,' she said, feeling, as she often did, that her own small stature put her at a disadvantage. 'I'll show you the room first, and then, if you like it, we can discuss terms.'

She had made enquiries on the rates currently charged, and was confident that what she had in mind was a reasonable sum.

'Oh, it's lovely!' Sarah exclaimed involuntarily, as Avril stood aside for her to enter the guest room. 'What a pretty paper!'

Avril relaxed a little. 'I've tried to make it more of a bedsit,' she said, 'and the bathroom across the landing will be for your sole use.'

Sarah walked to the window and looked out.

'It's lovely having all the trees along the road, and, of course, great being so near the school. It can only be – what? – a five-minute walk?'

'About that,' Avril agreed, adding, as Sarah turned back into the room, 'I think you'll find there's plenty of storage space, with the chest of drawers and wardrobe.' She paused but could think of nothing further to add. 'Is there anything you'd like to ask?'

'No, it looks absolutely fine, thanks.'

'Then let's go down and discuss the details over coffee. Did you say you're in Stokely at the moment?' she asked when they were settled with their coffee cups.

'Yes; I've been living at home while I was at college.'

'So this is your first teaching post?'

Sarah nodded. 'I'm really looking forward to it.' She paused, eying the photographs on the corner table. 'Do you live here alone?'

Avril was a little disconcerted; foolishly, she hadn't anticipated the question. 'I do now, yes. My husband and I separated at the end of last year.'

Sarah nodded again, offering no comment.

'My two daughters live in Marsborough,' Avril added, almost defensively.

'I wish I'd had a sister, but I was an only one.'

'Your parents will miss you, then.'

'There's only my father; Mum died when I was a baby. He brought me up, with the help of a string of housekeepers.'

He was to be congratulated, Avril felt, on producing such a self-confident young woman under what couldn't have been easy circumstances.

The business arrangements were concluded briskly and amicably. Breakfast would be served in the dining room at eight o'clock, and Sarah could have the use of the kitchen until seven in the evening if she so wished, to cook and eat her meal. The rent would be paid in advance, and a month's notice would be required on either side. Sarah accepted the figure quoted, again without comment, and it was agreed she would move in two days before term started, which would be just after Easter.

The entire interview was over in half an hour, and as Avril closed the front door, she was left with mixed emotions. The girl was down-to-earth, confident, and pleasant enough, but somehow Avril could not imagine herself warming to her. Still, it was a business arrangement and there would be no call to socialize.

She returned to the sitting room and began to load the coffee cups on to a tray.

The weekend in Tynecastle passed pleasantly. Max and his father spent a considerable amount of time together – which had been the point of the exercise – and he was also taken for a spin in Michael's new car, the painting of which had been agreed. The two young men had plans for Saturday evening, but Cynthia had booked for the rest of them to see the latest Alan Bennett play, which they all enjoyed. On the Sunday morning, Paul drove Rona and Max up to the moors for a bracing walk while Cynthia prepared lunch, and they flew back later that afternoon.

'Did Roland really seem better than when you last saw him?' Rona asked anxiously, as they drove home from the airport.

'I think so, though not as much as Cyn's reports led me to expect. Still, she sees him day by day, so is better able to judge. I wish he could get rid of that cough, but it seems the doctor's not too worried about it. One good thing – I persuaded him to show me the canvas he's working on, and it's powerful stuff. Quite up to standard, which was a relief. With his being below par, I was worried it mightn't have been, and nothing would bring him down faster than a waning of his talent. His work's all-important to him, and always has been.'

Gus, who'd been lodging at the vet's, gave them his usual enthusiastic welcome, and Max took him out for a quick walk while Rona unpacked.

'There's a message from Pops,' she told Max when he returned half an hour later. 'We're invited to lunch at the Golden Feather on Easter Saturday. Apparently it's Catherine's birthday, and her son and daughter-in-law will be there.'

'That's a fair hike to go for lunch; let's hope

it's a good one. We've nothing else on, have we?'

'Not according to the diary.' She paused. 'I hope Linz is OK about it.'

'Why the hell shouldn't she be?' Max demanded. 'Surely she's got over her sulks by now.'

Rona bit her lip, regretting her unthinking comment. Though wanting to defend her twin, she'd no wish to start an argument with Max. 'I'm sure she'll be fine,' she said quickly. 'She was when we had dinner with Pops, wasn't she?'

Max glanced at her, pulled her against him, and gave her a squeeze. 'Of course she was,' he said.

Rona wasn't left long in doubt about her sister's reaction. As she sat down at her desk the next morning, the phone rang.

'I see the extended family is reaching out its tentacles,' Lindsey said, without preamble.

'One way of putting it, I suppose.'

'How else? These people aren't claiming relationship with us, are they? Step-brother-and-sister-in-law or something?'

'Heavens, I'd never thought of that! I suppose, when Catherine becomes our stepmother, they will be.'

'God!' said Lindsey theatrically. 'As if life isn't complicated enough.'

Rona said cautiously, 'You don't sound in the

best of spirits after your weekend tryst. How did it go?'

'It went.'

'That's all you're going to say? You and Hugh aren't all lovey-dovey again?'

'Lucy,' Lindsey said acidly, 'ever the soul of propriety, put us in separate bedrooms at opposite ends of the landing.'

Rona laughed. 'I hope Hugh's feet didn't get cold!'

'He got cold feet, all right,' Lindsey answered tartly, 'but not from coming down the corridor.'

'You mean he didn't...?'

'That's exactly what I mean. What the hell's he playing at, Ro? He's been trying to get me into bed for months, and then, when the opportunity arises, he backs down.'

'But you've refused him up to now. Perhaps he's finally accepted it.'

'Then why invite me down in the first place?'

'I'd guess,' Rona said slowly, 'it was to make you feel exactly the way you're feeling now.'

'The crafty devil!' Lindsey said after a minute.

'Did you let him see you were miffed?'

'No, of course not. I've got *some* pride.'

'Then it'll be interesting to see what his next move is.'

'If he bothers to make one.'

'Oh, he will,' Rona assured her. 'Believe me, he will.'

'I'll keep you posted, but I have to go now;

92

I'm phoning from the office.'

'Linz – you will be there on the fifteenth, won't you?'

'Oh, I'll be there. I can't wait to meet my new relations.'

With which, sarcasm and all, Rona had to be content.

The next phone call, an hour or so later, was, to Rona's surprise, from Finlay Curzon.

'I persuaded my mother to unearth some old photo albums,' he said. 'There are several prints of my grandparents, and even a sepia one of Great-grandfather. I thought you'd be interested to see them.'

'Oh, I should,' Rona told him. 'Thank you.'

'I'll be coming into Marsborough later today. Perhaps I could hand them over then?'

'If it's no trouble, that would be great.'

'The thing is, they're fairly heavy; is there somewhere we could unload them straight from one car into the other?'

'That could be a problem; parking's quite tricky in town.' She hesitated. 'The simplest thing might be for you to bring them to the house. It's pretty central, and during the day it's easy enough to park outside.'

'Right, I'll do that. About three o'clock? I have the address from your letter.'

'Three would be fine; I'll see you then. Thanks very much, Mr Curzon.'

'Finlay,' he corrected, and put down the

93

phone.

Rona took out the family tree she'd brought back from Chilswood and spread it on her desk. His grandfather and great-grandfather, he'd said. That would be – her finger moved up from his entry – Spencer Curzon, the wearer, she remembered, of a watch and chain, and his father, George – who'd actually been the son of Samuel, founder of the firm. The albums would indeed be a gold mine.

The final call of the morning was from Avril. 'All fixed,' she announced with satisfaction. 'I become a landlady on Tuesday the eighteenth of April.'

'Well done, Mum! What's she like, your new lodger?'

'Her name's Sarah Lacey. She's all right, but she struck me as being very sure of herself. I don't think we'll have much difficulty keeping our respective distances.'

'Well, you don't want her in your pocket, do you?'

'Indeed I don't,' Avril agreed, though she added disconcertingly, 'She might thaw a little when we get to know each other.'

Thaw? Rona pondered when her mother had rung off. She'd thought Avril had simply wanted someone in the house, a goal she was on the point of achieving. Now, though, she wondered uncomfortably if, subconsciously, she'd been hoping for a surrogate daughter, someone who would come in from work and perch on the kitchen table, telling her about the day's doings. Which was not a landlady/lodger relationship at all, nor one, it seemed, that this Sarah Lacey envisaged.

Finlay rang the doorbell at exactly three o'clock.

'What a fabulous house!' he commented, when Rona answered it.

'We like it, yes. There aren't many rooms, but that's our fault; we knocked down walls to make space.' She paused, eying the car parked at the gate. 'Shall I help you carry in the albums?'

'No, don't worry, I can manage. I was just checking I had the right house.'

She waited while he returned to the car and retrieved six or seven large books from the boot.

'It's very kind of you to go to this trouble,' she told him as he came into the hall with them.

'No problem. Where would you like them?'

'If you'll leave them on the bottom stair, I'll take them up when I go.'

'Better, surely, if I carry them up for you?'

'Well – thanks.'

She led the way to the study and he followed her, laying the albums, under her direction, on a side table.

'You're well kitted out here, aren't you?' he remarked, noting the small fridge and electric hob.

'The kitchen's down in the basement,' Rona explained. 'This saves me having to run up and down two flights of stairs every time I want a drink.'

He walked to the window and looked down at the tiny paved garden with its statues and containers.

'Another good idea. Much easier to manage than grass.' He turned to her with a smile. 'Not thinking of selling, are you?'

She smiled back. 'Not a chance!' She opened the topmost album, to be confronted with a wedding group, circa 1900. 'I'd need permission to reproduce these in the article.'

'You have it. Ninety per cent of them are taken by family members, and the professional ones are out of copyright. I just thought it would help, to visualize the people you write about – as, presumably, one can with biographies.' He glanced at her. '*Do* you write biographies? My mother was wondering.'

'I do, yes, under another hat.'

'You didn't mention them in your CV.'

'They weren't relevant.' She glanced back at the album. 'There's rather a dearth of names, isn't there? The people who stick in the photos know so well who everyone is, they don't bother noting it down, which leads to a lot of frustration for their descendants.'

'I wouldn't be much help there, but my mother could fill you in. I suppose you'll be wanting to see her?'

'I'd like to see everyone who's willing, principally to gather as much family lore as possible.' She closed the album. 'Would you like some tea?'

'Thanks, that would be welcome.'

Gus was awaiting them at the foot of the stairs, tail wagging furiously. Finn went down on his haunches to stroke him, and Gus, embarrassingly effusive as always, licked his face.

'I'm sorry,' Rona apologized, taking hold of his collar and pulling him back.

'Don't be; I'm fond of dogs. We had one when I was married, but he was more my wife's really, and when we split, she was granted custody.' The quirk to his mouth made Rona unsure whether or not he was serious.

She pushed open the sitting room door. 'If you'd like to wait in here, I'll put the kettle on.'

When she returned minutes later with the tray, he was studying the group of modern paintings, displayed to perfection on the plain duck-egg walls. He turned as she came in.

'What an interesting collection.'

'They're my husband's; he's an artist himself.'

'Yes, you mentioned that. Are any of these his?'

'No, he's very chary of hanging his own work. We have a couple in the bedroom, but most of them are commissions, anyway.'

He looked about him at the marble fireplace, the antique side tables and comfortable sofas and chairs, the shelves of assorted books, and the richly curtained windows at either end. 'This is one of the rooms you enlarged? It's charming.'

She nodded. 'The back half was a dining room, but we prefer it this way. We always eat in the kitchen, even when we have people to dinner.'

'And, as you also told us, your husband's the chef,' Finn observed, seating himself at her invitation.

'It seems to go together; his arrangement of food on the plate is often worthy of a photograph.' She glanced at Finlay as she poured the tea. 'I told him how shocked you all were that I don't cook.'

'Thereby enhancing our reputation as dinosaurs.'

'Oh, I never implied that!'

'Chauvinists, then.'

'Look, I did apologize. I can't keep doing it.'

'There's no need. The fact that no women in the family *wanted* to join the firm is immaterial. I doubt if they were ever asked.'

'Were they strong personalities, those women? You said your sister is.'

'Well, as I told you, the earlier ones disappeared off the map – or at least the family tree – so I can't say, though my uncles might be able to enlighten you. I do know Grandma Florence was quite a tartar; my father used to tell us how she ruled the roost when he was young.'

'I look forward to seeing her photo. And your mother?'

'My mother was an opera singer in her youth, with the temperament that goes with it. We had to watch our Ps and Qs. Come to that, we still do! As to Aunts Sybil and Elizabeth, you'll have to ask my cousins. As far as Edward and I are concerned, they've always been pussycats.'

Rona stirred her tea reflectively. 'So you maintain none of the women wanted to join the firm; what about the men? Did they have a choice?'

'An interesting question. To the best of my knowledge there were no dissenters, but then the choice of careers on offer is pretty wide – accountancy, design, management, marketing, product co-ordinating – there's room for them all. And now we have computer-aided design, we need IT specialists as well.'

'You never had any doubts yourself?'

He shook his head emphatically. 'It was all I ever wanted to do, go to the factory with Dad. Edward and I used to pester him to take us in the school holidays, and we'd spend hours watching the different processes in action, particularly the painting and decorating. I still find it fascinating.

'But as I mentioned last time,' he continued, 'we might well have to revise our men-only attitude, since Edward's the only one of our generation to produce a son. Oliver and Sally have three daughters, Sam and Emma one, and

Nick and I have completely let the side down, with no children at all.'

'Has your sister any sons?'

'Three, yes. No justice, is there? We might end up press-ganging them!'

That there was time for both Finlay and Nick to produce sons of their own, was, Rona felt, not a point she could mention. The past was safer ground.

'So have there been any scandals in the last hundred-plus years? They always liven up a series!'

Finn laughed. 'Again, you'll need to ask the older generation, but to the best of my knowledge, we've all behaved admirably, apart from old George, who was considered a bit of a rake in his time.' He gave her a crooked smile, and she thought again how attractive he was. 'If there *are* any skeletons,' he added, 'I have a feeling you'll unearth them. It might be safer to confine you to writing about the firm, rather than the family. Only joking!' he assured her, seeing her startled glance.

'Your website's full of the firm's history,' Rona pointed out, 'but with all due respect, people are more interesting than plates! I think that's why the series has attracted so much interest; the firms and businesses I write about are household names, but no one knows anything about the people behind them, who founded them and built them up. It's the human element that's so intriguing; who married whom, how many children they had, and so on. And if there's a scandal buried somewhere in the past, so much the better. As long, that is, as it's far enough in the past not to hurt anyone still alive.'

Which, she thought soberly, hadn't always been the case.

Finlay got to his feet. 'Well, I promised to help you, and I shall, so let's hope you don't unearth too many skeletons. Now, I really must be getting back. Thanks for the tea.

'When are you going to pay us another visit?' he asked as Rona opened the front door for him.

'I'm not sure. I'll be spending the next day or two going through the albums and no doubt making out a list of questions. Then I hope to start on the family interviews, if that's all right, beginning with the older members.'

He took out his wallet and handed her his business card. 'My mobile number and email address. Let me know who you want to see, and I can advise you the best way to contact them.' He held out his hand. 'Goodbye, Rona. And good luck with the research.'

'Thank you. And, again, for the albums. I'll be in touch.'

She waited while he walked down the path, got into his car, and, with a raised hand, drove off down the road. Then she closed the door, feeling oddly flat. Were she not a happily married woman, she reflected, she could be in danger of falling for Finlay Curzon. And that was quite a thought. Unlike Lindsey, who, since her teens, had fallen in and out of love with monotonous regularity, there had only ever been two men who mattered in her life: Max, and Gavin Ridgeway, now married to her closest friend.

Which reflection didn't help with the present circumstances. There was no denying the spurt of excitement Finlay's presence evoked, and furthermore she suspected it was mutual. It was a situation that called for careful handling, and was one reason why she was in no hurry to return to Chilswood.

'You went all the way to Marsborough?' Edward said, with lifted eyebrow.

'It's not exactly the ends of the earth, and I thought the old family albums would interest her. Anyway, I wanted a word with Philip Yarborough at Netherby's. They've put in a large order for the Chiltern range.'

The fact that customers were usually contacted by telephone or email was glossed over by both of them.

Edward said neutrally, 'His wife's ill, isn't she? I heard she was with her parents in Norwich.'

'That's right; it's a mental illness, but she's doing well and he's hoping she'll be home in the summer.'

There was a pause. Then Edward said bluntly, 'You like her, don't you? Rona Parish?'

'That obvious?'

'To me, it is. She's an attractive girl, no denying it, and with plenty of character, to boot. But we've been dangling attractive girls in front of you ever since Ginnie left, and not getting any response. What's different about this one?'

Finn shrugged. 'We seem to be on the same wavelength, that's all. Don't worry, I shan't let it get out of hand. She's married, after all.'

'Ah yes, the absentee husband. Making her – what was the phrase Nick coined? – a class widow.'

'Absentee or not, his influence in the house is very noticeable. It's an amazing place they've got there; pure Georgian from the outside, and though they've altered the interior, it's still totally in keeping. There's definitely an artist's hand in it.'

Edward leaned back in his chair. 'So what's the next move?'

'She wants to interview Ma and the aunts and uncles. Then, no doubt, the rest of us. It's a family history she's after, rather than the firm's.'

'Well, you're the marketing man, but it can't do any harm, can it?'

'Of course not. On the contrary, it should do us a power of good. You know what they say about publicity.'

'That there's no bad?' Edward grimaced. 'Our forebears mightn't agree with you, but that's a closed book. As far as the articles go, I'd say we've everything to gain.'

'Which is why I'm giving her a helping hand,' Finn said, holding his brother's sceptical gaze.

'Fine. Let me know if there's anything I can do.'

Finlay nodded. 'Thanks for Friday evening, by the way. It was great.'

'Yes, everyone seemed to enjoy it, despite the spectre at the feast.'

'Nigel de Salis? I shouldn't lose any sleep over him. Relations between us are on a strictly business level and he *is* a good customer. Everything else is water under the bridge.'

'Let's hope there's never a flood tide,' Edward commented.

Six

Rona spent the next two days going through the Curzon family albums. In some instances she was able to attach names to anonymous figures by dint of their appearing on another page, duly annotated. The album she'd first glanced at, opening with the wedding group, wasn't the earliest chronologically, and to her delight she came across a faded print of Samuel Curzon himself. Though obviously taken in a studio, the outlines of the factory had been artistically sketched in the background. It was dated 1860. The unknown compilers of the albums, though sometimes negligent in the naming of their subjects, were meticulous in their dating.

She worked with the family tree open beside her, ticking names on it as she discovered corresponding likenesses. Some photographs were so faded that they'd need a lot of work to make them clear enough to reproduce, but then not many would be used in the articles anyway. As Finn had foreseen, their chief advantage was to her personally, in bringing to life the people she'd be writing about.

The most recent album covered a longer

period than the others, with only a few photos taken after the end of the 1950s. This could have been either because the Curzons became less interested in recording events, or because slides took over from prints at about that time. However, it did contain one of particular interest, showing three fair-haired children on a beach, squinting against the sun. It was labelled: *Edward, Jacqueline and Finlay. August 1969*. Rona studied it for several minutes. The two little boys, aged, she estimated, ten and six, were in swimming trunks, their legs caked with sand. Their sister, between them in size and presumably also in age, was wearing a large sun hat that left part of her face in shadow, and appeared more interested in her ice cream cone than in the photographer.

Rona flicked through the remaining pages, but there were no further pictures of the children, and in fact the last few leaves were left blank. There might, of course, be later albums, but she was aware of her disappointment. In particular, she'd like to have seen the woman Finlay had married and later divorced.

She clamped down on the thought, and was relieved when the phone on her desk broke the silence with its warbling.

'Ro? Reporting back as promised. Hugh phoned last night.'

'And?'

'Invited me out to dinner.'

'You're going?'

'Yes, though I turned down the first two dates he suggested. No point in seeming too eager.'

'*Are* you eager, though? To get involved with him again?'

'We're already involved.'

'To go further, then.'

Lindsey's sigh came over the wires. 'I admit I was annoyed he didn't even *try* to make a move at the weekend. If he had, I doubt if I could have held out. You know the effect he has on me.'

Not a satisfactory response. After a moment, Rona asked, 'And Jonathan?'

'Is anxious to continue as before.'

'And how do you feel about that?'

'God, I don't know. I'm tempted there, too.'

'So your conscience has gone into hibernation?'

'Only partially.' Another sigh. 'The trouble is that there are complications with both of them. What I could really do with is someone completely new.'

'Oh, yes; I'd forgotten the latest object of interest. Any more sightings of him?'

'No, but I think he'll be at a party I'm going to on Saturday.'

'Going to with whom?'

'It's not that kind of party. I'll go along by myself, then I'm not beholden to anyone.' Lindsey paused. 'How about the two attractive men you had lunch with last week?'

Rona bit her lip. 'One of them was round here

on Monday. He brought me some photo albums to look at.'

'Makes a change from etchings.'

'Lindsey, for God's sake!'

'All right, all right. No need to snap. I was joking, but it seems I touched a nerve.'

'Of course you didn't; it's simply that your one-track mind gets a bit wearing.'

'Beg pardon, I'm sure.'

Rona drew a deep breath. 'Sorry, Linz. I've been poring too long over these dusty books and am in need of some fresh air. You're not free for a cup of tea at the Gallery, I suppose?'

'Sorry, I can't. I've an appointment in ten minutes.'

'Never mind, I have to go out anyway. Gus needs his walk, and I must get the ingredients for tonight's dinner, or Max will kill me. Good luck with your men – all of them. Keep me posted.'

She put down the phone and stretched luxuriously. Then she pushed back her chair and ran down the stairs. Gus, asleep on the front door mat, looked up, tail wagging hopefully.

'Yes, we're going out,' she told him. 'And I hope I'll be in a better mood by the time we get back.'

The wind was strong and unseasonably cold, and Rona's head was down as she battled against it on her way back along Guild Street. Which is why she had no warning when someone suddenly catapulted out of a shop doorway, cannoning into her and knocking her shopping bag out of her hand. She stumbled and almost fell as Gus, taking avoiding action, succeeded in winding his lead round her legs. Then a hand caught her arm, steadying her, and a breathless voice exclaimed, 'Oh, I'm terribly sorry! Are you all right?'

She looked up into the concerned face of a young woman, who took the lead out of her hand, untangled it, and handed it back.

'*I'm* all right,' Rona said ruefully, 'but I doubt if my shopping is. There are eggs in there.'

The young woman bent down, retrieved the bag, and peered anxiously into it. 'I'm afraid the flour bag's split,' she said apologetically. 'I'm not sure about the eggs, but nothing's seeped out of the box. I really am most dreadfully sorry.' She opened her handbag and took out a purse. 'Let me pay you for the damage. It was entirely my fault.'

Rona shook her head. 'There's no need for that; it was an accident, and they're easily replaced.'

'Then at least let me buy you a cup of tea. I must do something to make amends!'

Rona, who by this time was more than ready for some tea, hesitated, and the girl, encouraged, went on, 'There's a café just along here, isn't there? I passed it as I went up the road.'

They were, in fact, almost opposite the iron staircase leading to the Gallery.

109

'Please!' her assailant insisted, adding with a little laugh, 'Apart from wanting to apologize, I'm a stranger in town, and it would be nice to have someone to chat to.'

There was something immediately engaging about her, and Rona found herself smiling back. 'You've talked me into it!' she said. 'The café's just up these steps.'

The Gallery was, as usual, crowded, but their arrival coincided with a couple vacating one of the window tables, and they were able to claim it.

'My name's Julia Teale,' the girl volunteered, as they seated themselves.

'Rona Parish.'

'I'm glad to meet you, Rona, even if the meeting itself left a lot to be desired. I'm notoriously clumsy; my ex always said I couldn't walk across a room without bumping into every piece of furniture.'

'There's no real harm done,' Rona said. Now that she had a chance to look properly at her companion, she liked what she saw. Julia Teale had soft dark hair that the wind had freed from the comb that had held it, so that tendrils curled down either side of her face. Her eyes were wide and deep blue, and her skin flawless. It occurred to Rona that hers was just the kind of face Max would like to paint.

The waitress took their order – tea and cakes for two – and as she moved away, Rona began, 'You say you're new to the area?'

'Yes, I only arrived yesterday. I'm still trying to find my way around.'

'Is this a permanent move, or are you just visiting?'

'Actually, it's my job: I work for a market research firm, and have to do some initial fact-finding. I'll be here for a week or ten days this first visit, depending on how things pan out. Incidentally, could you recommend somewhere reasonable to stay? I doubt if expenses will cover the Clarendon, which is where I spent last night.'

'Well, you did choose the town's premier hotel. There are several others dotted around. How central do you have to be?'

'No problem there; I have my car.'

'The Lansdowne and the Pierpoint are both in Alban Road, which runs across the top of Guild Street, or there's the Irving in Windsor Way, in the opposite direction. That's more of a commercial hotel, but perhaps that's what you're looking for?'

Julia made a little face. 'Between you and me, I hate *all* hotels. I spend far too much time in them, and they all seem totally soulless.'

Their tea arrived, and Julia, who appeared to have taken charge, passed the cake tray to Rona. 'Have you lived here long?' she asked.

'All my life, apart from a stint at university.'

'Lucky you. I should think it was a lovely place to grow up.'

'It was, yes. Where do you come from?'

111

'Oh, I'm like the Flying Dutchman. I never settle long anywhere, but I was born in Dorset, and my family are still there. My work takes me all over the place – abroad, quite often.'

'It sounds as though you're in the wrong job, if you hate hotels!'

Julia laughed. 'I love the job itself, so I have to put up with them.' She poured the tea. 'Anyway, what kind of work do you do, that leaves you free to shop at three in the afternoon? Or are you a lady of leisure?'

'No, I'm a freelance journalist, so I set my own hours. I've been working all morning, and needed a break.'

'You're on the local paper?'

'No, a glossy magazine. Out monthly, so it's not too hectic.'

'You mean like *Vogue* or *Good House-keeping*?'

'Not quite so high-flown; *Chiltern Life*. If you don't come from round here, you've probably never heard of it.'

'Afraid not, but I'll look out for it. Have you anything in the current edition?'

'Actually, yes; I'm doing a series on local businesses.'

'That sounds interesting. I'll certainly buy a copy.'

An idea had occurred to Rona, and she was wondering if it would be feasible. She bent to pick up her bag. 'Would you excuse me a minute?'

'Of course.'

In the cloakroom, she took out her mobile and dialled her mother's number.

'Mum, it's me,' she said, when her mother answered. 'When did you say your lodger's due?'

'Tuesday the eighteenth. Why?'

'But the room's ready now?'

'Yes. What is this?'

'I've just met someone who's here on business and who hates hotels. How would you feel about putting her up? She'll be here for a maximum of ten days, so she'll be out of the way before What's-her-name arrives.'

'Oh Rona, I really don't know...'

'She seems very nice.'

'She mightn't want to come.'

'I bet she'll jump at the chance. What do you think? It would break you in gently.'

'All right; you can mention it to her, and see what she says. As long as she's out before Easter.'

'Thanks, Mum. I'll ring you back.'

Rona returned to the table, to find Julia making friends with Gus, who was in his customary place underneath it.

'What a well-trained dog you have,' she said. 'What's his name?'

Rona told her. 'Look, I've had an idea,' she began. 'But you must say if it doesn't appeal to you.'

Julia straightened and looked at her enquiringly.

'My mother is just starting a bed and break-fast business. Her first guest won't be coming till after Easter, and as you hate hotels so much, I was wondering if you'd like to go to her? It's a very nice bedsit, complete with TV and every-thing.'

Julia's face lit up. 'Wouldn't she mind?'

'I phoned her just now. She says you'll be welcome if you'd like to go, but there's no pressure.'

'But Rona, that's *wonderful*! Thanks so much for thinking of it.'

'How long are you booked in for at the Clarendon?'

'Only last night and tonight. As I said, I was looking for an alternative.'

'Then suppose we meet at the hotel after work tomorrow, and you can follow me in your car out to Belmont. It's about a twenty-minute drive, if that's all right?'

'More than all right. I really am grateful – and I'm no longer sorry I bumped into you!'

'She tried again to pay for the eggs and flour,' Rona finished, after relating the incident to Max that evening, 'but of course I wouldn't let her. She's really nice, Max.'

'Just as well it wasn't Friday she bumped into you; you'd have had more expensive items in your bag.' And, at her blank look, he added, 'Barnie and Dinah are coming. Had you for-gotten?'

114

'Lord, yes, I had! What with concentrating on the Curzon project, and then all this, it had gone completely out of my head. Have you decided what we'll be eating?'

'I was thinking of sesame chilli prawns as a starter, followed by pork chops *en papillote*, with mushrooms and cream. How does that grab you?'

'Sounds delicious.'

'And some kind of roulade for dessert. I'm still working on that.'

'Almond and apricot? That always goes down well.'

'OK, fine. How about making a note of what we'll need? It'll save time later.'

'I must warn Julia to buy something for her evening meal,' Rona remarked as she sat down at the table with pen and paper. 'And to leave the kitchen clear for Mum from seven onwards. That's part of the deal. She has a lovely face, Max.'

'Your mother?'

'Idiot! Too bad she's not here longer, or you could paint her.'

'My workload's full enough at the moment. I still have to find a way of fitting in Michael's MG.'

'Just a thought,' Rona said. 'OK, master chef, my pen is poised. Shoot.'

By lunchtime the next day, Rona had extracted all she needed from the albums. She now had a mental picture of several of the dignitaries who'd built up the pottery, and had earmarked two or three photographs for use in the articles. There'd been no arrangement for the albums' return; presumably she'd take them with her on her next visit. In the meantime, she must get down to meeting those older members of the family who were still alive.

She stared for several minutes at Finlay's embossed card, propped up against her pen-holder. Better to email rather than phone, she decided; then he can email back with the details she requested.

She went online and typed quickly. *The albums have been a great help, thank you. I should now be most grateful to have contact details for your mother, and also for Mr and Mrs Charles, and Mr and Mrs James, Curzon. Perhaps you could let me know whether they'd prefer a letter or phone call in the first instance. Best wishes, Rona.*

His reply came within the half-hour. The Charles Curzons were apparently on the point of moving, and though he supplied the new address, he suggested she delay contacting them for at least ten days. The addresses and phone numbers of his mother and Uncle James were also given, with the opinion that, since they already knew of her involvement, a phone call was all that would be needed. He ended: *Please let me know if there's any other way I can be of help. Regards, Finlay.*

Deciding there was no time like the present, Rona lifted the phone and punched in the first number.

Elizabeth Curzon turned as her husband came into the room.

'The girl Sam told us about has just phoned; she wants to meet us.'

James raised an eyebrow. 'What girl is that, exactly?'

'The journalist,' Elizabeth said impatiently. 'You know, the one who's going to write about the firm.'

'So did you make an appointment?'

'Yes, for tomorrow morning. That's all right, isn't it?'

'As long as it doesn't go on too long; I'm playing golf at two. Why does she want to see me, anyway? It's not as though I'm actively involved any more.'

'It's the family history she's interested in, and memories of the old days.'

'Well, my memory's not what it was. Not sure I'll be much help to her.'

'That's nonsense,' Elizabeth said roundly. 'You and Charles have a wealth of stories about your father, and the innovations he introduced.'

James glanced at the grandfather clock, which was gearing up to chime midday. 'Talking of Charles, I wonder how he and Sybil are getting on.'

'No doubt we'll get a blow-by-blow account

over supper.'

'Awful upheaval,' James continued, 'moving house at their age. So much to sort through and throw away.'

'Perhaps we should be thinking of doing the same; "down-sizing", I believe they call it now.'

'Not on your life!' James declared. 'When I leave this house, it will be feet first.'

'Coppins sounds very pleasant,' Elizabeth said pensively. 'And the garden here really is on the large side.'

'Jackson keeps it trim enough, and you know you'd miss the fresh vegetables. In any case, the last thing we want to do is trot along in Charles's wake. He wouldn't thank us for it, mark my words.'

'There are other places beside Coppins,' his wife pointed out. 'I'm not saying there's any immediate rush, just don't close your mind to the possibility. If I'm honest, I'm beginning to find the stairs rather a trial. A bungalow or ground-floor flat might be a very sensible move.'

James drew his bushy eyebrows together, un-comfortable at this reminder of time passing. 'Shouldn't be surprised if Charles and Sybil have second thoughts in a month or two, and regret the move.'

Elizabeth didn't reply. She had planted the seed in his mind, and was content for the moment to let it germinate.

Julia was awaiting Rona in the lounge of the Clarendon. Beside her was a small wheeled suitcase and, laid on top of it, two cellophane-wrapped bouquets.

She stood up as Rona walked in, and handed her one. 'For you, and the other's for your mother,' she said. 'As an expression of my thanks.'

'Oh, Julia, they're lovely, but you really shouldn't have. Thank you very much.'

Julia pulled up the handle of her case. 'By the way, what's your mother's name? I forgot to ask.'

'The same as mine,' Rona replied, her nose still buried in the bouquet. 'Parish is my maiden name, which I use professionally.' She smiled. 'In fact, most of the time, to be honest. It's who I *am*.'

'Good for you. So what's your husband called?'

'Max Allerdyce.'

Julia frowned. 'That sounds familiar. Should it?'

'It depends. He's an artist, so he's occasionally mentioned in the press.'

'Perhaps that's where I've heard it.'

'I meant to say: you do realize Mum only does bed and breakfast?'

Julia nodded. 'I bought myself something for supper, in the hope I'll be able to cook it there.'

'That's a relief; I should have warned you. Yes, you'll have the use of the kitchen till seven. It has a table, so you can eat there too if you prefer, and keep the cooking smells out of your room. OK, let's go. I parked behind the hotel; I presume that's where your car is?'

Guild Street was snarled up with rush-hour traffic, and the first part of their journey was frustratingly slow. Rona, anxious that other cars might insert themselves between them, kept an eye on the rear-view mirror in case Julia fell too far behind, and was relieved, as Guild Street turned into Belmont Road and the traffic eased, to see she was still on her tail. From there, they were able to proceed at a more normal speed, and reached Maple Drive a few minutes later.

Avril seemed the more nervous of the two, Rona thought as she introduced them. It was an odd experience, seeing her mother and the house she'd grown up in through Julia's eyes, and she felt a stab of fierce protectiveness for them both. Julia, however, seemed delighted with everything, and certainly her presentation of the bouquet eased the situation. At Avril's invitation, it was Rona who went upstairs with her and showed her the room.

'I still think of it as Grandma's,' Rona admitted, 'but it's had a considerable revamp in the last month or two, bringing it much more up to date.'

'It's lovely,' Julia enthused. 'It feels like home already. I'm sure when your mother's proper guest arrives, she'll love it.'

'I'll leave you to unpack, then. But bear in mind that it's almost six o'clock. How long will your supper take?'

'Don't worry, I shan't blot my copybook on my first evening. I purposely chose a quickie for tonight. Goodbye, Rona, and thanks again. I'll be in touch.'

Rona went downstairs, sought out her mother, and kissed her cheek.

Avril seemed surprised but gratified. 'What was that for?'

'To say thanks for having her. She's sweet, isn't she?'

'She seems very nice, and it was kind of her to bring flowers.'

'As I said, knowing she's here for only a week or so will break you in gently, and give you a chance to pick up on anything that might need adjusting.'

'The marmalade pot will be christened tomorrow,' Avril said with a smile.

'Good! I'll think of it as I dig mine out of the jar! I must be going, Mum; I've an interview in the morning, and I need to list the things to ask.'

'The Curzons?'

'Some of them, yes. James and Elizabeth. Have you met them?'

'On a couple of occasions, but it was Charles who your father knew best.'

'What are they like?'

Avril considered. 'Elizabeth struck me as a bit

121

severe. Tall and thin, with very short grey hair. James, on the other hand, gives rather a bumbling impression, but that's just a front. Tom said he doesn't miss a trick.'

'Fine. Armed with prior knowledge, I'll know how to approach them. They're Sam's parents, aren't they?'

'That's right. According to Sybil, it was a difficult birth, and Elizabeth couldn't have any more children. It was quite a blow, I believe.'

'Lucky, in that case, that she had a son,' Rona commented, still critical of the Curzon criterion. She picked up her handbag. 'I'll phone you in a day or two, to see how things are going. And thanks again, Mum, for taking Julia in.'

'I'm sure we'll get along fine. In fact, from first impressions, I think I'll feel more at ease with her than with Sarah Lacey.'

Lying in the familiar bed in a strange room, Sybil felt drained to the point of exhaustion. The move had been a two-day operation, the men having completed a large proportion of the packing the previous day. But complications had arisen, since the contents of the house were to be split between a variety of destinations. Some furniture was to go to Oliver, some to Nicholas, and the pieces they were undecided about to a storage depot. Frederick's desk and a few other items were earmarked for the museum, and all that remained had come here to Coppins.

Even after such a wide dispersal, Sybil felt the flat was bursting at the seams, and at least a dozen packing cases were stacked in the garage, awaiting her sons' arrival at the weekend to help unpack them.

Despite her conviction of the rightness of the move, it had been depressing to see the old house stripped to its bones. The shapes on bare walls where pictures had hung gave it a forlorn air which, as they finally drove away, had brought tears to her eyes. It had, after all, been their home through good times and bad for the last forty years, and she was grateful to it.

She turned her head as Charles came into the room, feeling a stab of worry at his drawn face. She reached out a hand to him.

'All right, darling?'

'I shall be,' he replied, taking it in both his own, 'once we get settled in.'

'I hope you haven't overdone it. There was no need, you know, to help the men as much as you did.'

'Well, that young lad seemed a bit cack-handed and I didn't want the family heirlooms spilling out on to the path.'

Sybil smiled. 'I'm sure he knew what he was doing.'

Her eyes moved critically round the new room. Their bedroom furniture looked over-large in these surroundings, and it might well be necessary to replace it with smaller pieces. Time enough for that, though.

'Thank God for James and Elizabeth,' she said. 'That meal was our salvation. I couldn't even have found the pans, let alone cook.'

'Things will sort themselves out in the morning. But yes, it was good of them. Quite apart from the meal, it was a relief to be able to relax in a room where everything was in place and there was a conspicuous lack of packing cases.'

'You're not going to do any more tonight, are you?'

'No. I intend to have a long, hot bath, in the hope of forestalling any aches and pains tomorrow.'

'I was too tired even for that. I'll have mine in the morning.'

'Well, the worst is over, and at least we're here.' He bent over and kissed her. 'Goodnight, my love. Sleep well in your new home.'

'And you,' she murmured. But her eyes were already closing.

Seven

By the time the Trents arrived for supper on Friday evening, Rona felt she'd had enough of the Curzons for one week.

'I'm building up a comprehensive file on them,' she told Barnie and Dinah, as they sat over drinks while Max put the final touches to the meal. 'I went on a factory tour last week, and had lunch with the present generation. Since then, I've been immersed in old family albums. Some of them go back to the eighteen hundreds, but they came to a dead halt around nineteen-sixty.'

'Any worth reproducing?' Barnie asked.

'A few, yes; principally one of Samuel, the founder, looking very solid and prosperous in his frock coat. Then today, to round off the week, I went to Nettleton, to meet the James Curzons.'

'Were they amenable to your questions?'

'Yes, despite first impressions, they were quite forthcoming.'

Dinah laughed. 'Despite first impressions?'

'Well, they both looked rather fierce. James has thick, beetle eyebrows and a disconcerting habit of peering at you from underneath them, and when he speaks it's like a machine gun being rattled off.'

'Good heavens! And his wife?'

'Tall and thin, with a very lined face and severely short grey hair. However, she was much nicer than she appeared, especially when she discovered I was Tom Parish's daughter. She dug out a few photos of her own to show me, and once I'd persuaded them to open up, they'd lots of stories about James's father, Frederick, and Frederick's brother Spencer. Just the kind of thing I was hoping for. And on Tuesday, I'm seeing Mrs Hester and her daughter.' Finlay's mother and sister.

'And you want to earmark this article for September?' Barnie confirmed.

'There might well be two, as I warned you, so either August and September, or September and October would be fine. It seems sensible to tie in with the celebrations. They're bringing out a new line to coincide with them, but it's all very hush-hush.'

Barnie leaned back, staring reflectively into his glass. 'You know, ever since you mentioned the Curzons, I've had this niggling feeling at the back of my mind.'

'Niggling how?'

'Something I seem to remember hearing, way back, about rumours that were circulating at the turn of the last century.'

Rona leaned forward excitedly. 'What kind of

rumours?'

'That's what's niggling me.'

'Finlay did say one of his ancestors had been a rake. Could they concern him?'

'Possibly, but I might be mixing them up with another family.'

'Do try to remember, Barnie. It could be useful.'

He nodded. 'I'll give it some thought, and let you know if I come up with anything.'

'Will we be dining off Curzon this evening?' Dinah enquired, with lifted eyebrow.

Rona shook her head ruefully. 'We leave that to my future stepmother.'

'That reminds me, how are your parents? I've been wondering how they're getting along.'

'They're fine; Pops is happily settled in his flat, and Mum has started taking in lodgers. In fact, I've just slipped her an extra one; someone who's in town for a week or so, and hates hotels.'

Max appeared in the doorway, his face flushed from the stove. 'Ladies and gentleman,' he announced, 'dinner is served.'

Despite their lack of dining room, the kitchen table, with its white cloth, crystal and candles, was worthy of the highest cuisine, and with the lights at the other, business end of the room extinguished, an intimate atmosphere prevailed. Reflections of the candle flames flickered in the glass of the door like a host of fireflies, and outside, in the giant urns, the first spring bulbs

127

were beginning to appear.

Life, Rona decided, was good. She always enjoyed evenings spent with the Trents; though they were older than herself and Max, she felt more relaxed with them than with some friends their own age. Barnie was known at *Chiltern Life* for his short fuse, and was rumoured to rant and rave when copy was late, though Rona had never witnessed such tantrums. Over six feet, he towered above his diminutive wife, but what Dinah lacked in inches she made up for in personality; her wiry black hair was untameable, and her deep voice and rich laugh were a constant surprise, emanating as they did from so small a frame.

'I had an email from Melissa this morning,' she was saying. 'Sam's due to start playschool next term, and can hardly wait. He asks every morning if it's time to go.'

'Let's hope such enthusiasm lasts throughout his schooldays,' Max commented.

'I bet Mitch is glad his stint in the Gulf is over,' Rona said.

'Actually, apart from missing the family, he enjoyed it,' Dinah told her. 'He might well have to go back, and provided the children are a bit older when that happens, I think they'd all go with him. Mel liked it very much when she went out to visit. There's a good social life, and wall-to-wall sunshine can't be bad.'

'Except when it reaches the forties,' Barnie put in. 'But Mel and the kids would go home during the hottest months. However, that's pure speculation. As of now, they're all back in the U S of A, and glad to be together again.'

Talk continued as the wine was finished, the coffee drunk, and the candles guttered out.

When the Trents finally rose to go, Rona reminded Barnie of his promise about the Curzons.

'He thinks there were rumours about them, in the early nineteen hundreds,' Rona explained to Max.

'You'd better be careful, my girl,' Max warned her. 'If you uncover dark secrets about every family you interview, you'll soon run out of takers.'

Barnie laughed. 'He's got a point, Rona. Perhaps you shouldn't dig too deep.'

'Oh, nonsense! As you know, readers are all for a bit of spice, and anything that happened so long ago must have lost its sting. Perhaps the newspaper archives would have something.'

Barnie shook his head. 'Very doubtful. In those days, personal peccadilloes were respected as such, and the gentlemen of the press didn't intrude.'

'Well, I might have a look anyway, on the principle of leaving no stone unturned.'

'I was serious, you know,' Max said, as they went down to clear the table. 'You've created quite a few upsets, one way or the other, over the last year or so. You don't want to get a name for investigative journalism.'

'Nothing could be further from my thoughts,' Rona said lightly, opening the door for Gus to go out on the patio. 'Sorry, boy, that's the best we can offer this evening.'

Max shrugged. 'Don't say I didn't warn you,' he said.

The following morning, Rona phoned her mother.

'Just wondering how you're getting on with Julia?'

'Oh, she's a delight, Rona – a pleasure to have in the house. I'm trying to keep things on a formal footing, but it's difficult with someone so bubbly. She's always wanting to chat, and to be honest, I enjoy her company.'

'I thought you'd get along. Since you're relishing the experience, perhaps you should revamp my room for another guest!'

'Hold on, now. One at a time is quite enough, and Sarah looks like being long-term.'

'Glad all's going so well, anyway. Tell Julia I'll give her a buzz next week, and perhaps we can meet for lunch.'

As Rona replaced the phone, she marvelled yet again at the change in her mother. This time last year, such a conversation would have been unimaginable. And Pops was so obviously happier than he'd been for years. All in all, it seemed that the effects of the dreaded split had been more beneficial than otherwise.

* * *

At nine o'clock, as promised, Oliver and Nick Curzon arrived at Coppins to assist their parents in sorting out their possessions. Fortunately, the garage allocated to the flat, and in which the storage boxes were stacked, was only yards from their front door. It was also fortunate that the strong, cold wind of the last few weeks had mitigated, and the air was warm enough for both doors to be left open while the unpacking was in progress.

The brothers had devised a system whereby they unwrapped the objects out in the garage and their father carried them indoors to Sybil, who deposited them in the place allotted to them. Pieces with an undetermined position were rewrapped and placed in a separate crate.

'No point filling the place with stuff you've no use for,' Nick said breezily.

'You sound like your mother,' Charles remarked. 'She's been pretty ruthless about discarding everything she doesn't consider necessary. Personally, I'll all for hanging on to them.'

'We're not talking of throwing them on the scrap heap, Dad,' Oliver pointed out. 'What you haven't room for at the moment can join the rest in storage, till you've had time to consider what to do with them.' He paused, glancing at his father. 'Your collection of books, for instance.'

Charles bristled, as his son had known he would. 'I'm not parting with any of my books,' he declared. 'I've a little room here I intend to use as a study, and I'm arranging to have

131

shelves put all round the walls to accommodate them.'

'And in the meantime?'

'They can go on the floor in there.'

'Wouldn't it be better to leave them out here till the shelves are up?'

'No; this garage mightn't be completely waterproof, and I'm not risking any damage.'

'Fair enough,' Nick said resignedly, 'but they're pretty heavy, so Oliver and I'll take them in later. Let's get these boxes emptied first.'

'Coffee for the workers!' Sybil announced, coming into the garage with mugs on a tray. 'My goodness, what a lot still to find places for! I'd forgotten all about that pressure cooker. It looks as if I'll have to do another cull on the kitchen contents.'

'As long as you confine yourself to the kitchen!' Charles muttered darkly. 'You're sure you boys can't find room for anything else?'

'Nothing large, that's for sure,' Oliver said, as Nick shook his head. 'We could probably house a bit of china or glass, if there's any you don't need.'

'I'll bear that in mind,' Sybil said as she returned indoors.

'What's this about you foisting some girl on Mum at short notice?'

Rona settled back in her chair. 'And good morning to you, too, Linz.'

'Who is she, exactly? And, more to the point, why didn't you *tell* me? Mum was going on and on about her, and I hadn't a clue what she was talking about.'

'Sorry; things have been a bit hectic the last couple of days. Her name's Julia Teale, and I just bumped into her. Or rather, she bumped into me, in Guild Street, and we got talking. She's here for a week or so on business, and as she hates hotels, I thought it would break Mum in gently before she starts on the long-term.'

She paused, and when her sister made no comment, added, 'All set for the big night?'

'The party, you mean?'

'Aren't you due to meet Prince Charming again?'

Lindsey said irritably, 'I'm beginning to wish I'd never mentioned him.'

'Oh, come on! Your love life is a continuing soap opera, and I can't wait to hear the latest!'

'If you carry on like that, you won't hear anything at all. But, since you ask, yes, I am quite looking forward to this evening. I splashed out on a new dress at Magda's – and by the way, she was asking after you. Says she's not seen you for a while.'

Rona's friend, Magda Ridgeway, owned a chain of boutiques scattered round the county.

'I've been meaning to get in touch with her,' Rona said. 'How is she?'

'Fine; just back from foreign parts, attending fashion shows. It's to be hoped Gavin knows

133

how to cook.'

'Oh, he does,' Rona assured her.

'Ah yes, I was forgetting he was an old flame of yours. Did you make it a rule only to go out with men who could cook?'

'No, I just fell on my feet.'

'Whereas I—'

'Whereas you are having the time of your life, footloose and fancy-free. Don't expect me to feel sorry for you.'

'I'd swap the lot for a happy marriage,' Lindsey said, and Rona's heart twisted.

'I know you would, sis. Never mind, perhaps the handsome stranger will turn up trumps. When's the dinner date with Hugh, by the way?'

'Next Tuesday. I told him I was busy till then.'

'And Jonathan?'

'Still twisting my arm.'

'Well, at least you can't complain no one's interested.'

'Trouble is, it's never the right somebody.'

'It will be, one day.'

Her sister, Rona reflected after they'd rung off, was a prime candidate for an arranged marriage. Her taste in men was, in Rona's opinion, abysmal, and what she needed was someone disinterested who could stand back, assess what was in her best interests, and produce the right man out of a hat. Fleetingly she thought of Finlay Curzon, but immediately dismissed him.

With a failed marriage already behind him, he didn't make the grade. Nor, if she were honest, would she welcome him as a brother-in-law.

Max's call from the foot of the stairs was a welcome distraction. 'How about a spot of fresh air before lunch? Gus didn't get his evening walk last night.'

'Good idea!' she called back. 'I'll be right down.'

Perhaps after all, she thought as she shrugged on her jacket, the man at the party might be the answer to Lindsey's prayers. She could only hope so.

Jenny Bishop said worriedly, 'I still feel that if they're coming all the way to Cricklehurst, we should invite them here.'

'My darling girl,' Daniel said patiently, 'the *reason* they're coming, quite apart from the Feather's excellent reputation, is to save you travelling to Marsborough. If we entertain them here, you'll be completely worn out and undo all the benefit. Anyway –' he smiled at her teasingly – 'they're looking forward to a meal at the Feather; they wouldn't thank us if we switched it to here!'

She smiled unwillingly back. 'It'll be a bit of a strain anyway, won't it, meeting Tom's family?'

'No reason why it should. Ma's not said much about Lindsey, but I know she's fond of Rona, and likes her husband.'

135

'It's odd, to think you'll have stepsisters.'

'I rather like the idea. After being an only one, it'll be great having siblings, even if they're only "step".'

'You're right, of course. I'm being a wimp – sorry!'

'Don't worry, my love,' Daniel said wickedly. 'Put it down to your condition!' And ducked, as she threw a cushion at him.

Charles had an impressive collection of books, most of which were large tomes and awkward to carry, and after a morning's strenuous work, his sons were tiring. It had been agreed that, since the kitchen was still less than orderly, they'd all repair to the nearest pub for lunch, and they were more than ready for it.

'Only one more lot,' Nick said, passing his brother in the hall.

'Just as well; there's not much floor space left.'

It was in avoiding the pile of books nearest the door that Nick tripped, and the three top volumes of the pile he was carrying crashed to the floor. He swore under his breath, hoping his parents hadn't heard the noise, and, having gingerly placed the remainder of his load on the floor, bent to retrieve the dropped volumes. As he did so, he noticed a corner of paper sticking out from one of them. Curious, he opened the book and extracted the yellowing, folded sheet.

'What have you got there?' Oliver asked,

coming in behind him with the last batch.

'Not sure; it was inside this book. Looks like a letter.' He unfolded the fragile paper and ran his eyes down it.

'Good Lord!' he said softly. 'It's addressed to Grandfather.'

'Really?' Oliver, having deposited his load, came to look over his brother's shoulder. The sheet was indeed a letter, dated 23rd July, with the year unspecified. It read:

My dear Frederick,
Over these past days, I have come to doubt the wisdom of setting to paper the matter on which I wrote you last week. Lest it inadvertently fall into the wrong hands, creating all manner of problems, I beg you immediately to put it to the flame, and oblige
Your loving brother,
Spencer

'You never signed yourself *my* loving brother, when you wrote to me,' Nick said after a moment.

'You'd have clobbered me if I had. But what the hell's it about, Nick?'

'Something, it seems, that could have created "all manner of problems".'

'Let's see if Dad knows anything about it.'

They found their parents in the sitting room. Sybil was trying to decide how to position

137

various pieces of furniture, and Charles was engaged in pushing them around under her direction.

'Thank God you've come,' he greeted his sons. 'All this hard work is giving me a thirst.' He straightened, eying the paper in Nick's hand. 'What's that?'

'A letter. From Great Uncle Spencer to Grandfather.'

'Great Heavens!' Charles held out his hand, and Nick put the letter into it, watching as his father's brows came together.

'What the devil's it all about?'

'We were hoping you could tell us,' Oliver said.

'What have you found, dears?' Sybil, who'd been studying the current layout of furniture, came over and joined them. Charles silently handed her the letter.

'Well, well!' she commented when she'd read it. 'It sounds as if old Spencer had been indiscreet!'

'But about what? That's the point.'

'Probably gambling debts, or something of the sort.'

'Where exactly did you find this?' Charles enquired.

'It fell out of one of your books when I – was putting it down,' Nick replied. 'I think it was *A History of Ancient Porcelain*.'

'That belonged to my father,' Charles said slowly. 'He must have been reading it when the letter was brought to him, and used it as a book-mark.'

'But why would they write to each other?' Oliver demanded. 'Surely they worked together every day, as we do?'

'I believe Father was sent to another pottery for a while, to gain experience. That could be the explanation. Without an envelope giving his address, it's probably the closest we'll get.'

'Well,' Sybil said philosophically, 'their indiscretion died with them, so that's that. Now, how about some lunch?'

The walk in the park had given Rona and Max an appetite, and on their return, they'd had a larger lunch than usual. They were still sitting over coffee when Magda rang.

'I've been meaning to phone you for weeks,' Rona told her.

'Likewise, but I've been away a fair bit.'

'So I heard, from Lindsey. I believe she's been patronizing you?'

'Yes; she bought a gorgeous dress, and looks sensational in it.'

Rona hoped silently it would work its magic.

'The reason I'm ringing,' Magda continued, 'is that we were thinking, since it's a good forecast for tomorrow, it might be nice for us all to drive out somewhere for lunch. Are you free this weekend?'

'Yes, and that sounds great. I'll just check with Max.' She put her hand over the mouthpiece. 'Magda suggests the four of us have a day out tomorrow. OK with you?'

'Great idea.'

'Max says yes,' Rona relayed into the phone. 'How about Penbury Court? We don't need to go round the house, but the grounds should be lovely at this time of year, and there's a choice of eating places.'

'Sounds perfect.'

'It would be good for Gus, too, if you don't mind him coming. There are plenty of places he can run free.'

'We wouldn't dream of going without him!'

Rona laughed. 'In that case, we'll take Max's car; it has a wired-off section to contain him when there are back-seat passengers. What time shall we collect you?'

'Gavin won't appreciate too early a start – he values his lie-in on Sundays. How about ten thirty?'

'We'll be there on the dot, and can catch up on all the news then.'

As she'd intended, the party was in full swing when Lindsey arrived, and she was promptly handed a glass and welcomed into its midst. It was an odd fact that she and Rona had few mutual friends, so seldom attended the same functions. Many of her own were couples she'd met during her marriage to Hugh; others were connected with her work – business colleagues who'd become friends, and a few she'd kept in contact with since schooldays.

As she laughed and chatted to them, Lindsey's eyes discreetly searched the room, but there was no sign of the man who interested her. All she knew about him was his name – Dominic Frayne – but it had been mentioned almost as an inducement when she'd been invited to this gathering. Perhaps he'd been unable to come. She fought disappointment; she'd spent a fortune on this dress, and knew she was looking her best. It would be irony indeed if the person she'd most wanted to impress wasn't even here.

Then, suddenly, she saw him, and her heart jerked before abruptly plummeting. He was at the far end of the room, in a group that included, of all people, Jonathan and Carol Hurst. As though drawn by her gaze, he turned, looking directly at her, and her own eyes dropped as she joined with increased animation in the conversation about her.

Minutes later, a tap on her shoulder made her turn, to see the Hursts smiling at her, and, immediately behind them, Dominic Frayne and a tall, blonde woman in an oyster satin dress. Close to, Lindsey saw he was older than she'd thought – nearer fifty than forty, with a network of fine lines round his eyes. But the powerful magnetism she'd felt from across the room had intensified with his proximity.

'Lindsey, you look ravishing,' Jonathan was saying, his eyes conveying a deeper meaning. 'You've met my wife, of course, but I don't think you know my friends: Dominic Frayne and Carla Deighton – Lindsey Parish.'

Frayne inclined his head slightly, his eyes never leaving her face, and the woman beside him nodded coolly. Who *was* she? Lindsey thought in agitation; when she'd seen him before, he'd been alone. To her consternation, the crowd she'd been talking to had drifted away, leaving her with these two couples who both, for different reasons, made her ill at ease.

'What a fabulous dress!' Carol said warmly, but Lindsey, though she smiled acknowledgment, recalled the embarrassment of their last meeting, and couldn't meet her eyes.

'Lindsey looks good in everything,' Jonathan said gallantly, his eyes clearly adding, *and nothing!*

She felt her cheeks grow warm, forcing herself to reply lightly, 'Thank you, kind sir!' Things were not going at all as she'd hoped, and, to emphasize her isolation, someone claimed Carol's attention, and she too turned away.

Aware of her empty glass, Lindsey seized on a means of escape. 'If you'll excuse me, I'll just—'

But Jonathan took it out of her hand. 'I'll get you a refill. You three get to know each other.'

Damn it! Lindsey thought, annoyance coming to her rescue; she would not be intimidated by this couple, whose aloofness was now beginning to irritate her.

Her glance included them both. 'Do you live round here? It's strange we've not met before.'

It was Frayne who replied, and his voice, measured and quiet, carried an underlying note of authority. 'I bought a flat here relatively recently.'

No mention of Carla Deighton's living arrangements; perhaps they were synonymous with his own.

'For work reasons?' Lindsey persevered, when nothing further was forthcoming.

Frayne smiled, and her insides flipped. 'In a word, no. My activities cover a wide field, so where I live is immaterial. You work with Jonathan, I hear.'

How much had Jonathan told him? Lindsey wondered feverishly. It wouldn't surprise her if he boasted to his friends about their relationship.

'We're partners in the same firm, yes.'

Carla Deighton spoke for the first time. 'Have you lived here long yourself?'

'All my life.' And how provincial must *that* sound to this sophisticated couple. *Were* they a couple, in the fuller sense of the word?

'It seems a very pleasant town.'

Rightly or wrongly, Lindsey read condescension in the remark, but fortunately, before she could reply, Jonathan reappeared and handed over her glass.

'Thanks, Jonathan,' she said quickly. 'Now, if you'll excuse me, I must have a word with

Nicole and David.'

And, fighting tears of disappointment, she threaded her way through the crowd in search of her friends.

That night, Dominic Frayne filled Lindsey's dreams, his image seemingly seared into her brain: the thick mid-brown hair, streaked with grey; the groove between his brows, the enigmatic eyes whose message she couldn't read, and when she woke her pillow was wet with tears.

Well, that was a wasted exercise, she told herself as her eyes fell on the sea-green chiffon hanging from the wardrobe door. How naïve he must have thought her, asking whether his work had brought him to Marsborough, when obviously he was a tycoon of some kind. No doubt he and that cool, sleekly groomed companion of his had smiled over it later. No explanation had been offered of their relationship, but she was of the same mould and much more suited to him, Lindsey thought savagely, than a small-town solicitor. So – write the whole thing off to experience, and in future don't build your dreams on fantasies.

Yet even as she thought of him, a tightening of her insides warned her that his lack of availability had done nothing to lessen his attraction for her. Which, to say the least, was unfortunate.

* * *

'So what firm are you writing about at the moment?' Magda asked casually, as they sat over lunch in Penbury Court's Orchard Restaurant, it having proved, after all, too cool to eat outdoors.

'Curzon. Admittedly they're not based in Marsborough, but they're local enough.'

'That should be interesting. Gavin was at school with some of them, weren't you, darling?'

Gavin nodded. 'Most of them, actually, but I hardly knew the younger ones. Edward and Oliver were in my form.'

'Did you like them?' Rona asked with interest.

'Yes, I liked them, though they weren't particular friends of mine. Edward was very good at games, and in all the school teams. Have you met him?'

'Only over lunch in the directors' dining room. I'm hoping to interview him more fully later. I'd like to see them all, individually if possible, to try to harvest any stories they might have of the old days.'

'From what I remember, the "old days", as you call them, are described pretty comprehensively in the display boards at the museum.'

'I've not been there yet,' Rona admitted. 'I'm aware a lot of information's already available, but it's nearly all technical, and I'm interested in the human element.'

'They've got some anniversary coming up,

145

haven't they?' Magda asked.

'Their hundred and fiftieth, yes. We're hoping to time the articles to coincide with it.'

'Articles in the plural? It'll run to more than one?'

'I'm hoping so. It depends how much I can glean.'

'She'll glean plenty, believe me,' Max put in humorously. 'She's like a terrier at a rabbit hole when she gets going. I'm just thankful she's never likely to interview me!'

Rona half expected to find a message from Lindsey when they returned home, but the answerphone was ominously silent. Once Max had retired to the sitting room with the Sunday papers, she seated herself at the kitchen table and phoned her.

'Well?' she said instantly, when Lindsey picked up. 'How did it go?'

'Don't ask.'

'Oh, Linz! Wasn't he there?'

'He was there all right, but so was his very glamorous companion.'

'Uh-oh. Is he married, then?'

'They have different surnames, but so have you and Max.'

'They're a couple, though?'

'Presumably.'

There was a pause, then Rona said lightly, 'Well, to be frank, that hasn't stopped you before. Nor, for that matter, have wives.'

'I suppose I deserve that.' Lindsey paused. 'You'll never guess who introduced us: Jonathan.'

Rona drew in her breath. 'Hardly a promising start. Was *his* wife there?'

'Yes. Raving about my dress.'

'How did Jonathan act?'

'Flashing me eye signals as usual. I tell you, it was not a comfortable situation.'

'Oh, Linz, I'm so sorry. Never mind, there are more fish in the sea.'

'Yes.'

'You don't sound convinced.'

'The trouble is, Ro,' Lindsey said heavily, 'I still fancy him rotten.'

And Rona, with a sinking heart, could think of nothing to say in reply.

Eight

On Monday morning, Lindsey's phone rang, and she lifted it to hear Jonathan's crisp tones.

'Lindsey, I'd be grateful if you could slot me in for a working lunch today; there are a few things we need to discuss.'

Somebody was with him, she thought. She replied equally impersonally. 'I think I can manage that. Twelve thirty at the Bacchus suit you? I've some shopping to do, so you go on, and I'll see you there.'

He'd want to discuss Saturday evening, she thought. It would be interesting to hear what interpretation he put on it.

Accordingly, she left the office at twelve fifteen and dropped a suit into the dry-cleaner's as she made her way up Guild Street. She saw Jonathan as soon as she entered the wine bar; he was in one of the booths against the wall, and half rose as she joined him, patting the cushioned bench beside him. Lindsey, pretending not to notice, seated herself opposite.

'A business lunch, is it?' she enquired, with raised eyebrow.

'You could call it that, but first things first.

Let's get the ordering out of the way, then we can settle down to talk. What do you fancy?'

Lindsey ran her eyes down the menu. 'Cheese omelette and a side salad, please. And a glass of white wine.'

'Only a glass?'

'I need a clear head; I'm seeing a client who requires careful handling.'

The waiter approached, removed a pen from behind his ear, and wrote down their order with a total lack of interest. Lindsey's modest request was supplemented by Jonathan ordering a bottle of Sauvignon, with the request that it be brought at once.

'So,' he began, as the man moved away, 'what did you think of our Businessman of the Year?'

Deliberately, Lindsey feigned ignorance. 'And who might that be?'

'Dominic Frayne, of course. He's making quite a name for himself.'

'You surprise me. He didn't have much to say on Saturday.'

'Struck dumb by your beauty, perhaps,' Jonathan suggested facetiously.

'How do you know him?'

'He's just joined the golf club – don't ask me how, when there's a year-long waiting list – and everyone who is anyone is falling over themselves to meet him.'

'Why did you bring him over?'

'As a means of getting to you, of course. I couldn't just make a beeline for you, could I?

149

You looked totally gorgeous, by the way. I think even Frayne was impressed.'

Lindsey toyed with the roll on her plate. 'Who was the woman with him?'

'Carla? She's his personal assistant, and acts as his hostess when he entertains.' He grinned. 'No saying what else she "personally assists" him with, though if their relationship *does* go beyond the professional, it must be pretty relaxed. His name's been linked with several women since his last divorce.'

'His *last*?' Lindsey echoed. 'How many has he had, for goodness' sake?'

'Two that I know of. He's a serial womanizer, so bear that in mind if he tries to latch on to you.'

'Oh, I will.'

'Anyway, enough of Frayne; when am I going to see you? Tomorrow evening? I think I could swing it.'

'I'm not free tomorrow.'

He looked at her for a minute, then leaned across the table towards her. 'Lindsey, the fact that Carol nearly walked in on us doesn't change a thing. Can't you get that through your head? She doesn't suspect anything, honestly.'

This was the moment to end it, to prove to her sister that her conscience wasn't dormant.

But before she could speak, the waiter returned with an ice bucket and the bottle of wine, and the moment was lost. She would tell him, she promised herself. But not today.

Rona had set aside that Monday for research, which necessitated a fairly long drive to the county town of Buckford. Having made an appointment to see the Curzon archives, she spent the rest of the morning examining them, but as Finlay had warned her, the vast majority of their contents concerned the development of materials, and though it was interesting to see how now-famous designs and patterns had evolved, the process was in the main too technical to describe in her article. Even Samuel's journals, which she'd been counting on for a more personal aspect, contained virtually nothing of his private life.

After a dispirited lunch, she switched to newspaper archives, in the hope of unearthing the 'rumours' that Barnie had mentioned; but despite searching a fairly wide time span, from 1890 to 1910, she again drew a blank. As Barnie had said, people's privacy had been respected in those days – praiseworthy at the time, but frustrating for future historians.

All in all, it had been a wasted journey, but one that had had to be made. On the way home, she drew into a lay-by to stretch her legs and allow Gus a romp in a field, and it was as she was throwing a stick for him that her mobile rang, and she answered it to hear Julia's voice.

'Hi!' she said. 'How are things?'

'Boring,' Rona replied.

'Oh dear! Why, what are you doing?'

151

'I'm on my way back from Buckford, having been bogged down in archives all day.'

'You sound a bit down; could you do with cheering up?'

'Very definitely.'

'Then how about letting me take you out to dinner?'

'I'd love to have dinner with you, Julia, but I'll pay my own way.'

'That's not an option. The whole point is to thank you for arranging for me to stay with your mother. She's a darling, isn't she?'

It was the first time Rona had heard her mother described in such terms. 'I'm glad you're getting on so well,' she replied diplomatically. 'But really, there's no need to—'

'Not negotiable. And your husband's welcome to join us, if he'd like to.'

'That's sweet of you, but he has a class this evening.'

'Just the two of us, then. Where do you suggest we go?'

Gus was panting at her feet, waiting for her next throw, and Rona bent to pick up the stick. 'I'd say the best place is an Italian, just round the corner from where I live. Suppose you come to me first, and we can have a drink before we go?'

'Brilliant. Since you know the place, would you mind booking us a table? For what – about eight?'

'Fine; yes, I'll do that. The road I live in is

parallel to Guild Street. Turn off into Fullers Walk, just beyond where we had tea, and Lightbourne Avenue's the first turning on the right. I'm number nineteen, on the left about halfway along. If we're having a drink first, come about seven fifteen.'

'See you then,' Julia said, and the phone clicked in Rona's ear. Gus whined a reminder and, realizing she was still holding the stick, Rona threw it for him. It would be good to go out this evening – just what she needed after a frustrating day.

Feeling decidedly more cheerful, she made her way back to the car.

After booking the table, Rona phoned Max.

'Just to say I'm going out to dinner with Julia, so could you ring a little later this evening?'

'That the girl who's lodging with your mother?'

'Yes; you were invited as well, but I made your apologies.'

'Nice of her. Actually, I've some news, too; I've just heard from Jack Striker.'

'Your art school pal?'

'Yes; he's working in Spain at the moment, but he'll be in London for a couple of days, and wonders if I could join him for a meal on Friday.'

'Then go; it must be ages since you saw him.'

'It is; but it would involve staying the night. If Jack's anything like I remember, there'll be plenty of booze flowing.'

'That's not a problem, is it?'

'It'll cut into the weekend, that's all.'

'We've nothing special planned, and you'll be back – when? – mid-morning on Saturday?'

'About then.'

'Then enjoy yourself. Just don't get any ideas about moving to Spain!'

Max laughed. 'No chance of that. Thanks, love; and I'll delay phoning this evening till about eleven. OK?'

'Yes, I'm sure to be back by then. We're both working girls, after all.'

'Have fun,' Max said, and rang off.

Julia was delighted with the house.

'I've never lived in an old one,' she said. 'There's no doubt about it, they've much more character. Could I possibly have a look round?'

'Of course. I'll give you a guided tour.'

Everything met with her approval, from the spaciousness of the sitting room to the kitchen corner in the study. 'I can just imagine you, beavering away up here, fuelled by countless cups of coffee!'

She moved to the desk, and her eyes fell on the Curzon albums. 'What are these?' she asked curiously, opening the one on top.

'They're to help my latest project,' Rona explained. 'At the moment I'm researching the Curzon family.'

'Oh yes, Avril told me, when she put out the

154

marmalade pot.' ('Avril'! Rona registered, with a small sense of shock.) 'They've got an anniversary coming up, or something. Have you found out anything interesting about them?'

'Not particularly, but I'm meeting another two tomorrow. So far, I've only seen the present directors, and the James Curzons.'

'Are they someone's parents?'

'Sam's, yes. They were very helpful; it's the older ones who are most likely to remember previous generations.'

Julia was still flicking through the album. 'Isn't there some talk about a startling new invention?'

'That's right. It's all very hush-hush.'

'And this article you're doing will be part of the anniversary publicity?'

Her mother again, no doubt. 'I suppose it will,' Rona agreed. 'Well, you've seen just about everything, so how about that drink?'

'How's the job going?' she asked, as they returned to the sitting room.

'Slowly, but that's only to be expected. The firm I'm working for is hoping to run a series of management training courses here, and my job is to interest people in advance and find out how many would be likely to attend. I've been round several of the banks and businesses, and met with a fair bit of interest.'

'Will it mean making a return visit?'

'Almost definitely. A pity I shan't be able to stay with your mother next time!'

155

'And as you saw, we've only one bedroom, so we can't help.'

'I wouldn't dream of asking, even if you could. You've done more than enough already.'

At ten to eight, they set off on the five-minute walk to the restaurant.

'Dino's in Dean's Crescent?' Julia queried, as they turned the corner. 'Is that a coincidence?'

Rona laughed. 'My sister swears his real name's Fred Smith, but that's not quite fair. He's Italian all right, though I dare say "Dino" is stretching it a bit. No matter, he's a love, and his restaurant's my home from home.'

As always, Dino welcomed them effusively, leading them to Rona's usual corner table.

'This is a friend of mine, Ms Teale,' Rona told him. 'I've been singing your praises, so she's expecting great things.'

'*Signorina.*' Dino bowed in Julia's direction. 'I shall attend to you myself.'

It was a pleasant, relaxing evening. Julia kept Rona amused with her fund of stories about the people she had met and the places she'd been.

'You make me feel very provincial,' Rona complained humorously. 'Though I've been to a lot of different countries on holiday, I've never lived anywhere but here.'

'"East, west, home's best." Isn't that what they say?'

'No doubt, but I do seem to see a lot of it, especially with working from there.'

The meal over, they strolled back through the

156

mild spring dusk, Gus trotting at their heels. Julia had found a parking place not far from the house, and they stopped when they reached her car.

'Are you sure you won't let me make a contribution to the meal?' Rona asked again, but Julia shook her head emphatically.

'Positively not.'

'Then thank you very much; it was just what I needed. We must do it again, going Dutch next time.'

'I'll look forward to it. I'll give you a call in a day or two, to let you know when I'm leaving.'

Rona stood watching as Julia started the car and drove off with a wave of her hand. A glance at her watch showed it to be almost eleven – time for Max's phone call.

Gus had sat down during their conversation, and she gave a little tug on his lead. 'Come on, boy,' she said. 'Let's go home.'

Just before ten the next morning, Rona set off for her meeting with Hester Curzon. The photograph albums were in the boot, and she was hoping Hester could identify some of the unnamed people in them.

As luck would have it, when Rona had phoned to make the appointment, it had been Hester's daughter Jacqueline who'd answered, and, having arranged to see Hester at ten thirty on Tuesday, Rona had asked if her daughter would also be willing to be interviewed.

'I live and work in Woodbourne,' Jacqueline had told her, on her return to the phone. 'As you probably know, that's a twenty-minute drive from Chilswood. If you can get there by, say, twelve thirty, and don't mind interviewing me over lunch, I could see you then.'

It was arranged that Rona would park her car in the town centre multi-storey, and walk to Jacqueline's office. Killing two birds with one stone, Rona had thought with satisfaction.

Hester Curzon lived in a bungalow in a secluded close on the side of town farthest from the industrial site for which it was known. She opened the door herself, and Rona's first impression was of the grace with which she held herself. She was wearing a caramel-coloured suede skirt and black cashmere sweater, with black stockings and high-heeled shoes, all of which were a foil for her creamy skin and the pale gold of her hair.

'I see you've brought the albums back,' she said. 'There was no hurry, you know.'

'Actually, I was hoping you could supply some missing names.'

'Wasn't I as meticulous as I should have been? I'll do my best to rectify it.'

She led Rona into a bright, sun-filled sitting room, where two cups and saucers in Curzon china awaited them on a trolley, together with a jug of cream and a dish of shortbread.

'If you'd care to sit down,' Hester said, 'I'll bring through the coffee.'

158

Always alert to her surroundings, Rona took the chance of a quick glance round the room. On the mantelpiece stood a photograph of a middle-aged man bearing a faint resemblance to Edward, and on a side table were two matched wedding groups, one of Edward himself with his bride, the other of a fair-haired girl and a man in naval uniform. Jacqueline, no doubt. There was no record of Finlay's wedding, presumably because the marriage had been dissolved.

Hester returned with a silver coffee pot and seated herself next to the trolley. 'You've met my sons, I believe.'

'Yes, we all had lunch together.'

'They couldn't tell me if you're the Rona Parish who writes biographies,' Hester continued.

'I am, yes.'

'Then why waste time on magazines?'

Nonplussed by the question, Rona hesitated, and Hester quickly apologized. 'Forgive me, that was unpardonably rude. I enjoy your pieces in *Chiltern Life*, but – if you'll forgive me – anyone could do those. It takes real talent to delve into people's lives as deeply as you do in your biographies. You make your subjects really come alive.'

'Thank you.'

'So why have you deserted them?'

'I've not made any conscious decision, but they take a very long time, and the last one I started had to be abandoned, for reasons beyond my control. It was a lot of work done for nothing. Actually,' she added frankly, 'I think that's why I enjoy doing this series so much. Because I concentrate on the families rather than the firms, they end up being mini biographies.'

Hester nodded as she poured the coffee. 'But I shouldn't be quizzing you; you're the one with the questions. Shall we start with those albums? Take them over to the table in the window, where we can see them better. I'll bring your coffee.'

Rona had put markers between the leaves where clarification was needed, and for the next few minutes Hester went through them, in some cases adding a name under a photograph, at others puzzling unsuccessfully to remember who someone was.

'I'm not a great deal of help, am I?' she asked ruefully.

'Don't worry, it was only for interest. I enjoyed looking through them because they brought to life several names I've read about, but apart from one or two, I'm not intending to use them.' She looked up at the other woman. 'Finlay did say there'd be no problem about reproducing them?'

'None at all, use any you need.'

'The ones I'd like are all in the earliest album, so I can leave the others with you, and perhaps hold on to this one a little longer?'

'Of course.'

'It's very kind of you to let me see them.'

'That was my son's doing rather than mine. I'd forgotten about them, and it was he who went up in the loft and dug them out. Now, let's sit down again, have another cup of coffee, and you can begin asking your questions.'

They returned to their seats, and Rona's cup was duly replenished.

'Would you mind if I used my recorder?' she asked. 'It's hard to remember exactly what's said.'

'Of course; please do.'

She set it on the table beside her. 'Really, as I said, it's the family I'm interested in. How did they all strike you, when you first joined it? You must have realized you were marrying into a dynasty.'

'Oh, I did, and it was quite an ordeal, I can tell you, meeting them all for the first time. Fortunately, they were very welcoming, and I fitted in with no problem.'

'So you got on well with your parents-in-law?'

'Yes, though they were considerably older than my own parents. My husband was the youngest of three, and his elder sister was ten when he was born.'

'What were they like?' Rona asked curiously.

'Very Victorian, bless them. Florence was small and stout and ruled the family with a rod of iron. Spencer used to bluster a lot but had a heart of gold. He doted on his grandchildren, though Finlay was only three when he died.'

'He remembers playing with his watch and chain,' Rona said.

'Really? Imagine that!'

'And your husband's sisters? Were you close to them?'

'Not really. Mary, the elder one, seemed very old-fashioned to me. She'd been born in nineteen-ten, had never married, and still lived at home. She'd only have been in her forties when we met, but seemed years older.'

'And the other sister?'

'Janet never married either, but as she was only a year older than JS, I could relate to her more easily.'

'Did she also live with her parents?'

'No, she was headmistress of a boarding school and had her own flat.' Hester smilingly raised her eyebrows. 'We've strayed quite a way from the firm, haven't we?'

Rona flushed. 'I'm sorry if I'm being intrusive; it's my insatiable curiosity about people, and what makes them tick.'

'You're not intrusive at all. Believe me, I should tell you if you were. You warned me it's the family that interests you, so please continue.'

Rona hesitated, but, at Hester's encouraging nod, asked tentatively, 'I wondered about your father-in-law's brother; what was he like?'

'Frederick? He was very artistic, and a lot of

his patterns are still in use. His particular flair skipped a generation, but Samuel has inherited it. Aunt Charlotte, his wife, was an accomplished pianist, so we shared a love of music. I was very fond of her.'

'You were an opera singer, weren't you? Did you keep it up after you married?'

Hester shook her head. 'It would have been too disruptive to family life. I'd no regrets, though; I'd enjoyed my career, but it was time to move on, and in any case I soon became pregnant.'

'How did you meet your husband?'

The older woman's eyes went to the photo above the fireplace. 'Through mutual friends. He always said it was love at first sight, but it wasn't for me. JS wasn't what you'd call musical, but he attended almost every concert I gave, and always sent a bouquet of red roses backstage, even if he couldn't be there. Eventually he wore me down, and since I was genuinely fond of him, I accepted him. But it was a year or so before I fell in love.'

'And once you were married, you were accepted into the dynasty?'

Hester considered. 'To be honest, I always felt on the fringes. The factory was the centre of my husband's life, but I wasn't encouraged to take an active interest in it. My role, along with the other wives, was to be a showcase, decorating my home with Curzon figurines and dining off their china.'

Rona nodded. 'That's how it struck me. I told them so, over lunch, and they were quite indignant. They said no women had shown an interest in joining the firm.'

'I doubt if they were asked. Our principal duty, of course, was to provide sons. As I mentioned, my husband had two sisters but was the only boy, whereas there were two on the other side of the family. Though he got on well enough with both Charles and James, he always felt the odds were against him. That's why he was so delighted when we'd two sons of our own.'

'I hear there's a shortage of boys in the next generation.'

'That's true; so far, my grandson Harry is the only one. Finlay and his wife divorced, which was a great disappointment. We were very fond of Virginia.'

She stopped, looking across at Rona. 'You know, ever since you arrived, I've been trying to think who you remind me of, and of course, that's the answer – Virginia. Not that you *look* particularly like her, though there is a resemblance; it's more that you have the same mannerisms.'

Suddenly uncomfortable, Rona cast around for a change of subject. 'Has there ever been any – scandal in the family?' she ventured.

Hester laughed. 'I'm not sure you'd call it scandal, but old George was a bit of a rake in his time, running up extensive gambling debts, with an eye for a pretty woman, and so on. He got into one or two scrapes, I believe, which earned him a nickname – the Rogue in Porcelain.'

Rona smiled. 'George Meredith.'

Hester's eyebrows went up. 'Well done, my dear! Not many people nowadays recognize the quotation.'

'*The Egoist* was one of our set books at uni.'

'Well, our own George would have been about thirty when it came out, and at the height of his escapades, so, although it wasn't the interpretation Meredith intended, the name seemed apt. Unfortunately, it stuck with him for the rest of his life.'

'Thanks for that; it'll add a little colour.' Rona looked round the room, her eyes resting on the china ornaments on display.

'I see what you mean about being a showcase!' she said. 'You have some beautiful pieces.' She switched off the recorder. 'Thank you so much for your time, Mrs Curzon.'

'It's been very interesting, looking back over the past and seeing the old photographs again. I hope I've been of some help.'

Rona's route out of Chilswood took her past the pottery, reminding her that she must go back and visit the museum. Minutes later, she was clear of the town and, since there was time in hand, she stopped to exercise Gus. There being no readily accessible fields, she clipped on his

165

lead and walked with him along the side of the road, allowing him to stop and sniff the grasses as her mind went back over the interview just finished.

Despite being, as Hester had said, on the fringes of the company, it seemed that it was from the women of the family that she'd learn most about the various characters who had comprised it. Already, helped by their photographs and Hester's thumbnail sketches, the shadowy figures of the older generations were beginning to come to life. She'd have liked to know more about Mary and Janet, John Samuel's unmarried sisters, but doubtless never would.

The journey to Woodbourne took, as Jacqueline had estimated, just over twenty minutes, and she found the town centre car park without difficulty. She'd brought a bottle of water with her, and poured some for Gus into the bowl she kept in the car. Then, leaving the window slightly open, she settled him on his rug on the back seat, and set off for her next appointment.

Jacqueline Sturton was awaiting her in the foyer of the office building. Edward had said she was an accountant, Rona remembered. She was not as tall as her mother, and the long blonde hair in the wedding photograph had been shortened to a smart bob. Rona searched her face for resemblances to her brothers, but found none.

Woodbourne was an attractive market town

with plenty of open spaces and a well laid-out shopping area. As they walked along the wide pavement, she promised herself a look round after lunch. The restaurant they turned into was French, with red and white checked tablecloths and a generally rustic air about it.

'There's a set three-course lunch if you're hungry,' Jacqueline said. 'Otherwise, you can choose from the à la carte. Personally, I prefer something light midday; they do a quiche Lorraine to die for.'

'That sounds just right,' Rona told her.

'And a glass of house plonk, since you have to drive?'

'Perfect.'

Jacqueline placed the order in fluent French, then sat back in her chair. 'Right,' she said. 'How can I help you?'

'I'm trying to build a composite picture of the various family units. Your mother kindly lent me some albums, which were interesting.'

'Oh God!' Jacqueline clapped a dramatic hand to her forehead. 'Not me lying naked on a rug?'

Rona laughed. 'No; in the only one of you, you were eating an ice cream on the beach. But do you remember any of your older relatives? Anything that would help me to flesh them out?'

Like Finlay, Jacqueline remembered her grandfather, and there were stories, too, of Grandma Florence and her collection of lace caps. 'I think they'd belonged to her mother,' Jacqueline said. 'I used to love trying them all on, but I never saw her wear one herself.'

Unfortunately, Frederick had died the year she was born and Charlotte soon after, so she'd never known them.

'You married a naval officer, didn't you?' Rona said, as their quiches arrived, and, at Jacqueline's look of surprise, added, 'I saw the wedding photo at your mother's.'

'That's right, though he's no longer in the Navy. He's a retired Surgeon Commander, and now he has his own firm making surgical instruments.'

'You never thought about joining the family business?'

'No, I decided very early on that I wanted to do accountancy. Numbers have always fascinated me, and still do. As far as I was concerned, the pottery was a job for the boys.'

The ethic seemed ingrained into the whole family, Rona thought.

'What about your sons, when they grow up?'

Jacqueline smiled. 'That will be up to them. At the moment, they're five, seven and nine, so I can't say I've given it much thought.'

The recorder being useless in these noisy surroundings, Rona jotted down odd reminders in her notebook. It wasn't until they were sitting over coffee that she asked her question about scandals, hoping for more on the Rogue in Porcelain. When there was no reply, she looked up

168

to see Jacqueline thoughtfully stirring her coffee.

'*Have* there been any?' she prompted.

'A colourful past is a prerequisite for old families,' Jacqueline answered slowly, 'and ours is no exception. But stories get embroidered and exaggerated along the way, and I never paid them much attention.'

Rona felt a prickle of excitement. 'Until?'

'Until my father was dying. I was sitting with him, to give Mother a break; he had a high fever, and was tossing and turning and mumbling to himself. I thought he was delirious, but suddenly he spoke very clearly. Only a few sentences, but I've been puzzling over them ever since. Then he lapsed into silence, and died later that night. I asked my mother and brothers what he could have been referring to, but Mother was too upset to talk about it, and the boys dismissed it as delirium.'

Neither Finlay nor Hester had mentioned that.

'I heard there were rumours at the turn of the last century,' Rona prompted.

Jacqueline frowned. 'About what?'

'I don't know. I hoped you might.'

She shook her head. 'I'm sorry, I can't help you. I wasn't supposed to hear what I did, and I feel honour-bound not to repeat it.'

Rona saw her point, but it was doubly frustrating to find there might, after all, have been something, only to have the subject abruptly terminated.

169

'I must be getting back,' Jacqueline added, glancing at her watch. 'Nice to have met you, Rona, and I look forward to reading the article in due course. It will be interesting, as Burns said, to "see ourselves as others see us".'

They parted outside the restaurant, Jacqueline to retrace her steps, Rona to walk on towards an interesting-looking arcade. On the corner of it was a large store with the name *De Salis China and Crystal* painted above it, and her eye was immediately caught by the window display, entirely given over to Curzon. There were tea sets, dinner services, commemorative plates, ornamental vases and dozens of figurines, all shown to advantage on a series of satin-covered stands.

Almost without thinking, she pushed open the door and went in. Inside the shop, the display was more catholic, with several other manufacturers represented in a series of glass cabinets down the centre of the store. A wide staircase led to another floor, with a notice promising 'Much more upstairs!'.

A man approached her with a smile. 'Are you looking for something special, madam, or just browsing?'

'Just looking, really. You have the best range of Curzon I've seen for a long time.'

'We like to support local industry, and it's very popular, of course.'

'I'm particularly interested, because I'm writing an article about them, to tie in with their

170

anniversary.'

The man stiffened, staring at her with an expression she couldn't decipher. He moistened his lips, but before he could speak, a woman's voice cut in. 'Of course, we deal with their sales reps. We hardly know the family at all.'

Rona turned. The woman who had joined them was smiling, though her eyes were watchful and her tightly clasped hands indicated tension.

'This is my wife,' the man said, after a taut silence, 'and I'm Nigel de Salis. We own the store.'

'Rona Parish.' Feeling the atmosphere to be unaccountably tense, she went on to chat about the displays, while at the same time sizing up the couple in front of her. De Salis looked to be in his late forties; of medium height, he had thick, light brown hair, a broad nose and deep-set hazel eyes. His wife, probably a year or two younger, was thin rather than slim, the sinews clearly visible in her neck, and her hair, a sandy brown, was loose on her shoulders, in a style rather too young for her.

'Well, I mustn't monopolize you,' Rona said lightly. 'And I should be getting back to my dog; I left him in the car while I had lunch.'

'Nice to have met you, Miss Parish,' Mrs de Salis said, with another insincere smile, and her husband nodded.

It was a relief to be back on the pavement. What an odd couple, Rona thought. The man's attitude had changed noticeably when she'd mentioned writing about the Curzons. And why had his wife been so anxious to stress they barely knew them?

With a philosophical shrug, Rona dismissed them from her mind and returned to the car.

Nine

On her return from Woodbourne, Rona phoned Julia's mobile.

'I wanted to thank you again for last night,' she said. 'I really enjoyed it.'

'So did I,' Julia replied. 'It was great not to have to cook my own supper, for once!'

'That's the other reason I'm ringing; how about coming here for dinner before you go? I'm no cook myself, but my husband is, and I'd like you to meet him. He'll be away part of the weekend, but is Wednesday next week any good? You'll still be here, won't you?'

'That's sweet of you, Rona, but no, unfortunately I shan't. Ten days was the maximum I allowed myself, and that's up this weekend. I've told your mother I'll be leaving on Saturday.'

'That's too bad. Then we'll have to arrange it for your next visit. Any idea when that will be?'

'Not at the moment, but obviously I'll let you know. We'll keep in touch anyway, won't we?'

'Of course we will. In the meantime, good luck with your research.'

'And you with yours!'

'A penny for them?'

Lindsey looked up to find Hugh watching her. 'They're not worth it,' she said.

'They are to me.'

She sighed, looking about her at the softly lit restaurant. 'Sorry, not for sale.'

He reached over and put his hand on hers. 'Lindsey, when are we going to get back together?'

'Who said we were?'

'You know you're coming round to the idea.' He studied her face. 'You've been very subdued this evening; is the other fellow playing you up?'

She snatched her hand away, meeting his eyes defiantly. 'What other fellow?'

'Oh, come on! Your business colleague, Jonathan Whatever-his-name-is.'

'Hugh, I've told you—'

'And I know you too well to believe you. He's married, sweetheart, and he's going to stay that way. Give him up and come back to me. We can make it work this time.'

She looked at him, at his pale face and light blue eyes, his red hair. And though as always her pulses raced in his presence, another image superimposed itself: a strong, autocratic face, with a network of fine lines round the eyes and a firm, unsmiling mouth. She gave a little shudder.

'Is it because I didn't come to your room at

174

Lucy's?' Hugh persisted. 'God knows, I wanted to. I got as far as the landing a couple of times. But I'd promised myself I wouldn't rush you, and I didn't want you to think I'd an ulterior motive in asking you down there.' He paused, searching her downcast face. 'Would you have let me in, if I had?'

She didn't reply, and he prompted gently, 'Lindsey? Would you?'

'Probably,' she said in a low voice.

'Oh God!' he breathed. 'I can't win, can I? Don't you see what you're doing to me?'

She looked up then, unwilling to take all the blame. 'We're doing it to each other, Hugh. We both know if we did get together, things would start to go wrong within a few months. We're – temperamentally opposed – we grate on each other. All right, so we want each other like crazy, which is fine for the odd date, but not enough for any lasting commitment.'

There was a long silence. She'd said too much, she thought in panic, and again the spectre of Dominic Frayne rose in front of her, and with some sixth sense she knew with certainty that he'd be contacting her within a few days. She couldn't become involved with Hugh again, not when she was on the brink of a new relationship; it wouldn't be fair on either of them. And by 'either', she meant herself and Hugh. It didn't occur to her to consider Dominic Frayne.

Finally, Hugh spoke, but he was too late. 'If

175

those are the only terms on offer, I'll take them,' he said.

Blindly, she shook her head. 'Hugh, I'm sorry. I can't. Please will you take me home now?'

Rona phoned Lindsey the next morning.

'How did the date with Hugh go?'

'It was pretty sticky, actually. I – more or less gave him the brush-off.'

'Not, I trust, to leave the way clear for Jonathan?'

'Not for Jonathan, no.'

'So you're still hankering after that man at the party?'

'He'll be contacting me soon. Don't ask me how I know, I just do.'

Rona bit back an ironic retort. 'Free for lunch, to talk it over?'

'Sorry, no, and I'm working from home tomorrow. How about Friday?'

'I suppose I can contain myself till then,' Rona said drily.

She spent the rest of the day transcribing first the recording of her interview with Hester, then the notes she'd made over lunch with Jacqueline. Added to the anecdotes already gleaned from James and Elizabeth, the Curzon dynasty and its component parts were coming together nicely.

As she worked, her mind kept returning to John Samuel. What had weighed on his mind to such an extent that it had cut through the fog of delirium when he was close to death? Something he urgently needed to impart to the family, but had left too late? Or something he'd never have told them in his right mind? Or was the seeming lucidity merely a facet of his delirium, creating traumas where none existed? That, at any rate, was what his sons believed.

Rona stretched, easing her aching back. Then, glancing at the clock on her computer, she phoned Barnie. He should be back from lunch by now.

'The Curzons have a family secret,' she announced, as soon as they'd exchanged greetings.

'Is that a fact? And have you managed to ferret it out?'

'No.' She told him about John Samuel's undisclosed dying words. 'I was wondering,' she added, 'if it might tie in with the rumours you remembered hearing about.'

'*Thought* I remembered,' Barnie corrected her. 'As I said, it could have been another family altogether.'

'I doubt it, since it was the name Curzon that rang a bell. I looked in the newspaper archives, but couldn't find anything.'

'I warned you about that. In those days, there was respect for people's privacy, and newspapers didn't rush to wash everyone's dirty linen in public. Consequently, though rumours circulated, there was damage limitation; relatively few people heard them, so they faded harmlessly away.'

'Not entirely, it seems. You've not come up with anything more yourself? Barnie?' she prompted after he hesitated.

'I've a vague hunch it concerned a paternity suit,' he admitted, somewhat reluctantly. 'It would have been around the time the pottery was becoming well known, and possibly the claimant was after a share in the pickings.'

'Would there be any reference in their own archives, do you think?'

'Highly unlikely. Victorian society prided itself on its morals.'

'Hypocritically, as often as not.'

'Undoubtedly. Anyway, the whole thing's so vague, in my opinion it's not worth pursuing. Stick to the known facts, girl, that's my advice. We don't want any libel actions.'

'Advice noted,' Rona said.

'Ah, but will you take it?'

She laughed, and did not reply.

Finlay Curzon phoned that evening.

'I hear you've been doing the rounds of my family,' he said.

'I've made a start, yes.'

'Were the photo albums any use?'

'Yes indeed; it was good to be able to put faces to the names on the tree.'

'So – you're ploughing your way through the

Curzons. Who have you left?'

'Of the older generation, only Mr and Mrs Charles.'

'They should be ready to receive you next week. I gather the move went as well as could be expected.' He paused. 'When are you coming back to the factory?'

'Well, now that I've sorted myself out a little, I was thinking of tomorrow. Will the museum be open?'

'It will, yes, but it struck me you'd do better going round when it's closed to the public. Then you could spend as much time as you needed with each exhibit, without feeling under pressure. If Friday would be convenient, I could have it opened for you.'

'That's very kind of you. Are you sure it's no trouble?'

'None at all. Go to the Visitor Centre when you arrive, and someone will come and let you in. Then you can hand in the key when you're leaving. Would you prefer morning or afternoon?'

She was lunching with Lindsey on Friday, Rona remembered. 'Could we make it about three o'clock?'

'No problem. I hope the visit proves worthwhile.'

'Avril!'

Hearing Tom's voice, Avril turned with a smile, but it froze on her lips as she saw he was

179

not alone. Beside him, regarding her a little uncertainly, was a tall, well-dressed woman who could only be his lover. Coming so soon after their lunch together, when they'd been so normal and natural with each other, the feeling of shock was all the greater.

Tom was speaking, but she barely heard him as she rapidly assessed his companion. No beauty, then; Catherine Bishop's face was pale, her hair a light brown fading to grey, her eyes grey and steady. Then, as the introductions were completed, she smiled, holding out her hand, and her face lit up, causing Avril to revise her impression of plainness.

'How do you do? I've been wondering when we'd meet, as we were bound to.'

'How do you do?' Avril echoed faintly, frantically looking to Tom for assistance.

He smiled encouragingly at her. 'You're looking very glamorous,' he told her. 'Are you off somewhere special?'

Avril felt a wave of gratitude, to him, and also to Providence, that her first meeting with her replacement had not been while she was still in her dowdy, uncaring phase. For Catherine Bishop, if not glamorous, was meticulously groomed and had an air about her that made Avril want to square her shoulders and stand up straighter.

'Only to bridge,' she replied.

There was a slight pause, which Tom broke by saying, 'Are the alterations to the house finished now?'

'Yes, and I even have a PG.'

He raised his eyebrows. 'I thought that wasn't till after Easter?'

'It wasn't supposed to be, but Rona found me someone in the meantime. A nice girl, who's only here for a few days and has an aversion to hotels. Rona thought it would break me in gently.'

Tom smiled. 'And has it?'

'Yes, I'm enjoying being a landlady. She's leaving at the weekend, then I'll have ten days or so before the permanent guest arrives – a teacher at Belmont Primary.' She glanced at her watch. 'I'd better be on my way,' she added. 'My partner will be waiting for me.'

'Good to have seen you, Avril,' Tom said warmly, and Catherine nodded agreement.

'You too,' she replied, and, with a smile that embraced them both, she went on her way, heart hammering but pride intact. That was another hurdle over. The second meeting, when it came, wouldn't be nearly as fraught.

Catherine slipped her hand through Tom's arm. 'All right, my love?'

'Just glad that's over.'

'It passed off remarkably well. She's pretty, Tom. After all you told me—'

'I also told you she'd taken herself in hand.' He paused, then added almost apologetically, 'I'm still very fond of her.'

'So I should hope. You were together a long time, and she is, after all, the mother of your daughters.' She glanced sideways at him. 'Something's worrying you.'

'I still feel I let her down. Oh, don't get me wrong,' he added quickly. 'I've never been happier, and the last year or so with Avril was hell. But what made my leaving ten times worse was the timing – the fact that she was really making an effort to pull herself together. It felt like slapping her in the face.'

'Well, she seems happy and confident enough now, and I loved that suit she was wearing.'

He put his free hand over hers. 'What I really want is for her to find someone who'd make her as happy as you make me.'

'Perhaps she will,' said Catherine.

'So all in all,' Lindsey finished, 'the evening wasn't an unmitigated success. He looked so crestfallen, I almost relented.'

'Well, you have been playing him along the last few months,' Rona reminded her. 'It's no wonder he was getting hopeful. You even told me he was the best long-term bet.'

Her sister smiled faintly. 'I'm a calculating so-and-so, aren't I?'

'Your words, not mine.'

Lindsey shrugged, glancing out of the window at Guild Street, thronged with lunchtime shoppers. 'Why did you stipulate here, rather than the Bacchus?'

'Because it's nearer home, and as soon as I leave you, I'm driving to Chilswood.'

Lindsey raised an eyebrow. 'The attractive, unattached man?'

'*I'm* attached, Lindsey,' Rona said, a touch sharply.

'Whoops!'

'What do you mean, "whoops"?'

'Only that you get defensive, every time I mention him.'

'That's nonsense.'

'If you say so. So why *are* you going to Chilswood?'

'To visit the Curzon museum, in the hope that it's more personal than the archives. They were made up of original moulds, patterns, and so forth, which would have been of little interest to *Chiltern Life* readers.'

Lindsey reached for the wine bottle and, when Rona held her hand over her glass, refilled her own. 'Well, enjoy yourself,' she said.

It would have been more convenient if she could have left Gus with Max, as she had the last time she visited the pottery, but since he was going to London that afternoon, this was not an option.

As she settled the dog on the back seat and reversed out of the garage, Rona found herself wondering, despite her retort to Lindsey, if she would indeed be seeing Finlay today, and unwillingly admitted that she hoped so. She also wondered whether, if taxed, he might be more amenable than his sister to repeating his father's last words.

However, when, forty-five minutes later, she arrived at the Visitor Centre, there was no sign of him. She was expected, and one of the girls on reception walked with her across the court-yard to the museum entrance, where she un-locked the heavy doors and switched on the lights.

'Take your time, Miss Parish,' she said with a bright smile, 'and perhaps you'll hand the key in when you're leaving.'

'Of course. Thank you.'

The doors closed behind her, leaving Rona alone in the echoing spaces. The room in which she was standing was lined with glass cases containing a wealth of Curzon china, dating, according to the neatly printed cards, from the factory's earliest days, and she moved slowly along, admiring dinner services, Toby jugs, figurines, and mugs commemorating Queen Victoria's Diamond Jubilee. Alongside each item was a card slotting it into its place in history, or pointing out how the design had developed from that of previous items. As new procedures were introduced, these, too, were clearly and simply explained.

The display cases down the centre of the room, Rona discovered, held family items in-cluding several birth certificates – details of which she jotted down in her notebook – and a collection of hand written letters and invoices, some in the hand of Samuel Curzon himself, some that of his son George. There were also a couple of Samuel's journals similar to those she'd seen in Buckford, but though Rona scanned them thoroughly, there was little of a personal nature.

The main room led into another that had been given over to picture boards outlining the history of the firm, and embellished with black and white likenesses of the various family members. And as Finlay had told her, there was a representation of the full family tree, including the names of the wives and daughters omitted from the shortened version.

Although she'd seen Samuel's likeness in Hester's album, Rona was interested in those of his descendants, notably his son George and grandsons Spencer and Frederick. George the rake, she thought with an inward smile, studying the handsome, rather indulgent face with its full lips and incipient double chin. A few old photographs were also reproduced in appropriate sepia: the tenth anniversary of the factory, with Samuel centre stage surrounded by his workers, and a family group of George, his wife Ada and two young sons, both wearing sailor suits. It seemed that after his dalliances, he'd settled down as an exemplary paterfamilias.

At the end of the room, pushed unceremoniously into a corner, stood a magnificent old desk, its surface, though pitted with wear, still gleaming richly. It was possible, Rona thought, that some of the documents she'd just been reading had been written at it. She went up to it, running her hand over its scarred surface. On the right-hand side was a bank of three drawers, embellished with what appeared to be their original brass handles. The middle one, however, wasn't fully shut, giving the desk an odd sense of immediacy, as though its owner had left it only minutes before. Rona gave it a gentle push, but it resisted her pressure.

She frowned. Admittedly it was none of her business, but even if the desk wasn't part of the exhibition, it deserved to look its best. The drawer must have become misaligned, and should be easy enough to correct. Feeling slightly guilty, she pulled it open and, as she'd expected, saw that it was empty. Holding it by both sides, she manoeuvred it slightly from side to side, and tried again. Still it refused to close flush with the surface.

Rona hesitated, her interest now aroused. Something must be impeding its passage, possibly some odd scrap of paper caught in the runners. She opened the drawer to its full extent and, kneeling down, reached into the cavity and felt around with her fingers, encountering the dust of centuries, soft and thick on the runners. But nothing more substantial.

She was on the point of withdrawing her arm when, in a final sweeping movement, her fingers brushed against something on the back of the drawer itself. A piece of paper, by the feel of it, crumpled and hard to dislodge, since it had caught on some splinters of rough wood. Carefully, receiving a few grazes in the process, Rona prised it loose and, sitting back on her heels, looked down at the screwed-up ball in her hand.

Taking care not to tear it, she unfolded the flimsy sheet, feeling a shaft of excitement as she realized it was a letter. Perhaps, after all, she'd found something personal relating to the Curzons. Smoothing the paper with her hand, she read:

19th July
  My dear Frederick,
  I write to inform you that our worst fears are realized. It does indeed appear likely that Papa had a liaison with this woman, resulting in the birth of a child. I have come across papers showing he paid her a substantial sum of money 'in final settlement', and can think of no other explanation for this gesture.
  Her claim that, on the death of Mama, he actually married her seems too bizarre even to consider, save for one point: the pages of the Parish Register covering the month of the alleged wedding appear to have been removed.
  Whether or not Papa effected the removal, with or without the connivance of

the minister – long dead, alas – we shall never know. As things stand, therefore, the boy's claim to legitimacy – and consequently a share in the business – can be neither proved nor dismissed with any certainty.

I am at my wits' end to know how to proceed in this matter, and would greatly appreciate your opinion. When shall you be returning to Chilswood?

Your loving and troubled brother
Spencer.

Rona felt a wave of heat wash over her. Was this, then, the family secret that had so disturbed John Samuel? She read it again, occasionally stumbling over the spidery writing. A Tichborne Claimant, here in Chilswood?

What should she do? What would the family want her to do? Replace the letter where it had lain for over a hundred years, and hope its contents also remained hidden? But other people beside JS might know of the secret, and continue to worry about it. Wouldn't it be preferable to bring it into the open?

Almost absent-mindedly, she gave the offending drawer a push, and it slid sweetly into place, flush now with the front of the desk. A paternity case, Barnie had said. His memory had served him well, after all.

She got to her feet, carefully refolded the letter and slipped it into her bag, accepting that she'd known all along what course of action to take. She'd show it to Finlay; he'd know what to do with it.

She walked back past the picture boards, pausing for a moment to study the likenesses of Spencer and Frederick. How had the latter reacted to that letter? What, if any, action had they taken? Had Frederick deliberately hidden it, or had it become lodged there by accident, when the drawer was overfull?

Rona quickened her pace, hurrying through the long room with its glass cases to the main doors, and switching off the lights as she emerged into the afternoon sunlight. There was no one about as she made her way back to the Visitor Centre.

'I've finished in the museum, thank you,' she told the receptionist, handing over the keys. But before she could ask for Finn, she was informed that he would like a word with her. 'If you'll take a seat, Miss Parish, I'll tell him you're here.'

Rona sat down on one of the plush sofas, her mind busy and the letter seeming to burn a hole in her bag. Would he be angry that she'd taken it on herself to free the drawer? How would he feel about her knowing what she did?

'So there you are!'

His voice startled her. She'd been so intent on her musings that she hadn't noticed him approach.

'I've something to show you,' she said quickly, coming to her feet.

'Then I suggest you do so in comfort. I was hoping you'd have a cup of tea with me.'

'Oh – yes. Thank you.'

'And since I've had enough of my office for one day, we'll go into town. My car's just outside.' He put a hand under her elbow, led her out to it, and opened the door for her. Silently, Rona got in. She was aware of his curious glance, but small talk was beyond her, and he made no further comment as he drove out of the factory grounds and along the approach road, turning left at the juncture with the main road.

Minutes later, as they went down the High Street, he commented, 'We're in luck; there's an empty meter just outside where we're going.' She watched while he put some money in it, and came back to open the door for her.

'This place is renowned for its home-made scones. I hope you're hungry.'

Only when they were seated at a corner table and Finlay had ordered tea and scones for two, did he turn to her and say, 'Well, whatever you have to show me seems to have stolen your tongue.'

'I'm sorry,' she said. 'I can't think of anything else.'

'It must be important. What is it?'

Rona opened her handbag, extracted the letter, and handed it across, watching his face change as he read. When he looked up, he seemed stunned.

'My God!' he said softly. 'Oh, my God!'

'I didn't know what to do,' she said.

'Where did you find this?'

'In a desk in the museum.'

'A *desk*?' His face cleared. 'Oh, that would be Frederick's. It was at Uncle Charles's, and when they moved, he gave it and various other items to the museum. It wouldn't fit in the store room with the other pieces, so it was temporarily shoved in a corner. But I'm quite sure there was nothing in the drawers.'

'One of them wasn't properly shut,' Rona explained, 'so I put my hand in behind it, to see what was stopping it.'

'Good God.'

'I'm surprised no one thought of that before.'

'Well, for a start, it's closed properly all the years I've known it. It must have been jolted during the move.' He looked back at the letter. 'But this is – dynamite.'

'I know. Had you any idea about it?'

He hesitated. 'Family legends have grown up, but we've always taken them with a pinch of salt.' He glanced down at the letter. 'This looks pretty conclusive, though.'

Rona said awkwardly, 'Jacqueline said when your father was dying—'

'Yes. Poor old Dad. He was rambling about there being no proof, and our not admitting we knew anything, and the business being in danger if it got out. I suppose, in his feverish state, everything he'd ever worried about came

191

back to haunt him, magnified out of all proportion.'

So she hadn't even had to ask, Rona thought numbly.

'She said you and Edward dismissed it as delirium.'

He looked uncomfortable. 'Well, it was, of course, but we should have explained. I'd always assumed Jackie had heard the stories, but perhaps not. Still, Dad's death wasn't the time to go into it – Mother was distraught and none of us were thinking straight – and the subject never came up again.'

Their tea was brought and, as Finlay was lost in thought, Rona poured it. 'I feel dreadful,' she said in a low voice. 'Being responsible for bringing it to light, I mean. If you hadn't kindly let me look round on my own, I'd never have taken it on myself to free the drawer...'

Finlay read the letter one more time, then carefully folded it along its creases and put it in his pocket. 'I'll discuss it with the family,' he said. 'In the meantime, I'd be very grateful if—'

'Of *course* I won't say anything. To anyone.'

'Thank you.'

She took the scone he passed her, warm and crumbling and smothered in butter, and said hesitantly, 'Have you any idea who the woman might have been?'

'None. It seems Spencer and Frederick between them managed to contain it, in which case they'd have been unlikely to tell anyone else. As for the woman, it sounds as though she was handsomely paid to keep her mouth shut.'

He gave a harsh laugh. 'I was going to suggest showing you the family plot in the cemetery; I thought you'd be interested to read the headstones. But perhaps we've unearthed enough skeletons for one day.'

Rona said, 'Actually, I *would* like to see them, but now mightn't be the time.'

'If you mean because of the letter, after a hundred years or so, one more day won't make much difference. I need to sleep on it, then I'll have a word with Edward. If you'd like to go, this is as good a time as any. Provided, of course, you don't have to be getting home.'

'No, that's not a problem; my husband's away tonight. But I did leave my dog in the car. I should go and let him out.'

'We'll collect him en route to the cemetery; it's in the same direction.' He paused. 'Has your husband a class this evening?'

'No, he's gone to meet an old friend who's back in this country for a few days. He felt guilty about going on a Friday, but he'll be home mid-morning tomorrow.'

'You seem to live a very disjointed life,' Finlay remarked.

'It suits us,' Rona said defensively.

'I'm sure it does – I wasn't criticizing. It wouldn't suit me, though; I'd prefer to spend more time together than you seem to. Still, I'm hardly an authority on marriage, am I?'

'You could always give it another try.'

'I'd have to meet the right girl first, and then she'd have to be – available. Sometimes the two requirements don't go together.' His voice changed abruptly. 'Well, if you've finished, let's go and take a look at my ancestors.'

Ten

Finlay parked his car in the directors' slot and accompanied Rona to the public car park.

'If he needs some exercise,' he said, as she released a jubilant Gus from her car, 'we could walk to the cemetery. There's a shortcut across the fields.'

'That would be fine. I could do with some fresh air myself.'

Once out of the factory grounds, they turned right and followed the road for a hundred yards or so until they came to a five-barred gate opening into a field. 'It's a right of way, so we're not trespassing,' Finlay told her, 'and there's no need to keep – Gus, is it? – on his lead. I used to walk my dog here.'

When he was married, Rona thought. He'd told her his wife had custody.

They walked slowly and in silence, both busy with their thoughts, while Gus galloped joyously ahead, every now and then emitting a bark of sheer pleasure. They were, Rona saw, wending their way behind the factory in the direction of the town, passing over stiles from one field to another, until the church steeple was visible ahead of them. Clouds had overtaken the earlier sunshine, and a cool wind blew along the ridge of the hill.

'Warm enough?' Finlay enquired, emerging from his brown study.

'Yes, thanks.'

'It's not much farther, and the family plot will be sheltered from the wind; there's a high hedge round it.'

'Very exclusive!' Rona said.

'I'm just thankful they didn't opt for a mausoleum. The very name gives me the shivers. It would be as well to put Gus back on his lead,' he added. 'We're nearly there.'

Rona did so, and they descended the last, sloping field towards the cemetery and, beyond it, the church and the town of Chilswood. Back to civilization, she thought.

The churchyard was surrounded by a grey stone wall, and they walked round it until they came to the entrance alongside the church.

'St Barnabus,' Finlay told her as she paused to look at it. 'The oldest part dates from the fourteenth century, and as you can imagine, generations of the family have been christened and buried here, though not necessarily married.' He flicked her a ghost of his usual smile. 'The discounted brides tended to be married in their family churches, but they're buried alongside their husbands.'

They followed the path between ancient stones, some lying on their sides, most undecipherable; some adorned with marble angels, others movingly simple. Each one told a story, if only they could read it. The path curved round and now Rona could see a dark box hedge, some six feet high, encircling a portion of the ground. Curzon territory, she thought.

They went through an archway cut in the hedge, and she looked about her. A path in the centre led to a weathered bench, and on either side were neat rows of headstones. A large area near the entrance, though, was still laid to grass – awaiting new arrivals, she supposed.

'The earliest family members are in the main churchyard,' Finlay said. 'We'll take a look at them on the way out. The graves in this plot date from about 1790. The Curzons were landowners hereabouts long before Samuel founded the factory, and at some stage must have decided they warranted a place of their own. As you'll see, generally speaking, we're a long-lived bunch. My father was the exception, unfortunately, and there are a few sad little babies' graves.'

They walked together up and down the rows, Rona keeping Gus on a tight leash as they read the dates of birth and death and, on the earlier ones, flowery tributes to the departed. Each of the graves had a small area in front of the headstone, newly planted with spring flowers, and there was a heady scent of narcissus. However, the surrounding hedges gave a feeling of claustrophobia, their dark greenness seeming to absorb the light, and the impression was emphasized as the afternoon darkened with the threat of rain. Even Gus seemed subdued, and his feathery tail was still.

Looking up from one headstone, Rona saw that the bench at the back of the enclosure bore some kind of plaque, and walked over to read the inscription. But as she approached it, Gus growled softly, pulling back on his lead, and suddenly she stiffened.

'Finn!' she said, her voice strident. 'There's someone behind the bench!'

'What?' Finlay, who was still reading the epitaphs, looked up sharply, then came swiftly over to her. 'I can't see anyone.'

'Crouching or lying down,' Rona enlarged, indicating a dark shape, barely visible through the wooden slats. 'I wouldn't have noticed, if it hadn't been for Gus.'

'Stay here,' Finn ordered, and, moving forward, leant his hands on the back of the bench and peered over.

'It's a woman,' he said, surprise in his voice. 'She – seems to be asleep.'

'An odd place for a nap,' Rona said, her heart still pounding. 'There's barely room between the bench and the hedge. Perhaps she's ill?'

'Hello!' Finlay said more loudly, still leaning over the bench. 'Are you all right?'

There was no response, and he straightened, looking back at Rona. 'She's lying face down,' he said. 'I don't like the look of her.'

'Can you get at her?' The bench was cemented into position, and impossible to move.

'I'll have a go. I'm afraid of hurting her, but she seems to need help.'

He moved round the end of the bench, bent down, and slid his hands under the woman's shoulders. 'It's all right,' he said to her, 'we're here to help you.'

Getting a grip on her, he raised her upper body off the ground and started walking slowly backwards, pulling her clear of the bench. Instinctively, Rona moved closer, dragging the unwilling dog with her. Once in the open, Finlay gently lowered his burden and turned her on to her back.

For a measureless instant Rona stared down at the face now exposed – a lovely face, unnaturally pale and with eyes closed – and at the soft hair, loosened under who knew what horrific circumstances.

'*No!*' she said forcefully. Then, as her hands went to her head, '*No, no, no!*'

Finlay, whose own shocked exclamation had been masked by hers, turned a white face towards her. 'You *know* her?'

'Yes, it's Julia, a friend of mine. She's – oh, God! – she's lodging with my mother. We've got to *do* something!' she added urgently. 'Is she still breathing?'

Without hope, he put his hand close to her mouth, then placed two fingers on the side of her neck. He straightened, shaking his head.

'There's nothing we can do, Rona. It's – too late.'

'There must be *something*! Can't you try mouth-to-mouth?'

'Believe me, it's no use. Just – look at her.'

Steeling herself, Rona forced her eyes from the still face to the crumpled body. Julia's familiar jacket hung open, and a dark stain had saturated the blouse beneath it. She'd worn that when they went to Dino's, Rona thought mindlessly. 'Oh, God!' she said under her breath. Then again, a little louder, 'Oh, *God*!'

Finlay's voice reached her as if from a distance. '*How* do you know her, Rona?'

Something in his tone penetrated the fog in her brain, and she turned to look at him. 'Why?' she asked sharply. 'You mean you do, too?'

Finlay nodded heavily. 'She's Nick's ex-wife,' he said.

Rona stared at him for a moment, then shook her head decisively. 'No, you're mistaken. It's Julia Teale. She's been in Marsborough for the last week or so on business, but she doesn't know this area.'

Finlay shook his head, but before he could speak, they were startled by the shockingly incongruous sound of a mobile phone. Both reacted instinctively, feeling for their own, only to break off and say in unison, 'It's not mine.'

'It's coming from behind the bench,' Rona said. 'Her bag must be there.'

She started towards it, but Finlay put a hand

200

on her arm. 'No – we mustn't touch anything. Leave it for the police. I'll get on to them now.'

He flipped open his own mobile and nodded towards the bench. 'You'd better sit down. You've had a bad shock.'

When she didn't move, he took her arm and led her over, waiting until she seated herself before making his calls, first to the police, then to his brother Edward.

'Can you contact Nick?' he finished. 'He's been in Aylesbury this afternoon, but it's nearly six now, so he should be back. The police have asked us to stay till they get here ... What? Oh, Rona's with me. She's been at the museum, and I was showing her the family plot. She says she knows Julia ... God knows.'

The museum, Rona thought numbly. That earlier discovery had paled before this one. Gus put a tentative paw on her knee, whining softly, and she absent-mindedly stroked his ears.

'That sounds sensible,' Finn was saying into the phone, 'theirs is the nearest, certainly, but you'd better check with them first. I'll keep you posted.' He clicked his phone shut, put it away, and came to sit next to her.

'You're shivering,' he said, and, putting an arm round her, drew her against him. 'The police won't be long.'

She turned an anguished face towards him. 'How can I tell my mother?' she asked. 'She'll be expecting her home any minute.'

'Is there someone who could break the news

in person?'

Rona drew an unsteady sigh of relief. 'Lindsey,' she said. 'I'll ask Linz.'

'Is she a relative?' Finlay enquired, as she fumbled for her phone.

'My sister. My twin sister.'

He gave a half-smile. 'How little I know about you,' he said.

She reached Lindsey in her car, halfway home from work, and it was several minutes before she understood what Rona was saying.

'She's *dead*?' she repeated incredulously. 'The girl who's staying with Mum?'

'Just tell her that, Linz, as gently as possible. The details can wait.'

'What details?'

The effort of explaining was beyond her and, though her sister couldn't see her, Rona shook her head. 'I'll tell you later, too. Just say there's been an accident.'

'Ro, what is this? You said you found her; what happened? Are you all right?'

'Yes, but promise me you'll go to Mum straight away. She'll need you. Please, Linz.'

There was a moment's silence. Then Lindsey said flatly, 'All right, I'll do it. I can stay the night if necessary.'

'Bless you,' Rona said. 'I'll be in touch.' And rang off, before her twin could question her further.

The sound of approaching police sirens reached them, and Finlay stood up. Gus gave another

202

whine, and Rona slipped to her knees and gathered the dog in her arms, burying her face in his fur. Finn stood watching her for a moment. Then he went to meet the police.

Uniformed officers were first on the scene, and after giving an initial account of finding of the body, Rona and Finlay were driven to the police station, where more detailed statements were taken.

By the time they were free to go, the enormity of what had happened had seeped through the shock, and Rona wanted above all things to be alone, able to grieve for her friend in private. As they came out of the interview room, a group of men were talking and laughing in the foyer. Something about one of the voices was familiar, and she glanced across, encountering a suddenly alert pair of grey eyes. It was, she saw with sinking heart, the detective with whom she'd crossed swords in Buckford the previous year.

'My God, if it isn't Miss Marple!' he said loudly, and as faces turned in her direction, Finn, sensing her distress, took her arm and led her out to the waiting police car.

'We're going to Oliver and Sally,' he told her, when, having given the address, they'd settled in the back seat. 'You're not fit to drive home, and in any case your husband's not there. They'll put you up for the night.'

'Oh, I couldn't possibly—'

'It's all arranged. I phoned them while you were being interviewed.'

'But – Gus...'

'No problem, really, but it will mean going through the whole thing again. Sally'll be upset; she and Julia were friends. And they'll – probably want to know how you met her.'

'Why?' Rona asked rebelliously, still unconvinced of Finn's identification.

'It seems strange, that's all. And Rona: this business is quite enough for them to take in at the moment. We'll leave the news of the letter for now, OK?'

'OK,' she said.

The police car drew up outside a large detached house in a leafy avenue, and they got out, Rona shivering in the evening air. The rain that had threatened at the cemetery had started during their interviews, and seemed to have set in for the night.

'Thanks for the lift,' Finlay told the driver, who touched his cap and drove off. The front door opened as they reached it, and Rona found herself facing a tall, fair-haired woman who moved swiftly forward and put her arms round her.

'You poor love,' she said. 'What a terrible experience you've had.'

To Finlay, she added in a low voice, 'I should warn you – Nick's here. He insisted.'

'Fair enough,' Finn said tiredly. 'How is he?'

'As you'd expect.'

Sally released Rona and smiled at her. Rona saw that her eyes were red-rimmed, and beneath expertly applied make-up her face was pale.

'As you'll have guessed, I'm Sally,' she said. 'Come through.'

Rona had braced herself for a room full of people, sure that Edward and possibly his wife would be there. But as Sally led her in, it was only Oliver and Nick who rose to greet her, both of them white-faced. Finlay went straight to Nick and put a hand on his shoulder.

'I'm so sorry,' he said quietly, and Nick nodded.

'Have the police been in touch?'

'Yes; they want to see me in the morning. Not that I can tell them anything, God knows.' He bent absent-mindedly to pat Gus, who wagged his tail uncertainly and then, since no one spoke to him, trotted over to the fire and settled on the rug.

'Come and sit down, Rona,' Oliver said. 'This might help.'

He handed her a glass of brandy, and passed one to Finlay. Sally, who had seated herself on a low pouffe, clasped her hands together and looked at Rona.

'Finn says you knew Julia?'

Rona took a sip of brandy, feeling its warmth course down her throat. 'I did, yes, but I find it hard to believe—'

'—that she was Nick's ex,' Finlay finished for

205

her. 'I can't think why she didn't tell you.'

Sally frowned. 'Why would she?'

'Because they discussed Rona's history of the firm.'

'She'd obviously written me off completely,' Nick said, with an attempt at humour. No one smiled.

'How long have you known her?' Sally persisted.

'Only about ten days, but we'd seen quite a bit of each other. We got on really well.'

'And how exactly did you meet?' Oliver asked.

That question again. 'She bumped into me on Guild Street, and I dropped my shopping bag. The eggs broke, and—' She gave a little shrug. 'We had a cup of tea together, she told me she hated hotels, and as my mother has just started doing B&B, I suggested she went there.'

'She was lodging with your mother?' Nick interrupted.

'Yes. She was only there a few days, but Mum had become fond of her.'

'Finn said you discussed this article you're doing,' Oliver continued. 'Did she – make any comments about the family?'

Rona looked at him in bewilderment. 'It doesn't make *sense*,' she said. 'When she came to the house, she looked through the albums Finn had lent me, and asked questions about people, as though she'd no idea who they were.' She turned to him urgently. 'Are you *sure* this isn't a mistake, and she's not who you think?'

He shook his head sympathetically. Oh, Julia, she thought forlornly, I wish you were here.

Nick ran a hand through his hair. 'What on earth was she doing in the cemetery, of all places? Come to that, why was she up here at all? The last I heard, she was living in Reigate.'

Rona's hand jerked, sloshing the brandy in the glass. 'Reigate?' she repeated sharply.

They all turned to her, and Oliver said curiously, 'Yes; why?'

Rona shook her head tiredly; it was too complicated to explain, too convoluted for her brain to grapple with. All at once there seemed a dozen facets to Julia about which she'd known nothing.

Sally rose to her feet. 'Dinner's almost ready. And don't say you're not hungry,' she told Rona. 'You need something inside you, to keep your strength up. But first, I'll show you your room so you can freshen up.'

Rona also stood and Gus, asleep in front of the fire, raised his head. She motioned to him to stay. 'Are you quite sure this isn't too much trouble? I'm quite capable of driving home.'

'After that brandy?' Oliver smiled, and she protested no further.

The room Sally had swiftly prepared was large and comfortable, as was the old-fashioned furniture it contained. An elderly relative's, perhaps.

'I'm afraid we don't run to an en suite,' she apologized, 'but the bathroom's immediately opposite. It's free at the moment, but I'd advise you to stay in your room in the morning till the school rush is over.'

'Where are the children now?' Rona asked.

'Watching a DVD. They don't know what's happened yet, but they've been told not to come downstairs. It's almost their bedtime anyway; I'll settle them before serving dinner.' She gave a quick glance around the room, as though checking its amenities. 'I've put out a night-dress for you, and there are clean towels and a new toothbrush in the bathroom. I always keep a stock.'

'That's very kind of you.'

Sally smiled and nodded. 'Come down when you're ready,' she said.

Alone in the room, Rona lowered herself on to the bed. Nothing to unpack, nothing to put away. She'd feel better for a wash, but first she must phone Max. It was now eight fifteen, and there was no saying where he'd be.

Wherever he was, his mobile was switched off, and frustrated tears came to her eyes. She badly needed to speak to him. She left a brief message that she was staying overnight in Chilswood, and to phone her on her mobile when he had a chance. Then, holding at bay the myriad questions gnawing at her mind, she went to the bathroom.

The cold water revived her a little, and after

reapplying such make-up as she had with her, and brushing her hair with the silver-backed brush on the dressing table, Rona made her way downstairs.

All the doors were closed, and she hesitated, trying to remember which was the sitting room. The sound of voices drew her forward, and as she put her hand on the knob, she heard Finn say, 'Oh, and another odd thing: the police asked if I knew anyone called Nigel. God knows how they got on to him so quickly.'

'Good God!' Oliver's voice. 'Don't say he's still on the scene?'

Unwilling to eavesdrop, Rona pushed the door open and went in, and the conversation stopped abruptly.

'Have you everything you need?' Oliver asked her. 'Do say, if not.'

'Sally's thought of everything,' Rona assured him, but as talk restarted, her mind was elsewhere. Nigel. She'd heard the name recently. And on cue, she remembered the man in the china shop, who'd reacted so strangely when she mentioned the Curzons. Curiouser and curiouser.

'When I prepared this casserole, I wasn't expecting dinner guests,' Sally apologized as they took their places at the dining table. 'Fortunately I made double the quantity, so the children could have it tomorrow.'

'Now, it will have to be chicken nuggets!'

Nick said with a forced smile.

Rona looked at him curiously. Of them all, Julia's death must surely affect him the most, yet he seemed no more upset than the rest of them. She wondered when and why he and Julia had divorced, and whether Nigel de Salis had had any part in it.

Having not expected to be able to eat, Rona found to her surprise that she was hungry. A great deal had happened since she and Finn had sat over scones together.

Cheese, biscuits and coffee followed the casserole. Every time there was a lull in the conversation, Rona's mind slid back to that scene in the enclosure, Julia's pale face and the blood on her blouse. The knowledge that she was not only dead, but had been murdered, was grotesque, unimaginable.

Finn said suddenly, 'Rona, I meant to ask you; why did that policeman call you Miss Marple?'

Sally gave an amused laugh. 'Did he really?'

'You'd met him before?' Finn pressed.

'Yes, in Buckford. I can't think what he's doing down here.'

'But why Miss Marple?' Oliver asked.

'Because,' Rona answered reluctantly, 'I've – come across murders before.'

'Murders?' Nick repeated. 'In the plural? How many, for God's sake? You're not a crime reporter, are you?'

Rona shook her head. 'They've mostly been in the past,' she defended herself.

'Then why were the police involved?'

'Because in the Buckford case, there'd been a miscarriage of justice.'

'And you sorted it out?' Sally guessed. 'Good for you!'

'The police didn't appreciate it,' Rona said drily.

'I can imagine!'

Finlay pushed back his chair. 'Well, time's moving on,' he said. 'I'd better be getting home. Many thanks, both of you, for taking us in at such short notice.' He turned to Rona. 'Oliver will run you to the factory in the morning, to collect your car. I hope you manage to sleep OK.'

Stupidly, it hadn't occurred to her that he wouldn't also be staying the night. He'd been her rock for the past few hours, and she was reluctant to see him go.

'I must be going, too,' Nick said.

Sally said gently, 'Will you be all right? You're welcome to stay, if you'd like to.'

Nick bent and kissed her cheek. 'Sweet of you, Sal, but I'm better in my own bed. And first thing in the morning, I'll have to go and tell the parents. God knows what they'll make of this.'

As though anxious not to be persuaded, he bid them all a brisk goodnight and left without further ceremony. The rest of them had follow-ed him into the hall, and Sally was taking her leave of Finn when there were two simultaneous interruptions. A sudden wail came from above, and Sally, with a muttered apology, ran up the stairs to investigate. And in the same moment, the telephone in the kitchen started to ring.

Oliver said, 'I'll be in touch, Finn,' and hurried to answer it.

Finlay looked down at Rona. 'You'll be all right, won't you?'

'I'll have to be,' she said.

'If there's anything – oh, hell!' He pulled her suddenly against him and kissed her hard on the mouth. For a moment she clung to him, while unwelcome sensations surged through her. Then his arm dropped and she stepped back. For a long minute they looked at each other, both of them breathing heavily. Then Finn said abruptly, 'Goodnight,' opened the door, and disappeared into the night.

Rona put out a hand to steady herself. Her heart was hammering and she closed her eyes, fighting for control.

'That was Edward, wondering if there's any more news,' Oliver reported, coming back into the hall. 'I told him he'd just missed Finn, so he said he'd try his mobile. Now, would you like a nightcap before you hit the stairs?'

Rona gave him a shaky smile. 'I think I've had enough alcohol for one night, thank you,' she said, grateful that her voice sounded more or less normal.

'About this dog of yours; he's made short

work of the casserole Sally put down for him. Will he be all right in the kitchen overnight?'

'Yes, certainly; he's not allowed upstairs at home. But perhaps he could be let out in the garden for a minute or two?'

'Fine. I'll see to that – you look done in.'

'Thanks, Oliver. It's very good of you and Sally to put me up like this.'

'It's the least we can do, since we seem to have inflicted a family tragedy on you. Or ex-family, to be more accurate. Have you anything to help you to sleep?'

Rona shook her head. 'Only exhaustion!' she said.

'Let's hope that does the trick. Sally will bring you a cuppa when the bathroom's free, but as far as I'm concerned, there's no rush; the office is closed on Saturdays. You'll probably be wanting to get home, though?'

Rona nodded.

'Well, Sal does the school run, and gets back about a quarter to nine; so if you can be down any time after eight thirty, that'll fit in nicely.'

'The children go to school on Saturdays?' Rona asked, surprised.

'Yes, poor little devils, just for the morning; they have Wednesday afternoons off, in lieu. Damned inconvenient if we want to go away for the weekend, but there you go.'

Rona wondered whether to go and see Gus, but decided against it. He might expect to be taken home. In any case, she wasn't sure how

213

long her control would last, and needed to get to her room.

She had, in fact, just reached it when her mobile rang, and Max's voice said in her ear, 'And what have you been up to, while my back's turned?'

Rona said on a gasp, 'Oh, Max!' and burst into a storm of tears.

She didn't sleep, of course. At least, not until light was beginning to seep through the thin curtains. As she tossed and turned, her mind was divided between grief for Julia and the puzzles surrounding her death, and an obsessive replaying of those minutes in the hall with Finn. Hot with shame at her response, she could only hope it hadn't been apparent to him.

She was, finally, in a deep sleep when Sally tapped on the door, and came in to put a mug of tea on the bedside table. Rona started up, confused for a moment as to her whereabouts. Then it all came flooding back, and she gave a little gasp.

'It's a quarter to eight,' Sally told her. 'The bathroom's free, when you're ready, but have your tea first, while you come properly awake. I'm glad you managed to get at least some sleep.'

It occurred to Rona that in all probability, none of them had had much last night.

Max phoned again, just before she went downstairs.

'How are you, darling? What kind of night did you have? I wish to God I could have been with you.'

'Me too, but I survived. How soon will you be home?'

'Before you, that's a promise. What time are you leaving?'

'I've not had breakfast yet. Then I have to collect my car from the factory, but I should be back soon after ten.'

'How's Gus? Did he survive the night without his precious basket?'

'I've not seen him this morning, but I heard him bark a few minutes ago, when the post arrived.'

Max laughed. 'OK. See you later, then. Lots of love in the meantime.'

'You too,' she said.

With the phone still in her hand, she glanced at her watch. There was time to give Lindsey a quick call before she went down.

The phone was picked up at once. 'Ro? Thank God. I was just about to call you.'

'How's Mum?'

'Very shocked, as you'd imagine. She keeps asking what kind of accident it was, and of course I don't know the answer. Are you going to enlighten me?'

'Not at the moment, Linz.' She cut across her twin's indignation. 'Listen, I have to go down to breakfast now, then as soon as I can I'll be on my way home. Max will be back by the time I get there, and we'll both come straight to Maple Drive. Hang on till then, there's a love. Give my love to Mum, too.'

'Will do,' Lindsey said resignedly.

The three little girls were in the hall when Rona went down, dressed in their school uniform. Sally introduced them, but they all looked alike, and their names didn't register.

'I'm just going to run them to school,' Sally said. 'Oliver's in the kitchen and the coffee's on. I'll be back in ten minutes.'

Oliver stood up when she appeared, and she received an enthusiastic welcome from Gus. The morning paper was on the table, and, seeing her anxious glance, Oliver shook his head.

'It's not made the nationals yet, thank God. It'll be in the evening paper, though, and they had it on the local news.'

'What did they say?' Rona asked, dry-mouthed.

'The bare minimum. That the body of a young woman had been discovered in the churchyard of St Barnabus last evening, but her name couldn't be released pending formal identification.'

'Who'll do that?'

'Nick, I suppose, poor devil. Did she – look very bad?'

'No,' Rona answered with a catch in her voice, 'she looked lovely. Just as though she was asleep.'

'Thank God for that. Now, what can I get

you? Cereal? Toast? Afraid we only run to a cooked breakfast on Sundays.'

Rona settled for toast, and Sally was back by the time it was ready for her. By unspoken consent, the murder wasn't referred to again, but it was still a relief when Oliver suggested they make a move. Rona repeated her thanks, and Sally gave her a quick hug.

'When things get back to normal, I suppose you'll be wanting to interview me for your article?' she said.

'I will, yes; I'll give you a call, if that's all right?'

Then she was in Oliver's car, with Gus in the back, and all she could do was wonder if Finlay would be waiting for her at the factory. Part of her longed to see him, part of her dreaded the prospect.

They turned in the gates, and Oliver drove straight to the main car park, where her car stood almost alone. There was no sign of Finn.

Oliver waited while Rona settled Gus in his accustomed place, and gave her a quick kiss on the cheek before she got in herself.

'So sorry you were involved in all this,' he said. 'I hope, now you've given your statement, you'll be left in peace. And on a lighter note, let me know when you want to see me about the article.'

'I will, Oliver. And thank you again.'

With her heart beating uncomfortably fast, Rona drove out of the factory grounds. No one emerged from the office block to waylay her. No doubt Finlay felt that discretion was the better part of valour, and had wisely decided to put some time between their last meeting.

At the junction with the main road, Rona turned right, and thankfully settled back for the journey home to Marsborough.

Eleven

Max was waiting when, having garaged the car, Rona and Gus arrived at the house. He gathered her into his arms and held her tightly.

'I do choose my moments to be away, don't I?' he said into her hair.

'There was no way of foreseeing this.'

'Have you any idea yet what happened?'

'None. It's a complete mystery what she was doing in the cemetery, and Max – the most amazing thing – she used to be married to one of the Curzons.'

He frowned. 'And she never mentioned it?'

'No, though we talked about them quite a lot. And another thing; it seems she lived in Reigate. Remember? Where the mysterious handbag was found, with my name and address in it?'

'Coincidence, do you think?'

'I don't know, but the family kept asking how I met her, and it made me think. As I told you, she bumped into me, quite literally, in Guild Street. Suppose it wasn't an accident? Suppose she waited till I was approaching, then deliberately collided, as a means of getting to know me?'

'But with all due respect, my darling, why should she want to?'

'I've no idea, unless, in view of the secrecy about her marriage, it's tied up with the Curzons.'

'But how would she know you'd any connection with them, or care if you had?'

Rona shrugged helplessly.

'For that matter, how would she recognize you?'

'She had this address; she could have waited for me to come out and followed me. Still, there's no point in going over everything twice; I promised Linz we'd go straight round to Mum's to fill them in, so we can talk it through then.'

'We'd better leave Gus here, since he's not welcome at Maple Drive.'

Rona nodded. 'It could be OK, now Mum's more amenable, but today's not the day to test it. A word of warning: at the moment, she thinks Julia's death was an accident, though I think Linz suspects it wasn't. I'm not looking forward to telling them.'

'Come to that, I don't know much more myself. You weren't exactly coherent last night.'

'No. Sorry.'

'Heavens, there's no need to apologize. I defy anyone to be coherent, after what you'd just been through.'

And that, thought Rona painfully, was even more pertinent than he realized.

Avril and Lindsey were anxiously awaiting them, and Rona, seeing her mother's face, bitterly blamed herself for bringing Julia here.

'What happened, Rona?' Avril burst out, as soon as they were in the house. 'Were you with her? Did she suffer at all? It all sounded so vague.'

'Let's sit down,' Max said calmly. 'Then Rona can explain.'

They did so, Avril perching on the edge of her chair, hands clasped, eyes fixed on her daughter.

Rona said tentatively, 'Have you had the radio on this morning?'

Her mother and sister stared at her in surprise. 'No; why?'

'It doesn't matter.' With a heavy heart, Rona embarked on her story. 'To fill in the background, after Linz and I had lunch yesterday, I drove to Chilswood, to visit the museum at the pottery.'

Lindsey nodded impatiently.

'I – found a letter there that might be very important.' Though it didn't seem so at the moment. 'So I showed it to Finlay Curzon over a cup of tea, and he said he'd discuss it with the family. Then he suggested I might like to see their plot in the churchyard, with the graves of the people I'm researching.'

'I'm sure you could hardly wait,' Lindsey said.

221

'So we went there,' Rona continued, ignoring her. 'At the far side, there was a bench with a plaque on it, and when I walked over to read it, Gus started growling and pulling back, and I saw that – that someone was lying behind it.'

'Not *Julia*?' Avril interrupted.

'Yes, Mum. And she was – dead.'

Avril frowned, shaking her head. 'But you said she'd had an accident. I don't understand. What had happened?'

Rona took a deep breath. 'It wasn't an accident, but I wanted to tell you in person. She'd – been stabbed, I think. Either that or shot, I'm not sure, but her blouse was covered in blood.'

There was total silence. Lindsey was staring at her wide-eyed and Avril's hands went slowly to her mouth. Max reached over and took Rona's hand.

Avril said in a horrified whisper, 'You mean she'd been *murdered*?'

'I'm afraid so, yes.'

'God, Rona,' Lindsey said shakily, 'you do find them, don't you?'

'But why? I mean, who...?'

'I don't know, Mum.'

'So what did you do?'

'Finlay phoned the police on his mobile, and they came and took charge. We were driven to the police station to make a statement, and Oliver and Sally Curzon kindly put me up for the night. They didn't think I was in any state to drive, and Max was away.'

'That was kind of them,' Avril said mechanically. 'But this is – insane! A lovely, bubbly girl like that – who on earth would want to harm her?'

Rona said gently, 'It seems there are things we didn't know about Julia. For one thing, she used to be married to Nick Curzon.'

'And she didn't tell you, when you were talking about them?' Lindsey asked.

'No. And Linz: remember that handbag in Reigate? That's where she lived.'

'What handbag?' Avril demanded, seizing on the shift in subject as a break from more gruesome topics.

Rona explained about the phone call. 'I didn't tell you, because I thought you'd worry there was a stalker after me. But I have to say, the more I think about it, the more I'm wondering if Julia engineered bumping into me that time, as a means of getting to know me. Did she talk to you much about the Curzons?'

Avril looked surprised. 'She did bring them up once or twice, now that you mention it; because of the marmalade pot, the first time. And we speculated a bit about this new product they're bringing out.'

'But she never said she'd been married to Nick?'

'No, definitely not.'

'Did she ask any questions?'

'Yes, but about you as much as the Curzons. How you did your research, and whether you'd

223

discovered any personal things about the families you'd worked on.'

'And you told her I had,' Rona said flatly.

'Well, it's true, isn't it?'

Max hadn't spoken since Rona began talking, but now he leaned forward. 'I think you should tell the police all this.'

'All what?'

'That she asked questions about the Curzons, but never mentioned being related to them. It could be relevant. By now, the police will know she lived in Reigate, but not the connection with the handbag – if indeed she was the owner. That's another thing we should mention.'

'I hope DI Barrett's not in charge of the case,' Rona said in a low voice.

'Who's he?'

'An odious man I met in Buckford, when I was researching for the octocentenary.'

'Well, if he's based in Buckford, he's not likely to be,' Max commented.

'Except that I saw him at Chilswood police station.'

'In what way was he odious?' Lindsey asked curiously.

'Oh, he accused me of thinking I knew more than he did. As it happened, I did, and, through no fault of mine, he ended up with egg on his face.'

'Enough to endear you to him, certainly,' Lindsey agreed.

Avril's mind had moved on. 'Will the police

come here?' she asked nervously. 'Julia's things are still in her room. She was supposed to be going home today.' Her eyes filled with tears.

'They'll want to see everyone she's had dealings with,' Max replied. 'Even as we speak, they're no doubt trying to find out where she's been staying, so that's another thing we should volunteer.'

'As a matter of fact,' Rona said slowly, 'I think I mentioned that, during the interview, but it's all a bit of a blur. They knew by then that I knew her, and it kind of led on from there.'

'In which case, Avril, you can certainly expect a visit.'

Avril said bleakly, 'I wish Tom was here.'

Lindsey sprang up and put an arm round her. 'I can stay, Mum, for as long as you need me. I'll go home and pack a few things.'

Avril reached up and touched her face. 'Thank you, darling. That would be a great comfort.'

Max stood up. 'If you'll excuse me, I'll go into the next room and make that phone call. We don't want to be accused of withholding information.'

Lindsey turned to Rona. 'If you and Max are going to be here for a while, I'll nip home and collect some things to tide me over the next day or two.'

Rona nodded, and Lindsey, too, left the room. In the silence that followed, they heard her car start up and drive away.

Rona said quietly, 'I can't tell you how sorry I am I involved you in all this, Mum.'

Avril smiled tiredly. 'You thought you were doing us both a favour. And she *was* the perfect guest,' she added unsteadily.

Rona bit her lip. 'I bet she couldn't believe her luck, when I fixed her up here.'

Avril raised a hand protestingly. 'Don't judge her too harshly, dear. There could be all sorts of things we don't know.'

'That,' Rona said grimly, 'I don't doubt.'

Somehow, the morning crawled by. Lindsey arrived back with a suitcase, which she took to her old room. Max made himself useful by mowing the back lawn, and Rona helped Avril to make sandwiches for a late lunch.

When they'd finished, Rona said tentatively, 'If you don't mind, I think we'll make a move. Gus is on his own and he needs a walk. He's not had one since—'

She broke off. Since he'd romped in the fields on the way to the cemetery.

'You should have brought him with you,' Avril said absently, and Rona and Max avoided each other's eyes. 'No, you go,' Avril added. 'There's nothing you can do, and Lindsey will keep me company.'

'Thanks, sis,' Rona said quietly as they were leaving.

'No problem. Let us know any developments.'

226

'You too.'

They exchanged a quick hug, and Rona, glad the distressing visit was over, followed Max down the path to the car. Just what, she wondered apprehensively, were those developments likely to be?

As they'd feared, the case was reported in the evening paper.

The body of Julia Curzon, 36, divorced wife of Nicholas Curzon of the famous porcelain firm, was discovered by his cousin Finlay Curzon and a friend, in the family burial ground late yesterday afternoon. She had been stabbed once through the heart. The police are anxious to speak to anyone who might have seen Ms Curzon yesterday, or spoken to her on her mobile phone. The number to ring is...

Max had spread the paper on the kitchen table, and Rona read it over his shoulder.

'She was on the family tree I saw yesterday,' she said, 'but as her maiden name wasn't given as Teale, it didn't register.'

'Perhaps she's married again,' Max suggested.

'Another thing she just didn't happen to mention?' Rona asked bitterly.

'At least you're only referred to as "a friend",' Max said. 'Be thankful for small mercies.'

Later, Tom phoned, wondering if Rona had heard the news. 'I thought, with the Curzon connection, you might have met her,' he said.

'I found her, Pops,' she told him, and wearily had to go through the story again.

'Why did I ever suggest you contact that family?' he demanded vehemently, when she'd finished.

'Actually, we're even more involved,' Rona told him. 'Julia's been staying with Mum.'

'*What?*'

'I fixed it, because she didn't like hotels, and Mum had a lull before the proper lodger.'

'God, yes; Avril told us when we met her. But she didn't mention a name, and naturally I didn't make the connection. Is she all right? It must have been a terrible shock for her.'

'It was, yes, but she's coping. Linz is staying with her for a few days.' Rona paused. 'You said "us"; who was with you?'

There was a brief silence, then Tom said, 'Catherine. Didn't your mother tell you? We met her in Guild Street a couple of days ago.'

'Oh.' For once, Rona could think of nothing else to say.

The police arrived at eleven o'clock the next morning. Max, after breakfasting in his dressing gown with the Sunday papers, had gone up for a shower, and it was Rona who answered the doorbell. On the step stood two men, the taller of whom was, as she'd feared, Detective

Inspector Barrett. He was a lean, loosely jointed man with fairish hair, whose pale eyebrows and lashes gave his face a curiously undefined appearance, at odds with his penetrating grey eyes.

For a moment they eyed each other in a silence broken only by the sound of church bells. Then Barrett said flatly, 'So, Ms Parish, we meet again.'

'Against your express wishes, as I remember,' Rona returned steadily.

'Ours not to reason why. This is DS Bright, by the way.'

Rona and the quiet, dark-eyed man at his side nodded cautiously at each other, then she stood aside. 'No doubt you'd like to come in.'

'If we may.'

She led the way into the sitting room, and Barrett looked about him appraisingly.

'Certainly one up on a cottage in Mayhem Parva,' he commented grudgingly, and Rona caught the sergeant's puzzled frown.

'Please sit down,' she said.

They did so, Bright, who had taken out a notebook, opting for an upright chair against the wall.

'I've read your statement, of course,' Barrett began, 'part of which is corroborated by Mr Finlay Curzon. What interests me, though, is your relationship with the deceased. How, exactly, did that come about?'

Perfunctorily, Rona went yet again through

her meeting with Julia, arranging for her to stay with Avril, and their developing friendship. Barrett listened in silence until she came to a halt.

'Yet you maintain that never, in the time you spent together, did she tell you her real name, or that she'd been part of the Curzon family?'

'No, she didn't, even though she knew I was writing about them.'

'Have you any idea why not?'

'None.'

'Did she ever mention having been married?'

'I think she made some reference to her ex; that was all.'

Barrett sucked on his lower lip. 'Your husband reported an incident relating to a handbag. Can you elaborate on that?'

Rona did so, and he nodded absently. No doubt he'd already checked with Reigate police, and she wondered what conclusion they'd reached.

'You never taxed her with this?'

'I'd no reason to. It was only after her death that I learned she came from Reigate.'

'But you must have asked where she lived?'

Rona thought back. 'She just said she moved about a lot, but that her family was in Dorset.'

'And you now believe the handbag had some connection with her?'

'It seems highly likely, wouldn't you say?'

'Unfortunately, "highly likely" doesn't carry much weight with the police, Ms Parish. We

230

need concrete evidence before reaching a conclusion.' He leaned back, crossing one leg high over the other, and surveyed her malevolently. 'However, since you're not hampered by such niceties, perhaps you'd kindly tell us who killed her? It would save a lot of time all round.'

Rona flushed and did not reply.

'Ms Parish here has all the answers,' Barrett tossed over his shoulder in the direction of the sergeant, who kept his eyes firmly on his notebook. 'She's made a name for herself by showing up the police all over the county.'

'Not true,' Rona said quietly. 'But I didn't expect to see you so far from Buckford, Inspector.'

'Moved to Chilswood for family reasons,' he replied, 'but I reckoned it was still a safe distance from Marsborough. I'd forgotten how wide a territory you cover.'

'I didn't realize we had visitors,' said a cold voice from the doorway, and Max came into the room. Barrett hastily uncrossed his legs and stood up, as did the sergeant.

'DI Barrett and DS Bright, Chilswood CID, sir,' he said, in a completely different tone. 'We've been speaking to your wife about the recent suspicious death.'

'So I gathered.' Max's voice was still icy. Rona wondered how much he'd heard.

'You never met the deceased yourself, sir?'

'That's correct.'

Max stood waiting, his face impassive, and

Barrett's eyes dropped. 'I think we have all we need for the moment,' he said after a pause. 'We won't take up any more of your time.'

Max turned back into the hall and opened the front door. 'Good morning, officers,' he said evenly, and closed it behind them.

'Odious man, indeed,' he remarked to Rona. 'How long had he been giving you grief?'

'He was just warming up when you appeared.'

'Well, don't let him get to you. From what I heard, his manner was hardly professional. Any more of it, and I'll report him.'

'My knight in shining armour!' Rona said, and he laughed.

'Come on, we've wasted enough of the morning. Let's drive out somewhere for a pub lunch and a good long walk.'

Gus, picking up on the last word, looked up expectantly, tail wagging.

'You're on!' Rona said.

The police – though not Barrett and his henchman – also called at Maple Drive, searched Julia's room and interviewed Avril. According to Lindsey, who, fortunately, was there at the time, they'd asked what Avril knew of Julia's background – which was virtually nothing – and when she'd last seen her. Apparently she'd left the house at nine thirty on Friday morning, saying she'd be home about six and would cook Avril a special meal, since it was to be her 'last supper'. A strangely prophetic phrase, Rona thought with a shudder.

'I've persuaded Mum to go to the library as usual tomorrow,' Lindsey finished. 'I'll have to work myself, and it's better than her sitting around here by herself. No one's likely to connect her with Julia – as far as the public's concerned, there's no local link – and since it's only for the morning, it shouldn't be too much of a strain. In fact, it'll take her mind off things.'

Rona hoped she was right.

Now that the immediate shock was lessening, Rona's thoughts had begun to revert to the letter she'd found and, more personally, to her last encounter with Finlay. At best, it would make their next meeting embarrassing. Perhaps, she thought wryly, she should ask Lindsey's advice on the protocol in such circumstances.

Had events not overtaken them, she might well have confided in her sister, simply for the relief of being able to talk about it and thrash out her reactions. There was, of course, no question of things going any further; her main fear was that her instinctive response might have given him the opposite impression.

In the meantime, although she'd promised not to divulge the letter's contents, she wrote out as much of it as she could remember, glad of something far removed from present worries on which to exercise her mind. *Had* old George so

233

far defied convention as to marry his mistress, thereby creating all manner of problems for his descendants?

Rona was engaged in transcribing the notes she'd made in the museum – the task having been set aside for more pressing matters – when, on the Tuesday morning, the phone interrupted her. She half expected to hear Lindsey, but the voice that greeted her was not her sister's.

'Rona – hi! Tess here.'

Rona tensed. Tess Barclay, though a friend, was also a reporter on the *Stokely Gazette*, and she was instantly on her guard. Unnecessarily, as it turned out.

'Your cover's blown, chuck,' Tess informed her breezily. 'Been up to your old tricks, have you?'

Without hope, Rona played innocent. 'What do you mean?'

'Unearthing dead bodies all over the county.'

'Oh, Tess, you're not going to drag me into it, are you?'

'You're already in it, love,' Tess retorted. 'The mysterious "friend" who happened to be on the spot. Since when were you a friend of Finlay Curzon? Anyway,' she went on, mercifully not waiting for an answer, 'the case is hot news – and so, for that matter, are you, after all your previous doings. It's a wonder you've escaped thus far – sheer luck, if you ask me.'

'So how did you hear?'

'Our crime reporter has a nose like a blood-hound. Even looks like one, come to think of it. So how about helping out an old pal and giving me an interview?'

'I'd really rather not, Tess.'

'Oh, come on! A spot of publicity never hurt anyone, least of all a writer. Someone will be after you, that's for sure; it might as well be me. And you owe me, remember, over that other case.'

'It wasn't a "case",' Rona returned waspishly, 'and if *you* remember, the debt was paid in the form of a meal out.'

'Look, this is urgent and I haven't time to plead. Because of Easter, everything's brought forward and tomorrow's press day. So smooth down your feathers, there's a love, and give me a phone interview.'

'But you must know all the facts. I can't tell you anything new.'

'You can tell me what the hell you were doing in a cemetery in Chilswood on a Friday evening. Not, I presume, one of your usual haunts – if you'll excuse the pun!'

Reluctantly, and with as little detail as she could get away with, Rona went through her story.

'And you just happened to be with her ex's brother when you found her,' Tess mused. 'Isn't that rather stretching coincidence?'

Rona said woodenly, 'He was showing me the

235

family plot.'

Tess sighed. 'You're not being very helpful. You've forgotten to mention, for instance, that you knew the girl yourself, and that she was staying with your mother.'

Rona felt a spurt of anger. 'Where did you get that from?'

'The police were a bit more forthcoming than usual.'

'Bloody Barrett!' Rona said under her breath. 'What?'

'Nothing. But that proves my point – you already know as much as I do. Look, I'm sorry, Tess, I'm really not trying to be difficult.'

'You could have fooled me.'

'It's just that it's a bit too close to home, and I'd prefer to keep a low profile.'

'Not much chance of that, I fear. So – you're turning the spotlight on the Curzons. How are you finding them?'

'Very helpful,' Rona said steadily.

'This must have been a bit of a shaker, though. What about the one who was married to her? Know him?'

'I've met him, yes; it was a terrific shock for him.'

'I'll bet it was. *Entre nous*, and strictly not for publication, do you think he did it?'

'Oh, for heaven's sake, Tess! Of course he didn't!'

'Well, he'd certainly be *my* prime suspect.'

'One thing, Tess: say what you have to about

me, but *please* don't reveal she'd been staying with Mum. It has nothing to do with the case, and she's upset enough without everyone quizzing her about it.'

Tess thought for a minute. Then she said, 'OK, fair enough. If it gets out, it won't be through me.'

'Thank you.'

'That's another debt you've clocked up, buddy-buddy.'

'Supper anytime, at a restaurant of your choice.'

Thankfully, Rona put down the phone. So once again she'd be hitting the headlines, she thought resignedly. Well, it probably wouldn't make much difference.

That afternoon, Finlay phoned, and Rona felt her cheeks burn as she returned his cautious greeting.

'I hope you've managed to recover from that ghastly business last Friday,' he said hesitantly.

'Just about, I think. What about the rest of you?'

'The police interviewing has been pretty intensive, and obviously that's a strain, especially on the older generation.' He paused, then went on rapidly, 'Rona, before we go any further, I really must apologize for my behaviour the other night. It was – totally uncalled for.'

She said carefully, 'Don't worry about it; we were all under a lot of stress.'

'That's very generous of you. May I hope I'm forgiven, then?'

'Of course.'

'Then would you consider meeting me for a cup of tea? There are quite a few things we need to discuss, and it would be easier here; the press are everywhere in Chilswood.'

'You're in Marsborough?'

'Yes, I have some business to see to, but I'll have finished by about three thirty, if that's convenient? At the Clarendon, say?'

Rona hesitated. She'd not been to the hotel since traumatic events had overtaken them all at Christmas, but she couldn't stay away for ever, and afternoon tea was as innocuous a way as any of re-establishing herself there.

'That would be fine,' she said.

Twelve

Finlay was already there when she walked into the hotel lounge, and stood up to greet her. He was wearing a light grey suit and a blue tie that echoed the colour of his eyes, now watching her a little anxiously. He held out a hand, and she shook it.

'Thanks for coming, Rona.' He pulled out her chair, and they both sat down. 'I've ordered tea for two. I hope that's all right?'

'Thank you, yes.'

He sat back in his chair. 'Well, where do we start? The family have all been interviewed, poor Nick, of course, getting a particular grilling. No doubt you've also had the police round?'

She nodded. 'Sunday morning, no less.'

'What were they concentrating on?'

'How well I knew Julia, what she had and hadn't told me. I don't think I was much help.'

'You'd really no idea she'd been married to Nick? It seems incredible, if you were as friendly as you say, and she knew you were writing about the firm.'

'Exactly. You'd expect her to have at least

239

mentioned it, wouldn't you? To be honest, I feel rather hurt; it seems she wasn't being genuinely friendly, just using me to find out about your family.'

He frowned. 'Find out what? Hell, she knew us better than you do.'

Their tea arrived and was laid out on the table between them: sandwiches, scones with jam and cream, little iced cakes. When they were alone again, Rona said, 'Frankly, I don't know what she was after. My mother says she asked a lot of questions, about my methods of research among other things. And don't forget she was expecting to come back soon; perhaps, having done the groundwork, she meant to dig deeper then.'

She poured the tea, and handed Finlay a cup. 'Anyway, how are things going at your end? There haven't been any arrests, have there?'

'Not as yet.' He passed her the plate of sandwiches. 'Nick was steeling himself to identify her, but her brother came up from Dorset. Couldn't wait to get away again, according to Nick, who says he's a pretty useless character. He and his wife have never got on with Julia.'

'Had she no one else?'

'No, there were just the two of them, and their parents are dead.'

'It seems dreadful, that she's getting no support from her family. She was such a happy, friendly girl.'

Finlay pulled a face. 'We'll have to agree to

240

differ on that one.'

Rona was silent for a moment, then came to a decision. 'Could I ask you something?'

'Of course.'

'When we were at your brother's on Friday, I overheard you talking about someone called Nigel.'

'Ah. Yes.'

'Was it by any chance Nigel de Salis, who has the china shop in Woodbourne?'

Finlay stared at her. 'Good God, don't say you know him, as well?'

'Not really, no. But after I'd had lunch with your sister, I was passing the shop and noticed the wide range of Curzon in the window. So I went in. Mr de Salis came to serve me, but when I said I was writing about the family, his whole manner changed.'

'I bet it did,' Finlay said.

'So it *was* that Nigel? He knew Julia?'

'You could say so. He was the one she ran away with.'

Rona stared at him. 'But – he came back?'

Finn nodded. 'After about six months. His wife forgave him.'

'What did Julia do?'

Finn lifted his shoulders.

'She didn't try to make up with Nick?'

'I don't think so, but he wouldn't have had her back. The whole business hit him hard, and he was very bitter about it.'

Would Finlay have his own wife back, given

the chance? Rona wondered. And had she also gone off with another man?

She said quickly, 'Could Julia have been trying to get back at him in some way?'

'I can't imagine why; it was she who left him.' He passed his cup across for a refill, and Rona silently complied. 'It was a shock, I can tell you, when the police asked about Nigel; I'd no idea they were still in touch.'

'So I suppose he'll have been interviewed, too.'

'Without a doubt.'

'I wonder how his wife took that. She was very keen to stress they only dealt with your sales reps and didn't know the family.'

'Wishful thinking!' Finlay commented.

'Have they any children?'

'I believe so, yes. In their teens.'

'What a mess,' Rona said soberly.

'Murder usually is. And divorce, for that matter.'

She felt it safer to make no reply.

'About that letter,' Finlay went on after a moment. 'I spoke to Uncle Charles about it, and amazingly enough, another one came to light during the move.'

'From Spencer?' Rona asked eagerly.

'Yes. It seems to have been written after the one you found, regretting he'd been so explicit and asking Frederick to destroy it. They were all wondering what had been in the first letter, and I was able to tell them.'

'Was there any truth in it, that George had married that woman?'

'The jury's still out on that one. However, it's spurred Uncle to do some searching and see what he can unearth. Frederick was a bit of a hoarder; there are reams of papers and files and Lord knows what, that Uncle's had neither the time nor the inclination to go through. He says he was waiting for someone to write the family history, in the hope they'd do it.' He smiled at her. 'So perhaps it's up to you.'

'Are you serious?'

'I don't see why not. Who knows what else might be waiting to be discovered? Would you be prepared to take it on, if the rest of the family agree?'

'Like a shot!' Rona said. 'But surely, if this was what so worried your father—'

'I shouldn't put too much weight on that; as I said, it was only his illness magnifying things. I reckon this far down the line, its coming out can't do much harm.'

'But what about the child? Spencer was afraid he might claim an inheritance?'

'According to the letter, the woman had been given a once-and-for-all settlement. That, apparently, was the usual practice in such cases. So, if you're prepared to give it a try, and everyone's in agreement, let's go for it. They say that if you trace your ancestry, you're likely to find someone hanged for sheep-stealing, so let's see what we come up with. Anniversaries are a time for looking back, after all. Oh, and Uncle said to tell you they're happy see you whenever you're ready. That would be an opportunity to start the ball rolling.'

Rona told Max about the proposition on the phone that evening.

'Isn't that beyond the call of duty?' he asked.

'I'm quite happy to do it. You know how I love ferreting about in family history.'

'Will they pay you for it?'

'Heavens, it never crossed my mind. It's just an extension of what I'm already doing.'

'But it will save them the bother of sorting through all those papers, or paying an archivist to do it.'

'A more pertinent question is whether or not Barnie will allow me extra space. We could be looking at three articles, if something worth-while comes up. I'll have a word with him, once I've seen Charles Curzon and have a better idea of what's involved.'

'On your own head be it,' Max warned her.

'It usually is!' Rona replied. 'Oh, and by the way, I'll be featuring in the *Stokely Gazette* this week, thanks to Tess.'

She went on to relay that morning's phone call. 'Tess said the police had been unusually forthcoming. In other words, that blasted Barrett has been spilling the beans.'

'Well, it was bound to come out,' Max soothed her. 'I've been expecting it daily. Even if

244

your pals at Curzon avoided naming you, all it needed was the right question at a press conference.'

'Especially if it was Barrett who happened to be holding it.'

'Don't let him get to you, honey. In this instance, he'd only have been doing his job.'

'Wasn't that the Nazis' excuse?' Rona asked bitterly.

Lindsey phoned the next morning.

'Mum's been fussing about Julia's things,' she told Rona. 'They're still in her room, and she has to get it ready for the new girl, who's due on Tuesday. The only thing the police removed was her briefcase; they said her brother would collect the rest when he came to identify the body. Naturally we heard no more, and when I phoned to ask what was happening, they said he'd "declined" to take them, and that Julia's flatmate would come for them. Talk about passing the buck. Anyway, I explained the position, stressing that it wasn't up to Mum to clear the room so would they please chivvy the girl along; and the upshot is she'll be here in the morning.

'Which is the point of this call; Mum can't face meeting her, or seeing Julia's things being packed up, and I'll be at work, so she wonders if you'd come over and supervise proceedings. Would that be a problem?'

Rona's heart sank; it wouldn't be easy for her,

either, though it was possible she'd learn something from the flatmate. In any case, she'd no option.

'Of course I'll come.' Another instance of the brother's 'uselessness', she thought. 'A bit hard on the friend, isn't it? What's she supposed to do with the things? There must be a whole lot more at the flat.'

'Her worry, not ours,' Lindsey said succinctly.

'So what time is she arriving?'

'I don't know; the police have given her directions. Presumably she'll be coming from Reigate.'

'That's just off the M25, isn't it? Provided the traffic's not too bad, it should take under two hours, which would make it around mid-morning. No need to stay overnight, anyway.'

'For which we can be duly thankful. Her name's Deborah Phillips, by the way. Oh, and I'm moving back home tonight. Mum's over the worst of the shock, and preparing for this Sarah will keep her occupied, once Julia's things have gone. So – thanks for that, sis, and I'll see you Saturday, if not before.'

'Saturday?' Rona repeated with a frown.

'The family lunch in Cricklehurst. Don't tell me you'd forgotten!'

'With all that's happened, it had gone completely out of my head. Just as well you reminded me, though I suppose I'd have seen it in the diary. Shall the three of us go together?'

'Oh, definitely. Safety in numbers! Shall I

drive to your house?'

'No, don't bother; we can pick you up and go via the ring road. We're to be there at twelve thirty, so we'd better collect you soon after eleven, to allow for holiday traffic.'

'I'll be ready.'

Lindsey's second phone call came that evening, as Rona was awaiting Max's midweek return.

'Ro – guess what?'

'Tell me.'

'I've just got home, and there's a message on the answerphone from Dominic!'

'Ah, I'm favoured with a name at last.'

'He rang on Sunday; what should I do?'

'Wait for him to ring again.'

'But he left his number; he's probably been expecting me to call back.'

'Then let him expect a little longer; it won't do him any harm. What was the message?'

'That he'd like to see me sometime.'

'Fine. Well, it's not incumbent on you to answer that, is it? If he's interested, he'll be in touch.'

'But after all this time, he probably thinks *I'm* not.'

'"All this time"? It's only three days, Linz, and he waited over a week to contact you; you don't want to seem too eager.'

'Even though I am?'

'Especially if you are. And when he *does* phone – and he will – mind you don't apologize

247

for not getting back to him.'

'All right, I'll play it your way. But if I miss out over this, I'll never forgive you.'

The *Stokely Gazette* was lying on the mat when Rona came down the next morning, and she steeled herself to pick it up. Being a local paper, the murder was, as she'd feared, still front-page news.

'Hitting the headlines?' Max queried, joining her in the hall.

'That's what I'm checking,' she answered grimly.

Together, they read through the update, relieved to note Tess had kept her promise and Rona's name was mentioned only briefly at the end of the report:

> It has emerged that the unnamed friend with Finlay Curzon was the writer Rona Parish, who is engaged on a history of the family. Ms Parish, whose work regularly appears in *Chiltern Life*, has, through her researches, helped the police close more than one 'cold case' over the past year. It will be interesting to see if she's of equal assistance in a more immediate one.

'Barrett will love that,' Rona commented. She'd have preferred no mention of her previous exploits, but after all Tess *was* a journalist, and owed it to both the paper and her readers to pass on such information as she had.

'Should keep him on his toes,' Max agreed. 'All in all, though,' he continued as they went down to the kitchen, 'I reckon you've got off pretty lightly. Had she been so inclined, Tess could have made a much bigger story of it.'

Finlay Curzon sat gazing at the letter that had arrived with the morning post. Printed in clear block capitals, it was brief and to the point, and read: YOU KILLED HER, YOU BASTARDS, AND I'LL SEE THAT YOU PAY FOR IT.

He looked up at his assistant's worried face. 'I wondered when it would be my turn. No clues on the envelope, I suppose?'

Meg shook her head. 'Also block capitals, and the postmark was Chilswood. A first-class stamp.'

'The same as the others. You're hanging on to them, aren't you, the envelopes too? If there's any more trouble, the police might want to test the flaps or stamps for DNA.'

'Shouldn't they be informed?'

'We discussed it when the first one came, but there doesn't seem much point. In the circumstances, it's probably par for the course.'

'They can't be from the murderer, can they?'

'God knows,' Finlay answered wearily. 'Put me through to Edward, would you please, Meg?'

At ten o'clock, Rona left home, and drove to

her mother's house with a heavy heart. Gus, up to now an unwelcome visitor here, accompanied her; she felt in need of him.

'Best behaviour, now,' she warned him as she unlocked the front door, wondering when she'd last used a key to let herself into this house. She stood for a moment in the hall, feeling the emptiness enfold her, and the dog paused at her side, looking up at her enquiringly. From somewhere – probably the dining room – came the steady tick of a clock, and the fridge hummed tunelessly in the kitchen.

'Stay!' she ordered Gus, and reluctantly went up the stairs and into the guest room. At first glance, it looked no different from when her mother had shown herself and Lindsey the new decorations. But as she moved further into the room, she could see some personal items on the dressing table: a small leather travelling clock, a brush and comb, and a box of tissues, with a crumpled one bearing the imprint of a pair of lips.

Rona averted her eyes. Julia must have blotted her lipstick before leaving on her last, fatal journey. Why had she gone to Chilswood? Wouldn't she have been wary of bumping into her erstwhile relatives? Or, as Tessa clearly suspected, had she arranged to meet one of them?

Rona opened the wardrobe and surveyed the few clothes hanging inside: a raincoat, a short grey skirt, and a few blouses. On the shelves alongside were some items of underwear and an unopened pack of black tights, while on the floor beneath, two pairs of shoes and some bedroom slippers stood neatly side by side.

A fly was buzzing against the window pane, and Rona opened it to let it out. But despite her attempts to guide it, the fly refused to take the offered escape route, and eventually she gave up. She was still at the window when a small blue car drew up outside, and she saw that Deborah Phillips had arrived.

Rona took a step back and watched as the driver emerged from it, a slight figure with a mass of unruly brown curls. Then she ran down the stairs, and opened the front door just as her visitor reached for the bell.

'Oh!' The young woman looked taken aback. 'Mrs Parish?' she asked hesitantly.

'No, her daughter. She hopes you'll excuse her, but she's at work, so she asked me to meet you.'

Deborah Phillips's face cleared. 'You're Rona?'

'Yes – and you're Deborah.'

'Debbie.' She held out her hand, which Rona took. 'I was hoping to see you; I've heard so much about you from Julia.'

Her voice shook as she said the name, and Rona took her arm and drew her inside. 'Would you like some coffee before you start on the packing?'

'Thank you, that would be great.'

She followed Rona into the kitchen and sat down at the table while Rona filled the kettle. With her back to her visitor, Rona said quietly, 'I'm so very sorry about Julia. It's been an awful shock for us all, but it must have been far worse for you. Or would you rather not talk about her?'

She turned, surprising tears in Debbie's eyes. 'Actually, I want to. I want to know everything you can tell me about her time up here.'

Rona smiled ruefully. 'And I was hoping you could tell me.' She took down the cafetière and ladled coffee into it. 'When did she decide to come?'

'It was decided for her, about six weeks ago. She went where her firm sent her.'

'So it wasn't her idea?'

Debbie flicked her a glance. 'I think she suggested they might consider Marsborough. It would—' She broke off, and Rona didn't press her.

Instead, she said, 'If you know about me, you must have spoken to her while she was here.'

'Oh yes, several times. She – liked you very much.'

Rona poured boiling water on the coffee, then turned and leant against the counter. 'Debbie, did Julia know about me *before* she came up here?'

Debbie's eyes fell. 'I don't know what you mean.'

'It doesn't matter.' She took down two mugs

and put them on the table. 'Milk and sugar?'

'Just milk, please.'

Debbie watched as Rona depressed the plunger and poured the coffee. 'She was so grateful to you, arranging for her to stay here. It made all the difference.'

Rona didn't reply directly. 'How long have you shared a flat?'

'Since she came to Reigate.'

'When was that?'

'About eighteen months ago.'

'But you'd known her before?'

'Oh yes, since schooldays.'

'She was using the name Teale up here. Do you know why?'

'She always used it for work. Curzon was too well known, and she wouldn't revert to her maiden name, because it reminded her of her brother. Teale was her grandmother's name.'

A simple explanation, after all. And it seemed Julia really had come up here on business, even if she'd suggested it. That much was true, at least.

She said suddenly, 'Did she ever lose her handbag?'

Debbie looked at her in surprise. 'Yes, she did. How did you know?'

'I'll explain in a minute; can you tell me how it happened?'

Debbie took a sip of coffee. 'It was about a week before she came up here. We'd arranged to meet for lunch, and she arrived with a brand

253

new shoulder bag. When I commented on it, she said she'd been on her way to meet me when the strap of her old one snapped, so she went into a department store to buy another.

'When she'd chosen it, she handed over her credit card, and while the assistant was busy at the till, started to transfer things to the new bag – wallet, diary, keys, and so on. Then she was asked to punch in her PIN, so she dropped the old bag on a chair. The shop was crowded, and when she turned back, it had gone. The assistant was very upset and wanted to call the manager, but Julia told her not to bother. She'd removed everything of value, and would have thrown the bag away anyway. She told me all she'd lost was a favourite lipstick. "I wish whoever it was joy of it", she said.'

Another mystery explained, and, again, quite simply. Debbie was looking at her curiously.

'Are you going to tell me how you knew?'

'I had a phone call from the Reigate police, saying my bag had been handed in.'

Debbie stared at her. '*Your* bag?'

'Yes. Apart from a few cosmetic items, all that was in it was a slip of paper with my name, address and phone number on it. That's why I asked if Julia knew of me before she came.'

A dull flush spread over Debbie's cheeks. 'I think she did, yes.'

'How?'

'Through Nigel – the man she was in love with.'

'They were still in touch?'

'Oh yes; they met at every opportunity. He belonged to a London club and used that as an excuse for going there. Julia would meet him, and they'd spend the night together.'

It was Rona's turn to look confused. 'If they were still so fond of each other, why did they split up?'

'Because of the effect it was having on his family. The children were at an impressionable age and his wife couldn't cope. I believe she's a very nervy individual.'

'But how did *Nigel* know my address and phone number, and why ask Julia to contact me? At that stage, I'd never even met him.'

'I'm not too clear on that. She was very vague when I asked her, but I think it had to do with the family. The Curzons, I mean. Are you connected with them at all?'

'I'm writing an article on the firm, yes.'

'That must be it, then.'

'They're launching a revolutionary new line in the autumn. Perhaps he thought I'd know about it and be prepared to tell a friend; though what use it would be to him, I've no idea. It's not as though he's a competitor – he only sells the stuff.'

Debbie fidgeted uncomfortably. 'I'm afraid I can't help you.'

'No wonder it knocked the stuffing out of him, when I appeared in his shop as large as life,' Rona went on, thinking aloud. 'It must have been like the mountain coming to Mahomet.' She drew a deep sigh. 'Well, I wasn't much use to either him or Julia. I've no idea what the product is.'

Debbie said awkwardly, 'I don't blame you for being annoyed, but although admittedly she set out to meet you, she really did like you. Very much.'

'I liked her, too, and so did my mother.'

'Yes; Julia said she was very kind to her.' Debbie took a gulp of coffee. 'Have you any idea who could have killed her?'

'None at all.'

'I did wonder, if she was poking her nose where she wasn't wanted, if someone might have decided to stop her.'

Rona's mouth went dry. Not the Curzons, surely? 'I can't think who,' she said.

'What was she doing in the cemetery, anyway? It just doesn't make sense.'

'Actually, it's an ideal place to meet secretly. There's a high hedge round it, so except at the entrance, no one can see inside.'

Debbie stared at her. 'You know it? You've been there?'

Rona bit her lip. So after all her pleas to Tess, she'd given herself away. 'I was with Finlay Curzon when he found her,' she said.

'Oh God, no!'

'As I said, I'm writing about the firm and had been studying the family tree. He thought I might be interested to see where all the people

I'd been reading about were buried.' She looked at her visitor's distraught face. 'If it's any comfort, I'm sure death was instantaneous,' she added.

Debbie didn't reply, and Rona saw she was struggling to compose herself.

'When did you last speak to her?' she asked gently.

Debbie fished in her handbag for a handkerchief and blew her nose. 'She phoned on Friday morning. Then I rang back later, to ask her to collect something on the way home, but her phone was switched off.'

'How did she seem, when you spoke to her?'

'Fine. She said she'd be back in time for lunch the next day. I was expecting her, when the police arrived. I just couldn't—'

'How did they know to contact you?'

'From my message on her mobile – I'd rung from the flat. The police up here saw it was a Reigate code, and got on to the local station. They were very kind, the two who came to tell me, but then other officers arrived and went through the flat with a fine-tooth comb. They looked under her mattress, pulled out drawers, and went through all our books, cassettes and CDs, looking inside the covers in case anything was hidden there. I suppose they had to, in case there were any clues as to who might have killed her, but it was horrible.'

'It must have been.' Rona paused. 'Are you alone in the flat now?'

'For the moment, but as soon as the police give their permission, my cousin's coming to join me. She's been looking for somewhere, and I'm only too glad to have the company.' She put down her mug. 'Well, it's no use putting it off any longer. Let's get this over with.'

Rona led the way upstairs and motioned her into the guest room. 'There are a few things in the wardrobe,' she said, opening its door.

The sight of the familiar clothes was, finally, too much for Debbie, and she broke down, sobbing uncontrollably. Rona held her, letting her cry. She wasn't far from tears herself. *Who did this?* she kept asking herself. *Who in the name of heaven could have killed her?*

After a few minutes Debbie straightened and Rona, hastily concealing the lipstick-smudged tissue, passed her the box.

'Sorry,' Debbie said shakily. 'I've been dreading this.'

'I'm sure. Would you like me to help?'

At her nod, Rona wheeled the neat little suitcase out of its corner, lifted it on to the bed, and opened it. It was empty; if it had ever held anything of note, the police would have taken it. Between them and in silence, they laid the clothes carefully in the case, together with the items on the dressing table and the sponge bag Rona retrieved from the bathroom.

'What will happen to all her things?' Rona asked, as Debbie finally closed the case.

'She hadn't made a will, so as next of kin, her

brother will be the benefactor. But he made it clear he doesn't want her personal effects, so most of them will go to charity shops. I'll probably keep something as a memento – an ornament, or something like that.'

They went down the stairs together and Gus, who was asleep on the front doormat, looked up hopefully and wagged his tail. Debbie was too upset to notice him.

She handed Rona a card. 'My phone and mobile numbers,' she said. 'You'll let me know what's going on, won't you?'

'Of course I will.'

Brought together by the shared tragedy, they reached for and held each other's hand. Then Debbie went swiftly down the path, put the case in the boot, and got into her car. Two minutes later, the sound of her engine had died away.

Rona returned to the kitchen, washed up the cafetière and mugs, and put them away. Then she, too, left, hoping that the house was now sufficiently purged to welcome the new lodger the following week.

Thirteen

'Daniel?'

'Hi, darling.'

'Sorry to ring you at work, but I've just bought a copy of the *Gazette*, and it says it was *Rona* who found that body in Chilswood!'

There was a pause, then Daniel said incredulously, 'Are you sure?'

'Quite sure; I've read it twice. Do you think your mother knows?'

'She will if Tom does.'

'Strange they haven't said anything.'

'Not really; after all, what is there to say, other than what you've read? And we're seeing everyone on Saturday, so we'll hear it first-hand then. Sorry, love, I must go – there's a call on the other line. See you later.'

'See you,' Jenny echoed, and thoughtfully switched off her phone.

As Rona approached Marsborough, she became increasingly reluctant to return to the empty house. Her mind still circled round Debbie and Julia, and the tragedy that had overtaken them, and she felt in urgent need of distraction.

260

Reaching a decision, she used her hands-free mobile to call Max.

'I'm feeling restless. Any chance of joining you for lunch?'

He sounded abstracted. 'It's barely twelve o'clock, love, and I've just mixed some fresh colour. Can you give me an hour?'

'OK. I'll pass the time by looking round Netherby's, in the hope of finding something for Catherine. I've been to her bungalow, so I've some idea of her taste.'

Guild Street when she reached it was, as usual, lined with parked cars, and she drove slowly, searching without much hope for a space. Then, just ahead of her, a car pulled away from a meter, and she slid smoothly into its place. Furthermore, there were forty minutes on the clock, which should be ample for her purpose.

'Shan't be long,' she told Gus, who was asleep on the back seat, and set off in the direction of the department store. The lunch invitation had stressed 'No presents', but Rona had no intention of going empty-handed. On the other hand, she knew Catherine would be embarrassed by an expensive gift, and the challenge was to come up with a compromise.

The store was busier than she'd anticipated; and she realized belatedly that it was the school holidays, and children were stocking up on Easter eggs. After trying unsuccessfully to fight her way to a counter, she took the escalator to the second floor and the gift department proper.

There was the usual display of Curzon, but not, at the moment, wanting to underline her link with the firm, she moved instead to a cabinet containing a collection of crystal. And nestling at the back, she found what struck her as the perfect present: a small, delicately coloured paperweight.

The search had taken longer than expected, and time on the meter would be running out. Having paid for her purchase, Rona was relieved when the lift stopped right in front of her, and discharged a couple of people. She stepped inside and pressed the down button, her mind already moving ahead. She'd still be on the early side for Max, but she could stroll round the little garden with Gus, who would be glad of some exercise.

The lift stopped, and she was preparing to leave it when she realized they'd only reached the first floor. The doors opened, and to her consternation, Rona found herself face to face with Mrs de Salis, accompanied by two teen-aged children. The woman stiffened as she recognized her, and would have let the lift go, but the children had already stepped into it and perforce she followed.

'Good afternoon,' she said stiffly, and Rona, equally taken aback, smiled in acknowledgment, her eyes going to the teenagers. Dressed unisexly in jeans and anoraks, they slumped against the sides of the lift, their eyes on the floor. The girl's hair, a mousy brown, was drawn severely back and held in place by a rubber band. Her brother, tall and lanky and aged, Rona guessed, fifteen or sixteen, was, despite his spotty complexion, the better looking of the two, taking after his father rather than his mother.

Catching Rona's glance on them, Mrs de Salis said unnecessarily, 'My son and daughter, Aidan and Lorna.' They looked up on hearing their names, and their mother turned to them, completing the stilted introduction. 'And this is Miss Parish.'

Interest flared immediately on both their faces, and Lorna exclaimed, 'The lady who found the body?'

'Afraid so,' Rona answered, since the other woman seemed incapable of doing so. Both children were now staring openly at her, and she was relieved when the lift reached the ground floor, the doors opened again, and they were faced with a crowd of people waiting to enter.

'Have a good Easter!' she said fatuously, and made her escape.

'Mind if I join you, Ed?'

DI Barrett looked up. 'Be my guest,' he invited laconically.

Charlie Harris, a fellow DI, unloaded his tray on to the pub table – a brimming tankard and a plate of sausage and mash. 'How are things?' he asked as he sat down.

Barrett grunted and pushed away his own plate, where egg yolk was already congealing. 'If people *must* get themselves killed, why can't they have the decency to be Joe or Jane Bloggs? When the name Curzon hits the headlines, sparks fly.'

'That, I have noticed, though I've been pretty tied up with my own case. Has a motive been established?'

'Nope.'

'Weapon?'

'No sign of it, but Marshall says it was a flick knife. One of thousands on the market.'

'Couldn't be a random killing, could it?'

'With jewellery and money untouched, and in the middle of a bloody graveyard?'

'Perhaps not.' Harris reached for the mustard. 'OK, then, give us the low-down. Coming to it fresh, something might grab me.'

Barrett shrugged. 'Any contributions, etcetera. You know who found her, don't you?'

'One of her relations, wasn't it?'

'Accompanied by that bloody Parish woman.'

'Who's she, when she's at home?'

'A journalist, if you please. She queered my pitch up in Buckford a year ago, but that wasn't the first time she'd poked her nose into police business.'

'And what's she done now?'

'Isn't finding the body enough for you?'

Charlie Harris took a mouthful of sausage,

and said indistinctly, 'Hardly her fault, though. She wasn't *looking* for it, was she?'

'Who knows?' Barrett returned glumly. He took a long draught of beer, and wiped his mouth on the back of his hand. 'Point is, she knew the victim, even had her cosily tucked up at her mother's, would you believe. And her account of how they met was, to say the least, unconvincing.'

He leaned forward, arms folded on the table. 'And there's another thing, Charlie. Julia came from Reigate, and we contacted the nearest station to go and break the news to her flatmate. Which they did. But the mention of Buckford-shire rang a bell, and they came out with some cock-and-bull story about a handbag being handed in a few weeks back, with a name and address in it and little else. Like to guess whose name it was?'

'Surprise me.'

'None other than Miss Flaming Parish. They contacted her, but she denied all knowledge of the bag. Quite a coincidence, wouldn't you say?'

'Sure is. No doubt you questioned her about it?'

'We did, though to give him his due, her husband had beaten us to it. Their account tallied with the official report, and no further light's been shed.' He sighed heavily. 'And as if all that wasn't enough, we have lover-boy.'

'How did you unearth him?' Harris asked

with interest.

'He was considerate enough to leave a message on her mobile. A good hour, mind you, after the estimated time of death.'

'Well, he'd not have done that, would he, if he was the guilty party?'

'Double bluff? No, you're probably right; I doubt if he's bright enough.'

'And the message was?'

'How about having a drink before she "headed south"?'

'Was she about to?'

Barrett nodded. 'The next day. Pity she didn't leave earlier, and save us all a heap of trouble.'

'Who is this guy?'

'Name of de Salis; he owns a china emporium in Woodbourne. He and Julia fled the coop two years ago – or the marital nest, at least. They stayed in Woodbourne, and he continued to work at the shop all the time they were shacked up together. Not surprisingly, his wife threw a wobbler and the kids went wild, so he slunk back home with his tail between his legs.'

'And Julia?'

'Took off down south. Though it seems that wasn't the end of it, and they've continued to meet on the QT.'

'He admitted as much?'

'He'd no choice; we had him by the proverbial. But he was up to high doh that we'd tell his wife. Practically wet himself, begging us not to.'

Harris shook his head sadly at the perfidy of his sex. 'But to get back to Julia, what was she doing in this neck of the woods? Did she come up to see him?'

'Not primarily, though no doubt it was a fringe benefit. Believe it or not, she was on business. We went through her briefcase, and she'd had a clutch of interviews with banks and offices around Marsborough. According to her diary, she also met up with a couple of guys after office hours, which we're looking into.'

Charlie Harris wiped a piece of sausage round his plate to retrieve the last of the gravy. 'So if she was working in Marsborough, and de Salis was in Woodbourne, what the hell was she doing in Chilswood?'

'A very good question. Her car was found in the Brook Street multi-storey; ticket having expired 5.10 p.m. Friday – much the same time as she did. What we don't know, of course, is when she arrived and what she did before going to the cemetery. We've put out the usual request for info, but no joy so far.'

He straightened and finished the last of his beer. 'So there you have it, Charlie-boy. Something will emerge, if we keep hammering away. At least one person knows more than he's saying, that's for sure; so once we've seen them all, we'll bring them in a second time, and a third if necessary, till one of them cracks.'

'The best of British,' said Charlie Harris.

Having told Max about her meeting with Debbie, Rona reported her encounter at Netherby's.

'She looked ghastly,' she ended, helping herself to more cheese. 'Heaven knows, she was like a tightly coiled spring last time I saw her, but today she looked positively grey, and her eyes had sunk right into her skull.'

'That's what a philandering husband does to you,' Max remarked. 'Be thankful you haven't that problem.'

'Debbie says he and Julia never really split up, and met regularly in London. Maybe his wife knew. Even if she didn't, the mere fact that she was killed up here, in de Salis terrain, as it were, must have aroused her suspicions.'

'Perhaps she thinks hubby killed her.'

'He might have done, for all we know. For that matter, so might she.'

Max sighed. 'Oh, my love, why is it that you're constantly tied up with murders?'

'Well, you can't say it was my fault this time; I certainly didn't go looking.'

'You don't have to; murders seem to seek you out.'

Rona gave a little shudder. 'What a horrible thought! Especially when I came to be cheered up.'

Max laughed. 'Sorry. What are your plans for this afternoon?'

'I might try to make some appointments for next week. The Charles Curzons, for instance;

Finlay said they're prepared to see me now.'

'You're still intending to go through those papers for them?'

'Given the chance, yes. But I must let you get back to your painting.' She leant across the table to kiss him. 'See you this evening.'

'Yes, here's to a long weekend. I could do with a break, and I'm sure you could too.'

When Rona finally reached home, it was to find a message asking her to ring Finlay.

'Just to say I've spoken to Uncle Charles,' he told her, when she returned the call, 'and he's sending the family papers over to the factory. We're proposing to allocate you a room there, so you can spread them all out.'

'Thanks.' She hesitated. 'Finn, there's something you ought to know.' And she went on to relate the story of Julia's handbag.

'What an extraordinary thing!' he exclaimed, when she'd finished. 'So that's why you reacted to the mention of Reigate. Why didn't you tell me before?'

'Because although I immediately guessed it must have been hers, I'd no proof till I met her flatmate this morning.'

'Have you told the police?'

'Not that I've proof.'

'Don't you think you should?'

'Quite probably.'

'We always thought it strange, you know, that you just happened to meet her in the street. This confirms that she planned it, though God knows why.'

Rona paused, then asked indirectly, 'As a matter of interest, what terms are you all on with Nigel de Salis?'

'Terms? Business ones, that's all.'

'Nick too?'

'Fortunately, Nick doesn't have anything to do with him. De Salis is a good customer, though, and shifts a lot of our stuff. It was tricky for a while, but after he'd gone back to his wife, things gradually settled down. Naturally, we'd no idea he and Julia were still in touch, but in any case Nick had divorced her by then. Why do you ask?'

'I was wondering why the police questioned you about him, right at the beginning.'

'Perhaps his phone number was on her mobile.'

'Could be. Well, speaking of the police, I'd better ring them before I get into any more hot water.'

'Will Tuesday suit you, to make a start on the papers?'

'I was hoping to see your uncle and aunt then, but if I call at the factory first, you could show me where the room is, and everything.'

'Fine. See you then, and have a good week-end.'

As he rang off, Rona steeled herself to phone DI Barrett. No point in handing him an excuse to criticize her, she reflected, as she waited to be connected.

'Ms Parish.' The familiar, sarcastic voice. 'This is an unexpected pleasure.'

'I have *concrete evidence* for you, Inspector, that the handbag with my address in it belonged to Julia Teale.'

A pause, then, 'And that evidence is?'

'Her flatmate told me today that Julia had her bag stolen the week before she came here.'

'So why do you suppose she wanted to meet you?'

'I've no idea. Ask Nigel de Salis.'

Barrett's voice sharpened. 'We don't need your advice on conducting our enquiries. Mr de Salis has been questioned, and we're quite satisfied with his statement.'

'Fair enough; but if you're thinking she wanted to pump me about the Curzons, that doesn't make sense, since she obviously knew much more about them than I do.'

That appeared to silence him, at least for the moment. 'Very well,' he said at last, adding grudgingly, 'thanks for the information about the bag.'

'Always ready to help the police, Inspector,' Rona said crisply, and put down the phone.

Next, she rang the Charles Curzons and made an appointment for eleven o'clock on Tuesday morning, allowing her time beforehand to familiarize herself with her temporary accommodation at the pottery.

And now, she thought, stretching, she would

try to put the Curzons, one and all, out of her mind and enjoy the Easter weekend. Although, with the family lunch in prospect, there was likely to be, at the very least, some interested questioning.

'Is that Mrs Parish?'

'Yes, speaking.'

'It's Sarah Lacey. I've just seen the local paper. Is it – I was wondering – is the Rona Parish who discovered that body any relation?'

Avril's heart sank. Ever since she'd been able to think beyond Julia's death, she'd been worrying about how much to tell Sarah. How would she react, if she discovered the dead girl had been using her room? Suppose she cancelled their arrangement? She'd expected to have until Tuesday to work out the best approach, and the phone call caught her off-guard.

'She's my daughter,' she admitted reluctantly.

'What a terrible experience for her! Is she all right?'

'Yes, she's fine, thank you.' Avril hesitated, then, lest she'd made Rona sound callous, added, 'She's a journalist, you see, so she's seen such things before.'

'A crime reporter, you mean?'

'No, just – a journalist,' Avril said lamely. This was the moment to admit her own acquaintance with Julia, but the words stuck in her throat. Perhaps, she thought cravenly, she'd wait till Sarah had arrived and settled in. Then she mightn't be as likely to pack her bags again.

'You're all set for Tuesday?' she asked.

'Yes, that's the other reason I'm ringing; I expect to be there late afternoon, if that's all right?'

'Fine. I look forward to seeing you.'

Avril replaced the phone with a feeling of reprieve. Before Tuesday, though, she must work out the best way to apprise Sarah of the facts.

'Lindsey Parish?'

Lindsey went still. 'Yes?'

'Dominic Frayne.'

'Hello,' she said weakly.

'Hello.' A pause. 'I tried to get you earlier in the week.'

No apology, Lindsey reminded herself. 'I was at my mother's.'

She closed her eyes, measuring her heartbeats and praying her sister's strategy was the right one.

'Well,' he continued after a moment, 'it's now rather short notice, but I wondered if you'd like to spend Saturday in Paris?'

'Paris?' she repeated uncertainly.

'I have a small plane and go over whenever I can; it's no more hassle than flying to Birmingham. We could have lunch, look at some galleries if you like, or walk in the Bois de Boulogne. Then have dinner, and fly home. What do you say?'

Oh, damn! Damn, damn, *damn*!

273

With an effort she concealed the depth of her disappointment. 'It sounds lovely, but I'm afraid I can't. We have a family lunch on Saturday.'

'Couldn't you excuse yourself?' A note of irritation.

'No; it's a bit complicated, but it's my future stepmother's birthday, and we're meeting her family for the first time.'

'I see.' Clearly, he didn't.

'I'm sorry,' Lindsey said, and waited with crossed fingers. Make or break time, she told herself; if he rang off without suggesting another date, she'd never hear from him again.

'Are you free on Tuesday evening?' he asked abruptly, and she breathed a huge sigh of relief.

'Yes, I think so.'

'Then we could at least have dinner, albeit in less exotic surroundings.'

'I'd like to. Thank you.'

'Very well. I'll call for you at seven thirty.'

'I live at—'

'I'll find you,' he said, and rang off.

Lindsey lowered herself slowly into a chair, her heartbeats nearly suffocating her. Easter in Paris! If only she'd been free to go with him! But at least he'd suggested an alternative. She reached for the phone, then stopped herself. Max would be home, and she didn't want to appear foolish. She'd tell Rona on Saturday.

Good Friday. Somehow, Avril had been expect-

274

ing to spend it with one or both of the girls. But she must be reasonable, she told herself; they had their own lives to lead, and they'd all be meeting at Rona and Max's for Sunday lunch.

Sunday lunch. The phrase was laden with memories, layer after layer of them, the earliest going back to when the girls were young, and were allowed, once a month, to choose the weekend joint. Rona always chose beef, she remembered, and Lindsey lamb. There would be roast potatoes and two vegetables, with either Yorkshire pudding, mint or apple sauce, depending on the meat. And dessert was invariably served with fresh cream – the only meal of the week so blessed.

Later, Sunday lunches had become less happy affairs. During her slide into irritation and depression, she knew the continuing tradition became an irksome duty which her daughters – not to mention her husband – would happily have foregone, but to which she had clung doggedly, as to the last remnants of happier days. And now it had come full circle, and it was she who received the invitation.

With a sigh, Avril went into the kitchen to prepare her lunch, eying almost malevolently the single pack of hot cross buns lying on the table. Times were when two or three packs would not have sufficed. On one occasion, she remembered, the twins had made them during a cookery lesson at school. Lindsey's had turned out very creditably, while Rona's were a total disaster –

perhaps contributing to her lifelong dislike of cooking.

Cheese on toast, Avril thought, starting to prepare it. And there was a piece of salmon for this evening. The rule of no meat on Good Friday still held, though it wouldn't have occurred to her to go to church. And this afternoon she planned to put the final touches to Sarah's room.

Sarah's room, she repeated to herself. Not Julia's. She must forget Julia had ever been here, had perched on this table on her return from work, making Avril laugh with her impersonations of the pompous men she'd met. Julia, who, when pressed to report anything lacking in her room, had suggested a small kettle and tray might be useful, so tea or coffee could be made without going down and disturbing Avril. That had already been put into effect, and it was Sarah who would benefit – Sarah, who was most unlikely to perch anywhere, or to regale Avril with tales of her day.

Slowly, insidiously, the tears spilled down her cheeks, and Avril wept yet again for the young woman who'd met such a brutal end.

Jenny Bishop awoke on the Saturday morning with a vague feeling of malaise. The prawns they'd had last night? she wondered. She lay on her back, letting her thoughts drift while her hands, splayed on her stomach, savoured the movements of the child inside her.

Daniel stirred. 'Cup of tea?' he offered sleepily.

She felt the bile rise in her throat. 'Not at the moment, thanks.' God, she hoped she'd be all right for the lunch. It would be tricky enough meeting her future relatives, without wondering if she'd time to dash to the ladies'. Catherine was so anxious all should go smoothly.

Of course she'd be all right, she told herself firmly. Mind over matter. It worked every time. She reached out a hand to her husband.

'Could I change my mind about the tea?' she asked.

As arranged, Max and Rona collected Lindsey soon after eleven, and the early departure proved a wise decision. The roads were clogged with traffic and there were constant hold-ups, partially explained by there being several garden centres along their route – a magnet for family outings on holiday weekends. Rona wondered how her father and Catherine were faring.

In fact, they arrived just as Rona, Max and Lindsey were getting out of their car, and they walked together to the main entrance of the restaurant. It opened into a bar-cum-foyer, where people studied the menu over drinks as they waited for their tables.

A young man stood up and waved, and Catherine led the way to join him. Introductions were performed, and Rona took immediate stock. Daniel Bishop was tall and thin, and although he had his mother's smile, there was little resemblance between them. He was, frankly, better looking than Catherine, and there was something engaging about his slightly unruly hair and easy charm. Rona decided she approved of her prospective stepbrother.

Jenny, on the other hand, who had also risen awkwardly to her feet, did not, Rona thought, seem at her best. She looked pale, there were shadows round her eyes and, since she wasn't very tall, her seven-month pregnancy seemed to make her top heavy.

They all seated themselves, more drinks were ordered, and gifts exchanged. Tom had given his privately, but Lindsey produced a bottle of champagne, Daniel and Jenny an amethyst brooch, and Rona and Max the paperweight. All were exclaimed over with delight, amid protestations that they shouldn't have bothered.

'Have you been here before?' Daniel asked Rona, who was sitting next to him.

'Only once, soon after Max and I were engaged. It doesn't seem to have changed much.'

'If it ain't broke...' Daniel said. 'Jen and I come roughly once a month. It's great to be within walking distance – no bother about driving home after drinks, or having to phone for a taxi.'

'Yes, we've a restaurant near us that has the same advantages.'

Daniel hesitated, then said in a low voice, 'I

278

hope you won't think it a cheek, but I wanted to let you know how fond we are of your father.'

Rona looked at him, surprised. 'That's nice of you.'

'I mean it. Ma's a different person; he's made her come alive again. I hadn't realized till now just how lonely she must have been since Dad died. I couldn't be happier they've come together.'

'And to return the compliment, I'm very fond of Catherine,' Rona replied. 'It was awkward at first, because I met her before she and Pops became an item and liked her enormously. Then there was a difficult phase...'

'I know. It must have been hard not to resent her, on your mother's behalf.'

'Still, that's behind us now. Mum's made a new life for herself and seems happy, and you only have to look at Pops and Catherine to see how well suited they are.'

They were interrupted by the maître d' approaching to say their table was ready. As they rose to follow him, Rona saw a spasm pass over Jenny's face, and made an instinctive move towards her. But Jenny caught her eye and smilingly, almost imperceptibly, shook her head. Then Daniel took her arm and they all went through to the restaurant.

Rona was glad to see Lindsey was seated next to Daniel. Exposure to some of that charm should help soften her attitude towards the extension of the family. Having omitted to look at the menu in the bar, they now proceeded to discuss their choices. Jenny, apologizing for the fact that she wasn't hungry, announced she would just like some soup, and Rona caught Daniel's anxious glance. They gave their orders, wines were selected, and talk resumed again. And it was Jenny who brought up the subject Rona had been expecting.

'We saw your name in the paper,' she began. 'It all sounded very gruesome.'

'It was, yes,' Rona agreed quietly.

'How did you come to be there?' Daniel asked, and she launched resignedly into an explanation of her connection with the Curzons, and her prior meeting with Julia.

'So you actually *knew* her?' Jenny exclaimed. 'That makes it all the worse. What a coincidence, though, that she should turn out to be related to the Curzons, when you were writing about them.'

Coincidence was hardly the word, Rona thought ruefully, but she didn't elaborate, nor did she embark on the story of the handbag. She'd given an adequate explanation, and she didn't propose to expand on it.

The meal progressed, and conversation became less formal as they started to relax with each other. Pops looked ten years younger, Rona thought fondly; retirement from the stresses and strains of the bank, together with his new life with Catherine, had obviously paid dividends. Her eyes moved to her sister, chatting animatedly to Daniel. There was something about Linz today, some inner excitement that Rona couldn't quite fathom. When they had a moment alone, she'd ask the reason for it.

While the rest of them worked their way through the courses, Jenny, having managed barely half her bowl of soup, toyed with her bread roll and smilingly insisted she was fine, just not hungry. Since she was clearly embarrassed at not taking a full part in the meal, nobody pressed her, but Rona noticed Daniel's constant glance in her direction, and found herself sharing his anxiety.

The crisis came as they were finishing coffee. Jenny made a sudden movement, said hurriedly, 'Please excuse me a moment,' and, as she started up from her chair, gave a little cry and bent over, clutching her stomach.

'Darling, what is it?' Daniel was instantly at her side and Tom, too, was on his feet.

Jenny's face had blanched, but she attempted a smile. 'Sorry, I'm all right now. It was just—'

But she was unable to finish. Another wave of pain washed over her and she gasped for breath.

'Where's the nearest hospital?' Tom demanded briskly, as, between them, he and Daniel helped her from the room, anxiously followed by Catherine.

'Stokely.' Catherine's face was as white as Jenny's; Tom knew she was remembering their headlong dash through the darkness, to be greeted with news of a miscarriage. Oh God, he thought, please not again.

'No time to wait for an ambulance,' he said. 'We'll take her ourselves – we can be there in twenty minutes.' Then, to Jenny, 'Sit down here for a minute, while I bring the car round.'

As he hurried outside, Max, Rona and Lindsey, unsure what to do for the best, joined the group in the foyer.

Daniel turned to Catherine. 'It's the baby, isn't it, Ma?' he said in a low voice.

'It could be a false alarm,' she answered steadily, 'but Tom's right, she needs to be in hospital.'

'There's a list of what she'll need on the pegboard in the kitchen. Could you possibly get it together and bring it over?'

'Of course.'

Max said, 'We'll drive you to the house, then on to Stokely.'

Lindsey, who'd been keeping watch at the entrance, said suddenly, 'The car's here.'

Two minutes later, with Daniel in the back seat next to Jenny, Tom had driven off, and those who were left looked at each other in disbelief. Rona put an arm round Catherine. 'Don't worry,' she said. 'If it's *not* a false alarm, seven-month babies are fine nowadays.'

Catherine nodded. 'The main worry, though, is when she lost the last one, they couldn't stop the bleeding, and she nearly died herself. That's what'll be uppermost in Daniel's mind.'

282

Max, deciding no comment he could offer would be appropriate, turned to practicalities. 'I'll settle the bill, then I'll bring our car round.'

Catherine roused herself. 'Oh, Max, I can't expect you to do that. Tom—'

'Don't worry, we can sort things out later.'

The next hour or so seemed totally unreal. Rona and Lindsey helped Catherine gather the necessities required – an easy task, since most of them were laid out ready in the spare room. Perhaps Jenny had had a premonition she mightn't go full-term. Within fifteen minutes they, too, were on the road to Stokely, a journey passed for the most part in subdued silence.

On arrival at the hospital, they found Tom in the relatives' room. He came quickly to them, taking both Catherine's hands in his.

'Daniel's with her,' he said quickly. 'They've confirmed she's gone into labour, but apart from the fact that it's several weeks early, all seems to be progressing smoothly.'

Catherine nodded, her face tense. She turned to the others. 'Thank you so much for coming to the rescue,' she said. 'There's really no need for you to stay – Tom will be with me, and of course we'll let you know as soon as there's any news.' She gave a tight little smile. 'I'm sorry the lunch party ended so dramatically.'

Rona kissed her. 'Perhaps your grandchild will share your birthday,' she said.

* * *

283

At eleven o'clock that evening, Tom phoned to say that Jenny had had a little girl half an hour earlier. She weighed only four and a half pounds and had been put in an incubator, but seemed to be holding her own. Jenny was exhausted, but delighted with her tiny daughter.

'Are you and Catherine coming home?' Rona asked.

'Yes, and Daniel too; there's no accommodation here. He'll be back first thing in the morning, and will let us know how things are.'

'Give everyone our love and congratulations,' Rona said.

It was only as she turned out the light that she remembered she'd not asked Lindsey the cause of her secret excitement.

Fourteen

Avril heard the news when she arrived at Light-bourne Avenue the next day. Talk of Daniel and Jenny had taken her by surprise; it had never occurred to her that Catherine might have children – indeed, she'd never given the matter any thought. Now, suddenly, they were thrust, fully formed, into her consciousness, together with the realization that the son would be step-brother to her own daughters. It was not an idea she found comfortable.

'So Pops will be a step-grandfather!' Rona ended with a laugh.

'Which, the way you two are going, seems likely to be as close as he'll get!' Avril retorted, with a return to her old sharpness. Then, seeing the look her daughters exchanged, she flushed. 'I'm sorry,' she said quietly, 'that was uncalled for. It took me by surprise, that's all. I hadn't realized – Catherine – had a son.'

Who would also be Tom's stepson, and she liked that thought even less. Though he'd never said so, she'd always suspected he regretted not having a son; now, by default, he'd been pre-sented with one – another reason to resent

285

Catherine.

Max, who'd been down in the kitchen putting the last touches to the meal, appeared in the doorway to announce it was ready – a welcome interruption to the conversation. He escorted Avril downstairs, but Rona put a restraining hand on her sister's arm.

'Are you going to tell me why you're glowing like a hundred-watt bulb?'

Lindsey smiled. 'I meant to yesterday, but events took over. Dominic did ring back, and guess what, Ro? He wanted to take me to Paris for the day! He has a private plane, apparently.'

Rona gazed at her wide-eyed. 'Well done, sis! This time you've netted yourself a millionaire!'

'The only drawback was it was for yesterday; he was quite put out that I wouldn't renege on the family lunch, but when I stuck to my guns, he invited me for Tuesday instead.'

'There!' Rona exclaimed triumphantly. 'What did I tell you? So you're going to Paris on Tuesday?'

'Not to Paris, no, just out to dinner. But he *is* rather special, Ro, private plane or not.'

'It sounds to me as though he's used to having his own way, so be careful you don't always give it to him,' Rona advised, as they went down to lunch.

By tradition, there were two occasions each year when the entire Curzon family gathered for lunch. One was Christmas Day, the other

Easter Sunday. This year, it was to be held at Edward and Anna's house in Nettleton, and tables had been laid end to end to stretch the full width of the conservatory. Anna had placed the six children at one end, knowing they would want to escape as soon as possible. She'd considered the option of seating them at a separate table, but there were two disadvantages: firstly, Harry would refuse point-blank to be classed as a child and placed with his sister and four girl-cousins; and secondly, without the children and in the absence of Jackie and Bill, who were abroad and not really Curzons anyway, the adults would number thirteen.

A ridiculous superstition, Anna had chided herself, but with all the trouble at the moment – sabotage at the factory, the advent of anonymous letters, and, worst of all, poor Julia's murder – she didn't want to take any chances.

And now, after *potage bonne femme*, followed by roast lamb and all the trimmings and a choice of desserts, the children had indeed left them, Harry to escape to his room with a DVD and the little girls to open Easter eggs in what was still called the playroom. Coffee was on the table, and Edward had produced liqueurs.

'A lovely meal, dear,' Elizabeth said with satisfaction, sitting back in her chair. 'Easter wouldn't be Easter without roast lamb.'

Charles gave a slight cough, and, as he'd intended, they all turned to him. 'I know these occasions have always been purely social,' he began, 'but since James and I retired, we're seldom all together like this, and I feel we should take the opportunity to discuss some matters that concern us. If Edward and Anna will allow?'

Anna, whose heart had sunk, murmured the anticipated consent, as did her husband.

'First of all, this ghastly murder. There don't seem to have been any developments over the last few days. I'd ask you all to rack your brains and see if you can come up with any reason at all why Julia should have been in Chilswood, let alone at the cemetery.'

Finn said thoughtfully, 'There seems to be a connection with Rona Parish, but neither she nor I knows what it is.'

'Explain!' James barked, and Finlay related the story of Julia's handbag.

'But that doesn't make sense,' Sybil protested. 'Why would she want to meet Rona Parish?'

'I've been wondering about this ever since she told me on Thursday,' Finn replied. 'I doubt if Julia herself was interested in us, but she was still in touch with Nigel de Salis, remember.' He flung an apologetic glance at Nick, who was staring into his coffee.

'I fail to see the significance,' Charles said.

Finlay raised his shoulders. 'So do I, but I've a feeling there is one. Rona says she went into their shop after lunch with Jackie, and both de Salis and his wife reacted to hearing she was writing about us.'

'Embarrassment, probably.'

'She thought it was more than that.'

Sybil said, 'She's coming to interview us on Tuesday. We could sound her out then.'

'There's something else,' Charles told them. 'I was going to bring it up later, but since Miss Parish has been mentioned, this might be the appropriate place. One way or another, she's become much more involved in our affairs than we'd anticipated when we agreed to her articles. For instance, she found that letter in Father's desk, she's about to go through the family papers – a task long overdue – and she knew Julia personally, not to mention being present when her body was discovered.'

James looked at his brother from beneath beetle brows. 'So? What are you leading up to?'

'I think we should tell her about Genesis.' He looked round at their startled faces. 'I did mention the possibility earlier, but I promised to discuss it with you all, since any decision must be a joint one.' He paused. 'I've a feeling Genesis lies behind a lot of the trouble we've been having. Certainly such sabotage as we've had has been aimed at it, and if Julia *were* interested in us for some reason, all that's changed since she left is the announcement of this new line we're about to produce.'

'And what good would it do her to know about it?' asked Hester.

'She could pre-empt us by selling the story to

the tabloids,' Sam suggested.

'No!' Nick looked up at last. 'She'd never do that. Julia had a lot of faults, but she was never vindictive.'

'To reply to your question, Hester,' Charles resumed, 'I've no idea what advantage it would be. But this Parish girl has a good brain by all accounts, and if we present her with all the facts, she might make some connection that's escaped us. Her parents are friends of long-standing, which predisposes me to trust her, and it goes without saying there'd be an embargo on publishing anything before the anniversary.

'So, I'm asking you to support me in this decision. Is anyone definitely opposed to it?'

There was some murmuring, but no direct answer. 'Then I'll go down the table and ask each of you in turn. I must stress you're perfectly free to object, and if we all agree the objection's valid, we won't go ahead. So – Oliver?'

'As long as she keeps quiet about it, I've no objection.'

'James?'

'I suppose so,' grumbled James.

'Finlay?'

'OK by me.'

'Sam?'

'No objection.'

'Edward?'

'If you think it's best.'

'Nick?'

'I'll go with the flow.'

Finn imagined Rona's reaction to none of the women being consulted. But then none of them was privy to the secret of Genesis; it had been very tightly guarded. Until now. It was, he thought, to the women's credit than none of them had voiced a complaint that an outsider should be informed of it ahead of themselves.

Charles drew in his breath. 'Very well. I take it, then, that I have the agreement of you all that, with the strict proviso that it mustn't be disclosed prior to the anniversary, Rona Parish should be told about Genesis. As Sybil said, she's coming to interview us on Tuesday; I shan't make a final decision until I've met her, but I don't expect to have any reservations. If she meets my criteria, I'll tell her then.'

Rona was about to leave the house on Tuesday morning when Tess phoned.

'Not claiming your free meal already?' Rona teased her.

'No; in fact, I might have forfeited it.'

'Why? You played fair; I've no complaints.'

'The trouble is, someone else at the paper picked up on it. He went through back numbers and has done a thorough reconstruction job on your crime-solving career to date.'

'Oh, no!' Rona groaned.

'I tried to remonstrate, but didn't get any-where. It's been given the go-ahead and will appear on Friday. Rona, I'm so sorry. If I hadn't mentioned you in the first place—'

291

'Don't blame yourself,' Rona said wearily. 'You wouldn't have been doing your job if you hadn't.'

'I really do feel awful about it. At least let me buy you the meal.'

'We'll go Dutch,' Rona said. 'Thanks for the warning, anyway. I'll keep my head down for the next week or so.'

Rona arrived at the pottery just on nine thirty, and was shown up to Finlay's office. He stood up, holding out his hand, and as she took it, she had an unwelcome flash of that moment in Oliver's hallway. The attraction was still there, however well they held it in check.

'Reporting for duty,' she said brightly. 'Or at least, reporting to be given my assignment.'

'There are more papers than I realized,' Finn apologized, 'and frankly, the best place for a lot of them is the bin. If you come across any you feel aren't worth keeping, I'd be grateful if you could put them on one side, so we can flick through them before consigning them to the shredder.'

'Perhaps you should hire a bona fide archivist,' Rona suggested, remembering Max's comment.

Finn grimaced. 'You're right; we've a damn cheek, expecting you to go through them for nothing.'

She flushed. 'Not at all; I'm used to doing research for my articles. I only meant—'

292

'But you're *not* used to being asked to judge the merit of what you find, irrespective of its interest to you, and I'd no right to suggest it. A fee would definitely be in order.'

'I really wasn't—' Rona began again, but again was interrupted, this time by the telephone. She distinctly heard Meg Fairclough's voice say, 'A call for you, Finlay. She wouldn't give her name.'

Finn frowned. 'Put her through, then.'

There was a pause, a click, a voice, and Rona saw him suddenly straighten. *'Ginnie!'*

She turned and walked quickly over to the window, heart pounding. Though she'd put as much distance between them as possible, she couldn't blot out his voice.

'It's good of you to phone ... Yes, it has, rather ... No, they're no nearer finding the culprit ... Nick? He's all right, though of course it's been a terrific strain, on all of us.'

There was a longer pause, and when he spoke again, his voice had subtly altered. 'You're sure? Yes, of course I would. Very much ... I'll wait to hear from you, then. Goodbye.'

Rona remained at the window, staring unseeingly into the courtyard below. For several seconds silence stretched between them, then Finn said with an effort, 'Sorry about that. What were we saying?'

She turned and came back to the desk. His face was flushed and his hand shook as he shuffled some papers.

'You were about to show me where I'll be working,' she said.

He glanced up, meeting her eyes. 'As you'll no doubt have gathered, that was my ex-wife. She's been abroad for two weeks and has only just heard about Julia.'

Rona nodded, unsure what to say.

'She's – coming up to see us.'

'That's nice,' Rona said carefully.

'Yes. Right; the room you'll be using is two doors down.' He held the door open for her and she walked past him, turning left down the corridor. The room he showed her into was much the same size as his, but with the radiators off, the air felt chill. It was equipped with two desks, phone, fax and computer, and on one of the desks was piled a motley collection of binders, files and old, torn envelopes with their contents spilling out. Several cardboard boxes, also in danger of overflowing, stood on the floor beside it, together with some concertina files.

'You see what I mean,' Finlay said.

She did. 'I won't know where to start,' she said with a little laugh.

'If you'd rather not tackle it—'

'No, I said I'd do it, and I will.' Aware of the constraint still between them, she added with a forced laugh, 'Who knows what secrets I might unearth?'

'If you're sure, then. How soon can you start?'

'Tomorrow morning?'

'Excellent. I'll make sure the heating's turned on.'

She had the impression he wanted to be rid of her, to be free to consider the implications behind his wife's call. Well, she'd no intention of detaining him.

'Till tomorrow, then,' she said, gave him a tight little smile, and walked out of the room, along the passage and down the stairs.

So the unknown Ginnie had graciously offered to come and see 'them' (for which, read Finn), no doubt adding a cautionary, *If you'd like me to?* To which he'd replied, *Yes, of course I would. Very much.* Heaven knows, that was clear enough. What wasn't clear was why they'd ever parted in the first place, since he was obviously still in love with her. Hadn't his mother told her she resembled Ginnie? Obviously, that had been the source of her attraction for him.

So what was the problem? She hadn't *wanted* that awareness between them; it was unsettling and wrong, and they'd both known it would go no further. Why, then, was she left feeling as though all her rabbits had died?

With an exclamation of annoyance, she started the car.

A brisk walk with Gus helped clear her head, and by the time she reached Nettleton, Rona had put the episode behind her. Coppins, to which Charles and Sybil had recently moved, was a handsome old house at the end of a short drive. She'd been told the Curzons' apartment was at the far end on the right, and she drove into one of the spaces marked Visitors' Parking, and went to ring the bell.

Sybil opened the door to her. She was plump and silver-haired, wearing a heather tweed skirt and lilac cashmere jumper. Very different, Rona thought, from Elizabeth's severity.

'Come in, my dear,' she invited, leading Rona into the small hallway and through to an attractive room running along the back of the house. Charles, tall, straight and white-haired, with a small moustache, came forward to meet her.

'Miss Parish. Your father has told us a lot about you.'

Rona smiled at him. 'It's always a little un-nerving to hear that.'

'It shouldn't be. Sit down, sit down. Sybil has the coffee on. You must forgive the odd boxes dotted around; we're still trying to find places for things. We've disposed of an inordinate amount, to our sons and the factory museum—' He broke off. 'But you know that, of course. You've seen the old desk, not to mention what it contained.'

'Yes, I'm – sorry about that; I wasn't trying to pry, just to get the drawer to close.'

'Finlay told you we found another letter? Extraordinary, that after all these years they

296

should turn up within a week of each other.'

'I understand the contents weren't a total surprise?'

Sybil returned with the coffee tray, and Charles stood to help her. 'We're talking about Spencer's letters, my dear.' Then, to Rona, 'Yes and no. The story of the paternity claim became part of family lore, but it consisted largely of guesswork and overheard scraps of gossip, since neither my father nor Spencer ever spoke of it. Out of loyalty to George, I presume, and possibly – less admirably – watching their own backs.'

'And the missing parish records?' Rona queried delicately, accepting the cup of coffee.

'I'd say she stole them herself, to give credence to her story.'

'You don't think there's a remote chance your grandfather *might* have married her?'

'Not the slightest,' Charles declared robustly. 'She was a scheming little minx, by all accounts – one of the factory workers – and blatantly out for what she could get. Admittedly Grandfather had earned himself a reputation —'

'The Rogue in Porcelain,' Rona supplied.

'You've heard that, have you? Yes, well I dare say it was warranted in his youth. But at the time we're speaking of, he had two adolescent sons and a thriving business. There's no way he'd have allied himself to a woman like that.'

'She was only good enough to sleep with? *Droit du seigneur*, and all that?'

Charles shot her a swift look. 'I'm not condoning his behaviour, but men can be fools, Miss Parish; you'll be aware of that. A pretty face, open flattery, and they fall like flies. In mitigation, my grandmother had been unwell for the last ten years of her life, bedridden for five. That would have played into the girl's hands, and even though George would have been more than twenty years her senior, he was still a handsome man.'

'What happened to her and the child?'

'I've no idea, but I'm confident they were taken care of.'

'Would you have any objection to my including this in the article? As part of the family history?'

Charles stroked his moustache thoughtfully. 'Will Julia's murder be featured?'

'Since it's common knowledge, yes. I'm sorry.'

Sybil said sharply, 'I wish they'd stop hounding poor Nicholas. The police are treating him as their prime suspect, and the press follow him everywhere.'

Charles said, 'You knew Julia, I believe?'

'For just over a week, yes.'

'Finlay thinks she planned the meeting with you.'

'Yes.'

Sybil said gently, 'You liked her, didn't you, dear?'

Rona nodded, not wanting to discuss Julia

298

with those so obviously hostile to her. As though reading her mind, Sybil went on, 'However we might feel about her, what happened was a tragedy she didn't deserve. Her death has shocked and saddened us, naturally, but we can't regard it as a family bereavement. Not after what she did to Nicholas.'

Charles cleared his throat. 'Well, if all this is to be recounted in gruesome detail, no one's likely to bat an eyelid over George's past shenanigans. If you weren't a young lady, I'd say publish and be damned.' He paused. 'And there's another matter you must have been wondering about.'

Rona raised her eyebrows enquiringly, glad they'd moved away from the subject of Julia.

'This new line we're bringing out; Genesis, as we refer to it.' He moved to the mantelpiece and took down a small figurine Rona had noticed earlier. It was an exquisite model of a young girl leaning dreamily against a tree. She was holding a spray of blossom, each petal painstakingly detailed, and above her, individual leaves hung realistically from the fragile branches.

'This is Genesis,' Charles said. 'Here, take it.'

'I'm not insured!' Rona protested laughingly. 'It must be worth a bomb.'

'At the moment, it's priceless. That's the only piece outside the factory.' He handed it to her, and she turned it carefully over in her hands. It was a work of art, and she would have loved to possess it, but she was unsure in what way it differed from other pieces of Curzon.

Charles, seeming to sense her puzzlement, smiled. 'Come with me,' he said, and, to her surprise, led her into the kitchen.

'Now,' he said, 'drop it.'

Rona stared at him uncomprehendingly. *'What?'*

'I think you heard. Drop it. Or, if you prefer, fling it against a wall.' He waited a moment longer, and when she made no move to obey him, took it out of her hand and himself hurled it on to the tiled floor.

Instinctively, Rona closed her eyes, bracing herself for the sound of smashing china. There was none. When she dared open them, the ornament was lying, totally undamaged, on the floor. She turned to see Charles's smiling face.

'I don't understand.'

'What we've invented, my dear, is nothing more nor less than unbreakable china. Drop it on the floor, and it bounces. You could drive a steamroller over it, and it would do no damage. Try it for yourself.'

He bent to retrieve it, and again handed it to her. Still reluctant, she examined it carefully, but could see no evidence of its rough treatment. Each blossom and leaf remained intact. Holding her breath, Rona dropped the figure on to the tiles and, incredulously, watched it bounce.

'It's – unbelievable,' she said.

'It's taken years of research to develop,' Charles told her, 'and although the public in general will be overjoyed, not to mention collectors of fine bone china, fellow manufacturers mightn't be so happy. In the short term, their trade will slump as everyone rushes to buy Genesis. And, of course, if china is unbreakable, it will not need replacing; one dinner service given as a wedding present will last for life. No chips, no breakages. Oven, freezer and dishwasher proof.'

'Why are you showing it to me?' Rona asked.

'So that it, too, can be mentioned in your article. To balance, perhaps, what's gone before. However, I must impress on you the total secrecy surrounding Genesis. No one – positively *no one* – is to hear about it prior to its announcement. Your magazine, due out, I've established, a day or two later, will be highly topical but will not pre-empt it. And the same strictures apply to you, my dear,' he added to Sybil, who had followed them through, and whose exclamation of shock Rona had dimly been aware of when the priceless piece was dropped.

'None of the other wives know, nor does the general workforce. Only the directors, senior managers, and those involved in production, and they're all sworn to secrecy.'

He fixed Rona with a severe look. 'I'm putting you on your honour to adhere to this.'

'Of course I will,' she answered quietly.

301

Sybil said worriedly, 'It will cause a lot of ill-feeling, surely, among your competitors.'

'Only, as I said, in the short term. They'll immediately be hell-bent on producing their own versions. By means of osmosis, once something new is invented, in no time it's being manufactured worldwide. We're the first, that's all.'

They returned to the sitting room and Sybil refilled their coffee cups.

'I hear you've nobly offered to sort through the family archives,' Charles remarked. 'I hope you've reached a satisfactory financial arrangement.'

'Finlay did mention it, but—'

But they'd been interrupted by Ginnie's call, and it wasn't her place to mention it.

'I'll see to it. Only right you should be recompensed for your time. I've flicked through the boxes myself, but it's mostly ephemeral correspondence, from what I could see. Not really worth keeping, but my father was an inveterate hoarder. If you can sort it into reasonable shape, we'd all be grateful and you might possibly find a few nuggets of interest.'

It had been an eventful morning, Rona reflected as she drove home, but its two most outstanding occurrences had both, for different reasons, to be kept to herself.

'Max? What the devil has that wife of yours got herself into now?'

Max smiled to himself. 'Hello, Father. How are you?'

'Never mind me, it's Rona we're all concerned about.'

'No need to be, I assure you. If you're referring to the body that was found, she was merely an innocent bystander.'

'But they're saying she knew the girl in question?'

'Who's saying?'

'*I* don't know,' Roland Allerdyce returned testily. 'The amorphous and ubiquitous "they". Cynthia heard it somewhere. Did she or didn't she know her?'

'Yes, briefly. But that doesn't put her in any danger.'

'How do you know that?' his father barked. 'Has a motive for the death been established?'

'No, but—'

'Well, then. This girl might have seen something she shouldn't have while she was actually *with* Rona.'

'Hey!' Max protested. 'What are you trying to do? Put the fear of God into me?'

'I'm trying to ensure you look after her. You seem to be taking this very lightly, if I may say so.'

'Father, it's her work, and it would take a better man than I to keep her from doing it.'

'Don't say I didn't warn you.' A pause. 'Why don't the pair of you take a break? Come up here for a week or so, till the thing blows over?'

'We can't get away at the moment, but we'll certainly bear it in mind.'

'It's the moment I'm concerned about,' his father said darkly.

Fifteen

DI Charlie Harris raised his tankard. 'Confusion to our enemies,' he toasted.

Barrett followed suit. 'I'll drink to that.'

'So how's it going?'

'Frankly, it's not. We're no further forward than when we last spoke. Everything we've managed to get so far is negative.'

'Such as?'

'Oh, the usual. Checking hospitals to see if anyone's been in with a suspicious cut – the killer might have been wounded if Julia put up a struggle. Laundries and dry-cleaners asked about blood-stained clothing. You know the kind of thing. We drew a blank all round.'

He sighed disconsolately and drank some beer. 'Then both de Salis and his missus were likely suspects, but—'

'His missus?' Harris interrupted.

Barrett nodded. 'Her more than him, actually. She's pretty screwed up, and if she learned her old man was still seeing Julia, I can see her putting the knife in. Literally. Had to scrap that idea, though; both were safely and irrefutably ensconced in their shop till five thirty, and went straight from there to a parents' evening at their daughter's school. Cast-iron alibis, damn them.

'Then we had hopes of one of the guys Julia met after work, but he turned out to be in the clear.'

'Which presumably leaves you with the ex-husband?'

'Exactly; always the most likely bet. As luck would have it, he wasn't at the factory that afternoon; he'd driven to Aylesbury for a three thirty appointment, but the bloke had got his dates mixed and was in London. That checks out, by the way.'

'So what did he do instead?'

'Took the opportunity to buy himself some underwear, and was able to supply receipts. Then went for a cuppa before driving home.'

'Back to the pottery?'

'No; he reckoned it wasn't worth going into the office. The clothes receipt confirms the time he was in the store, but no one remembers him in the café, which according to him filled in half an hour or so. That thirty minutes could be crucial in fixing the time he arrived back in Nettleton, where he lives. For that matter, since no one saw him at his flat, there's no proof he didn't make a detour to Chilswood.'

'What motive would he have?'

Barrett shrugged. 'She could have asked him to meet her, tried to make a comeback, and he lost it. Word is it was an acrimonious divorce. Or, contrariwise, he might have *thought* she wanted him back, been amenable, then discovered she didn't, and regarded it as a second betrayal.'

'But in either case, would he have gone to meet her armed with a knife? Seems unlikely.'

'Granted it would be more plausible if a pen-knife had done the damage. Unless, of course –' Barrett brightened momentarily – '*she* was the one who'd brought it, thinking for some reason she might need to defend herself. Surprising how often the victim's killed with his or her own weapon.'

He finished his beer. 'But as it stands at the moment, we've only Curzon's word for what he did between three thirty and six, when his brother phoned to give him the news.'

Harris shook his head sympathetically. 'Ever wish mobiles hadn't been invented?'

'Do I ever? Time was when you knew where someone was when he answered his phone.'

'So what's your next step?'

'Another round of questioning and continuing enquiries, both here and in Reigate. In the meantime, the press are on us like a pack of wolves, thanks to the victim being a Curzon.'

'Perhaps,' Harris suggested wickedly, 'you should enlist the services of your journalist friend.'

'Don't even joke about it. I'm expecting her to turn up any minute with the culprit's head on a platter.'

'Figuratively speaking, I trust.'

'Either way would suit me,' said Ed Barrett.

Lindsey arrived back from lunch to find Hugh waiting on the street outside the office. Her mind had been so totally centred on the evening ahead that for a moment she stared at him blankly.

'Don't you recognize me?' he asked shortly. 'I shouldn't be surprised, it's so long since I saw you.'

'Hugh! What are you doing here?'

'It seemed to be the only way to get hold of you. You've not returned any of my emails or phone calls.'

'I'm – sorry,' she said. 'I've been busy.'

She moved aside to let Jonathan enter the building, ignoring his conspiratorial wink, though she saw Hugh flush, and guessed he'd seen it.

He said with heavy irony, 'If you have your diary or Filofax to hand, perhaps I can make an appointment.'

'Hugh, I haven't time for this. My lunch hour's over and I must get back to work.'

'It will take two minutes.'

With bad grace, she fumbled in her shoulder bag for her diary. If this evening went well, Dominic might suggest a further date, and she didn't, she thought uncharitably, want to be bogged down with Hugh.

She flipped open her diary and turned back a couple of pages. 'We had dinner two weeks ago today,' she told him. 'Hardly a lifetime ago.'

'It is, when I want to make love to you.'

'Sh!' She glanced about her anxiously, seeing a passer-by's mouth twitch. 'A lot has happened in the interim.'

'Ah yes. I saw Rona'd got herself in the news again.'

'I went to stay with Mum for a few days,' Lindsey said coldly. 'Not that I have to account to you for my movements.'

He sighed. 'Why do we always get off on the wrong foot?'

'Because you have two left ones. I can meet you for lunch tomorrow,' she added quickly, to cut off further conversation. 'Will that do?'

'Faute de mieux.'

'Well, it's all I can offer at the moment. One o'clock at the Bacchus?'

He held her eyes for a long minute. Then he said levelly, 'I'll be there,' turned on his heel, and walked away.

The doorbell rang at three thirty, and Avril, who'd been on edge since lunchtime, hurried to answer it. To her surprise, Sarah was not alone on the doorstep. Beside her stood a tall, balding man in casual clothes, who was regarding her with interest.

'Hello, Mrs Parish,' Sarah said. 'Meet my dad. He insisted on giving you the once-over.'

'Not true,' corrected her father calmly. 'I was coming to Marsborough anyway, and thought I'd like to see where Sarah will be spending the next few months.'

He held out his hand with a smile. 'Guy Lacey. I'm grateful to you for offering my daughter a home.'

'Anyone would think,' Sarah remarked acidly, 'that I was twelve years old, and starting boarding school.'

'Well, you *are* going to a new school, poppet.'

She flung him an exasperated glance, and Avril laughed. 'I don't know why we're standing on the doorstep. Do come in. If you take your things straight up, Sarah, your father can see your room. Then perhaps you'd like a cup of tea?'

Sarah opened her mouth – to decline, Avril suspected – but her father got in first.

'We would indeed. Thank you.' He lifted the case again, and followed Sarah up the stairs, while Avril hurried to the kitchen to switch on the kettle and put the batch of scones she'd made in the oven to reheat. She liked what she'd seen of Guy Lacey, the latent humour in his eyes and his easy manner. He obviously had the measure of his headstrong daughter.

When they joined her minutes later in the sitting room, he stood for a moment, looking about him appreciatively, then walked over to the corner table and studied the family photographs.

'Twin daughters?' he enquired, and, at her nod, 'Bet they were a handful!'

'They had their moments,' Avril conceded.

'They went to Belmont Primary, by the way.'

'We drove past it on the way here. It looks nice and spacious – plenty of windows. I've a thing about light.'

'Comes of being an electrical engineer,' put in Sarah drily, and he laughed. Then, glancing back at the photos, he grew serious. 'And it's one of them who had that nasty experience in Chilswood?'

Avril's heart started pounding. So that was why he'd accompanied Sarah. And, in doing so, forced her hand; she could no longer remain silent about her own role.

'Rona, yes,' she answered, trying to keep the tremor out of her voice. She squared her shoulders, and looked straight at Guy Lacey. 'If you'd like to sit down,' she added, 'there's something you should know.'

After Sarah's initial exclamation, they sat in silence as she told them of Rona's meeting with Julia and her brief stay in Sarah's bedroom, and the silence continued when she'd finished speaking.

Then Guy Lacey turned to his daughter. 'Any comment, poppet?'

'It's a bit – unnerving,' Sarah said.

'It's not as though anything happened in that room,' Avril put in anxiously.

'No, but it still brings it home rather.'

She steeled herself to say, 'If you've changed your mind about coming here, I shall quite understand.'

Lacey said quickly, 'Oh, I'm sure there's no question of that, is there, Sarah?'

The girl hesitated a moment, and Avril held her breath. Then she said, 'Not really. The room seems very comfortable, and it's so convenient for the school.'

Her father added, 'It's good of you to be so frank with us. Thank you. I hadn't realized your daughter actually knew the victim. That must have made it much worse for her – and, of course, for you.'

'Yes.' Avril drew a deep breath. 'Well, now we've got that out of the way, I'll bring the scones in, and we can have tea.'

As the meal progressed, her liking for Guy Lacey increased. There was a family resemblance between father and daughter, she noted; Sarah had inherited her father's grey eyes, though the expression in them was quite different, and they had the same shaped mouth. He wasn't as bald as Avril first thought; although his forehead was high, his hair – dark and generously sprinkled with grey – was still plentiful over the top and back of his head. She guessed he was in his mid to late fifties, but the casual clothes – open-neck shirt, sweater and jeans – made him seem younger. Tom, she remembered, had refused point-blank to wear jeans after turning fifty – mutton dressed as lamb, he called it.

Eventually, Lacey put his plate on the coffee table and stood up. 'I must be on my way. That was great, Mrs Parish, thank you. It's good to have met you, and I hope there are no further traumas for either you or your daughter.'

Sarah went with him to the door, and Avril collected the tea things together. The conversation she'd been dreading was behind her, and she still had her lodger. For the moment, that was enough.

Oliver Curzon rang his cousin's doorbell just after six, and it was answered by Emma.

'Hi, Oliver; come to collect Millie?'

'Got it in one.'

'Come in. They're upstairs playing a board game at the moment. They were running wild, but I decided that after a large tea, it was time to settle down a bit.'

'Quite right, and I'm glad about the large tea. Millie's fussy about her food, and Sally was hoping she wouldn't get a request for pasta the minute she was over the doorstep.'

'Little chance of that. Go through to the sitting room; Sam's there.'

She went to the foot of the stairs and called up. 'Victoria! Uncle Oliver's here; could you both come down, please?'

The anticipated wail of protest greeted her. 'We're in the middle of a game, Mummy! Can we finish it?'

'If it doesn't take too long.'

Emma joined the men in the sitting room. 'Could they have a few minutes' grace to finish their game?'

'Fine by me,' Oliver agreed.

'Time for a beer, then,' Sam said firmly. 'How about you, darling?'

'Not at the moment, thanks.'

As her husband went to get it, Emma said, 'You must be desperately worried about Nick. How's he coping with all this?'

Oliver looked grave. 'With difficulty, I think; especially since both the police and the press keep on at him.'

'The press?'

'They're always asking if he's any comment, and flashing cameras at him. And the police are worrying like terriers at that visit to Aylesbury, going over and over what he did when the customer didn't show, what time he got home, etcetera.'

Oliver reached up and took the glass Sam handed him. 'Thanks. We're talking about Nick. Ironically, it's the fact that he wasn't anywhere near Chilswood that's counting against him; if he'd been at the factory with the rest of us, there'd be no problem.'

'They're bound to come up with something sooner or later,' Sam said comfortingly.

'Then let's hope it's sooner,' returned Nick's brother.

Two hours later, when Victoria was in bed and they'd had their meal, Sam flicked a glance at his wife.

'What's the matter, love? You're very quiet this evening.'

'It's nothing,' she said evasively.

'This business with Julia getting you down? Unfortunately, all we can do is weather it till something breaks.'

Emma gazed into the fire. 'Why did Oliver say Nick wasn't in Chilswood that afternoon?'

Sam looked at her in surprise. 'Because he wasn't; he was in Aylesbury.'

'Yes, but after that.'

'He went home. Em –' Sam leaned forward, suddenly anxious – 'what is it?'

She looked up at him, her eyes wide and frightened. 'Oh, Sam, I saw him! In Chilswood.'

Sam went still. 'That afternoon? You couldn't have.'

'But I did! I was on the kerb waiting to cross the road, and he drove past. He didn't see me – he was looking straight ahead – but he passed within feet of me.'

Sam moistened his lips. 'What time was this?'

'About five o'clock. I'd just dropped Victoria off at Brownies.'

'Why haven't you mentioned it before?'

'To be honest, I'd forgotten all about it. Naturally it didn't seem important at the time, and it only fell into place when Oliver said he hadn't been near Chilswood. And he had.'

She looked worriedly at her husband's tense face. 'What shall we do?'

* * *

Lindsey lay immobile in bed, her eyes wide open in the dark. Whatever she'd expected from the evening behind her, it was nothing like the way it had panned out.

The first surprise had been the chauffeur-driven car, the second, the information that they were driving to London for dinner at the Savoy. She'd been expecting to be taken to either the Clarendon or Serendipity, the new restaurant everyone was talking about, and she'd had a moment of panic that she wasn't smartly enough dressed. But that was Dominic's fault for not briefing her. He was wearing a clerical grey suit, white shirt and blue silk tie and looked, she thought, very suave and elegant.

'How did the family lunch go?' he asked, as the chauffeur turned out of the drive into Fairhaven, the cul-de-sac where she lived. So he'd not forgotten being turned down in its favour.

'Dramatically,' she replied. 'One of the party went into labour and had to be rushed to hospital.'

'Good heavens! I hope you'd all managed to eat first?'

She laughed. 'We had, yes, except for the prospective mother, who wasn't hungry.'

'And did all go well?'

'I think so; the baby's two months premature and is in an incubator, but they seem hopeful of her chances.'

316

'I'm sure she'll be fine. My daughter was in an incubator for ten days,' said Dominic Frayne.

Lindsey was momentarily silenced. Two divorces, OK, but there'd been no mention of offspring. 'How many children have you?' she asked, trying to sound equally nonchalant.

'Three; two from my first marriage and one from my second. All independent now, thank God. Have you any yourself?'

Again she was taken by surprise. 'No.'

'You have been married, though?' And, at her nod, 'I thought that's what Jonathan said.'

So they'd been discussing her. What else had Jonathan told him?

That was the end of any personal discussion. He had been courteous and attentive, and she'd made him laugh a couple of times, but even on the way home, and despite the privacy afforded by the screen separating them from the driver, their conversation might have been between total strangers.

And that's what they were! Lindsey thought in frustration. Prior to that evening, they'd exchanged only a couple of sentences, and when he dropped her back at her flat, she felt she knew him no better than when they'd started out. How Dominic himself would evaluate the evening, she had no idea.

Avril had been a little concerned that, since school didn't start till Thursday, Sarah might be at a loose end the following day, while she herself divided her time between the library and the charity shop. Nor had she established the weekend routine; she certainly didn't want the girl hanging round the house.

On both counts, however, her fears were quickly put to rest. At breakfast the next morning, Sarah announced she was going into Marsborough, to shop and meet an aunt for lunch.

Possibly seeing Avril's relief, she added with a smile, 'Dad warned me that in a B&B you're expected to be out of the house between nine and five, though I might be back slightly earlier, depending what there is to do after school. And in case you're worrying about weekends, I shan't be in your way then, either. Until I make more friends here, I'll be going home Friday to Sunday evenings, if that's all right?'

'Of course,' Avril said awkwardly, 'but don't feel you have to go out. Your room's a bedsit, after all.' And marvelled at her own hypocrisy.

The girl was making an effort to be accommodating, she thought, as Sarah left the house half an hour later, and they'd soon feel more relaxed with each other. The fact that there'd been no awkward initiation period with Julia was best forgotten.

Since she would be working all day in the room allocated to her, Rona again dropped Gus off with Max. The task ahead filled her with a mixture of anticipation and trepidation; there had seemed no order to the piles of paper awaiting her, but by the end of the day, she should have a better idea of what they contained and how to set about sorting them.

There was no sign of Finlay when she arrived at the pottery, and it was Meg Fairclough who took her up to the room. The boxes and folders were as she'd last seen them, but at least the room itself was warm and welcoming.

'Let me know if you need anything,' Meg told her. 'I'll bring you a cup of coffee at ten thirty, and the directors have invited you to join them for lunch.'

'Would it be very ungracious to decline?' Rona asked. 'To be honest, I'd much rather have a sandwich up here and get on with the work.'

'Just as you like, of course. I'll make your apologies and bring you up something from the canteen.'

The next few hours passed slowly and laboriously, punctuated by the arrival firstly of coffee and later of a tray bearing a warm Cornish pasty and a bowl of fruit salad. Rona's hands were soon black from the accumulated dust, and her nostrils filled with the musty smell of old paper. Bills, scrawled designs for patterns, and letters, letters, letters – none of which, in her opinion, were worth keeping, except as historical examples of the formal exchanges between family members.

By three o'clock, her back was aching from bending over the boxes, and she had four or five separate piles of papers on the carpet. Although she'd originally hoped to sort them into date order, this proved virtually impossible, since only in official correspondence was the year given. At this stage, it was also impossible to separate those she felt could be scrapped; time enough for that when she knew exactly what she had.

Meg Fairclough, coming in with a cup of tea and a biscuit, found her on her hands and knees.

'How are you doing?' she asked, setting them down on a clear surface.

'Slowly,' Rona replied.

'Anything of interest?'

'To the family, yes, but not for my purposes.'

'I suppose that's only to be expected,' Meg said, and Rona was forced to agree.

At four thirty she decided to stop for the day, and, leaving the sorted piles on the carpet, went down the passage to wash the dust off her hands. Feeling slightly less disreputable, she returned to the room to collect her bag, and it was as she was leaning across a half-emptied box to reach it that something in the box caught her eye – handwriting that she recognized.

With a sudden flare of interest, Rona lifted the file that partially obscured it, to retrieve a torn scrap of memo in Spencer Curzon's hand. Seconds later, she turned and ran up the corridor to Finlay's office and knocked urgently on the door.

There was a pause, then his voice called, 'Come in,' and she flung the door open.

He was not alone. Standing beside him in the centre of the room was a slim, dark young woman, whose hand was on his arm. For a minute, all three of them stared at each other. Then Finn said, 'Rona! This is Ginnie, who—'

'Yes.' Rona forced a smile, which was briefly acknowledged. Clearly she resented the intrusion.

Finn turned to his ex-wife. 'And this is Rona, whom I was telling you about. She's doing a great job sorting through a century of accumulated rubbish, in the name of research.'

His eyes dropped to the paper in her hand. 'What have you got there?'

Before she could reply, Ginnie said quickly, 'You'll want to discuss it. I'll see you later, Finn.'

He half raised a hand to stop her, but she walked quickly out of the room, closing the door behind her.

Rona, feeling the wind had been taken out of her sails, went on standing there.

Finlay smiled at her. 'Well? What have you found?'

Silently, she moved forward and handed it to him, watching his face change as he read:

Had the de Salis woman in again, still main-

taining Papa had fathered her child and trying to extort more money. Word has reached me she's begun styling herself Curzon, but I swiftly scotched that. If she—

'Good God!' Finn said softly. 'Where did this come from?'

'One of the boxes. There can't be any mistake, can there? I mean, there couldn't be two families in the area with that name?'

'I'd say it's pretty conclusive.' He smiled. 'Well, you've lived up to your reputation by solving our family mystery for us. Well done. I wonder if Nigel knows; odd, that his affair with Julia should be following family tradition.'

'So what happens now?'

'Well, I'll let everyone know, of course, though we won't want it broadcast outside the family. Washing dirty linen and so on.'

'But your uncle said I could use it in the article.'

'That was before we knew her name. Check with him, by all means, but I suggest that if you use the story, you keep the woman anonymous. We don't want a libel case.'

He was waiting for her to go, she realized, as he had been after Ginnie's phone call. Since she'd come back into his life, everything else had been put on a back burner.

'Will you be here tomorrow?' he asked.

'Oh yes; it'll take several days to go through everything, even once. Then there's the final sorting. Do you want to keep that?' she added, nodding at the paper in his hand. 'Or shall I put it with the rest?'

He glanced down at it. 'I'll hang on to it for the moment, to show Edward. Thanks very much, Rona.'

Damn it, she thought as she made her way to the car park; she'd slaved all day over their blasted papers, and when she finally found something of interest, it had been taken from her. But she wouldn't give up 'the de Salis woman' and her story without a struggle.

'Wonderful news, Tom!' Catherine told him on the telephone. 'Daniel's just called to say the baby's to be allowed home tomorrow.'

'Excellent! So no doubt you'll be hot-footing it over to Cricklehurst?'

'I shall indeed. She'll need a lot of extra care for a while, but at least they'll all be under the same roof – a proper family. And they've finally chosen a name – Alice Catherine.'

'A little namesake for you – that's nice.'

'Isn't it sweet of them? She'll be known as Alice, of course. Oh, Tom, I'm so relieved everything's going well, after all the trauma last time.'

'So now you can relax and enjoy your grand-daughter. Give Jenny my love. Once the novelty's worn off, I'll come over with you, but for the moment the four of you need to be alone.'

'I knew you'd understand,' Catherine said gratefully.

'I gather from your side of the conversation that your sister has a new man,' Max observed that evening.

'Yes; a different kettle of fish, this one. Chauffeur-driven car and a private plane, if you please.'

'Poor old Hugh will have his nose out of joint; there's no way he can compete with that.'

'Lindsey says he's still hanging in there. Yesterday, he waited for her outside the office.'

'I can't think why she doesn't put him out of his misery,' Max said. He topped up her glass of vodka. 'No more news on the murder, I suppose? I had Father on the phone, worrying about your involvement.'

'He really needn't.'

'That's what I told him, but he seems to think I should be keeping more of an eye on you.'

Rona smiled. 'He's living in a different century, bless him.'

'I told him that, too, after a fashion. All the same, you do seem to land yourself in it. You won't take any chances, will you, love?'

'I'll be fine,' she said.

Sixteen

Rona spent the next day again sorting through papers, but found nothing of note. Having dug down to Spencer's stratum, as it were, she came across several other missives from him, but all were of an impersonal nature. It seemed that, apart from the memo she'd passed to Finlay, discretion had finally stayed his hand, more was the pity.

As before, she elected to have a working lunch in her room, only half admitting that part of the reason was to avoid Finlay. It looked very much as though his marriage was getting back on track – and good luck to them. She just didn't want to join in the celebrations.

Another day should finish the initial sorting, she thought, sitting back on her heels and surveying the rapidly emptying files and folders; and then, to be honest, she'd have had enough. Apart from the de Salis connection, none of it had any relevance to what she'd be writing about, nor did it shed any light on the family itself, but at least she'd satisfied herself on that score.

Again, she stopped at four thirty, and set off

for home feeling slightly flat. Halfway through the journey, she phoned Lindsey at the office. 'Doing anything this evening?'

'No.'

'Like to come to Dino's with me?'

'Why not? Only problem is there's a board meeting in half an hour, and I'm not sure how long it'll go on.'

'Phone me when you're ready to leave. There shouldn't be any problem getting a table.'

Having collected Gus from Farthings, Rona took him for a long walk in Furze Hill Park, glad of the empty spaces around her and the wind blowing through her hair after the musty confinement of the last two days.

Lindsey didn't phone until seven.

'That was quite a session, wasn't it?' Rona commented.

'Par for the course. They're a long-winded bunch.'

'Like to come here first, or shall we meet at Dino's?'

'Let's go straight there. To be honest, I'm feeling a bit frazzled and don't want to be late home.'

'OK. See you in fifteen minutes.'

To Rona's relief, Lindsey seemed to have forgotten her teasing about the 'attractive men' she'd met; Dominic Frayne must have wiped them from her mind. They were both glad to relax after a tiring day and give themselves up to comfort food and Dino's cosseting, making idle conversation and content just to be companionably together.

The last time she'd been there was with Julia, Rona thought at one point, but clamped down on the memory, refusing to allow it to dispel her present well-being.

'Don't fall asleep on the way home,' she warned her sister, when they parted on the pavement outside the restaurant.

'That's why I went easy on the booze. I'll drive back with all the windows open, and have a nightcap when I get there.'

Glad a fifteen-minute drive didn't separate her from her own bed, Rona walked slowly home, Gus trotting at her side. It was only nine thirty, and Max wouldn't phone before ten, when he'd tidied up after the evening class. She decided not to wait downstairs for his call, but to go straight up, and take it in bed. Like Lindsey, she needed an early night.

Her first thought, when the persistent ringing woke her, was that she must have fallen asleep while waiting for his call, though she'd a vague memory of speaking to him. Nevertheless, when she scrabbled blindly for the phone, it was Max's voice that reached her.

'Sorry if I woke you, darling – it's gone seven, by the way – but I've just heard. There's been a fire or some sort of explosion at Curzon.'

'What?' She sat up in bed, the last strands of sleep evaporating. 'When? Was anyone hurt?'

'I don't know. It was in the early hours, so presumably only the security staff would be there.'

Rona was struggling to grasp the situation. 'How bad is it?'

'Pretty extensive damage, from all accounts.'

'Genesis!' she gasped, making a horrified connection. Hadn't Edward said there'd been sabotage before?

'What did you say?'

'The new line: has it been destroyed?'

'I haven't heard, but I should think it's too early to say; they're not able to get into the building yet.'

Her mind raced, taking in the worst-case scenario. Suppose it was all lost – the long years of research – the triumphant announcement coinciding with anniversary celebrations – the wonder of the delicate, indestructible model she'd held?

'Oh, Max!' There were tears in her voice.

'Switch on the TV and see for yourself; they're still showing it. The fire's out, but the whole area's been cordoned off, and the fire investigation team are standing by to move in once it's cooled down enough. One thing's for sure, though; you won't be sorting any papers there today.'

Rona monitored the television and radio bulletins all morning, restlessly moving from one room to another; even the details of her previous exploits in the *Gazette* failed to distract her. Genesis wasn't her only worry. Had the museum survived, with its earliest records of the firm? And the shop, where she'd bought the marmalade pot? What about the papers she'd laboriously been sorting? And the rooms she'd seen on her tour, where potting, slip casting, decorating and glazing were carried out? Could the firm survive, if all that was destroyed?

Various phone calls punctuated the morning – from both parents, Barnie, Lindsey. But no one contacted her from Curzon, and she felt it would be intrusive to try to reach them.

Towards midday, it was announced that a night watchman had died in the blaze and another was in hospital with severe burns. There was still no word on damage to the buildings and their contents.

Shortly afterwards, Max phoned again. 'We're going to Tynecastle for the weekend,' he announced. 'I've booked the flight, so put a few things in a case and I'll collect you at four o'clock.'

'It's not your father, is it?' Rona asked in alarm.

'No, it's you, but I'm acting on his advice: you've been too tied up with this blasted family, and with the fire on top of everything, you need to get right away for a couple of days. OK?'

'OK,' she echoed meekly.

* * *

And the weekend away did give her a different perspective. She listened to all the latest reports, but she wasn't continually on edge, waiting for Finlay or Charles to phone. For the rest, Roland looked better than on their last visit a month ago, and Max had to admit to his nephew that he'd not yet started on his painting of the car.

They went for long walks on the fells with Cynthia and Paul, and had a couple of pub lunches. On the Saturday evening, Charles Curzon was interviewed on television, and Rona ached with sympathy for him. Speaking calmly and gravely, he voiced his deep regret at the death and injury to his staff, paid tribute to both men, and offered condolences to their families.

Only when the interviewer pressed him on 'the secret new line we've all been eagerly awaiting' did Charles state, still in the same measured tones, that it had been totally destroyed.

Rona put her hands to her mouth while the interviewer expressed conventional regret, adding, 'Then can you now tell us what it was?'

Charles lifted his chin and met the man's eyes. 'I'm afraid not. This is a severe set-back, admittedly, but as soon as the damage is cleared up and we're able to get back into the factory, work on it will begin again. Perhaps –' a bleak smiled touched his mouth – 'in time for the next anniversary.'

Seeing the tears in his daughter-in-law's eyes, Roland asked gently, 'You've met this man?'

She nodded.

'And did he tell you about the product?'

She hesitated, and Roland said quickly, 'That was unfair of me. Forget I asked.'

'I feel desperately sorry for them all,' Rona said unsteadily. 'They've worked so hard on this, and were so excited by it. And heaven knows, they've had enough trouble over the murder, without this.'

'Do you think it was arson?' Cynthia asked.

'Probably; there've been attempts before.'

'But this time a man has died, so it would be murder. Again,' she added, looking with compassion at Rona's stricken face.

'They say things go in threes,' Paul said grimly. 'Let's hope it doesn't follow in this case.'

On their return home on Sunday evening, Rona hurried to check the answerphone, certain that by now there'd be a message from Finn. There was not. Max, coming into the kitchen behind her, saw her frustration as she turned away.

'Be fair, love,' he said. 'They've a hell of a lot on their minds at the moment. Their whole livelihood could be at risk, which is a darn sight more important than some article you're writing.'

She nodded miserably. He was right, of course. All the same, she resolved that if she'd

331

not heard from one of them by five o'clock the next day, she'd put her scruples aside and phone Finlay.

The following morning, Rona set about sorting the notes she'd made on her interviews, and found, slightly to her surprise, that she already had enough for one article; all being well, her conversations with the younger directors and their wives should provide sufficient material for a second. It was sad, though, that she would not, after all, be able to end with the crowning glory of Genesis.

She worked steadily all morning, and was considering stopping for a lunch break when, at last, the phone on her desk rang, and she snatched it up.

'Finn?'

There was a pause, then a woman's laugh. 'In a manner of speaking. It's Polly, Rona.'

The receptionist at *Chiltern Life*.

'Hello, Poll. How do you mean, in a manner of speaking?'

'Well, I presume you were expecting Finlay Curzon? I've a message from him. He phoned us because he's lost your number.'

Along with everything else? Rona wondered. 'And what's the message?'

'He said there's been a development and he'd like you to meet him, but it would be better if at this stage you weren't seen together.' She hesitated. 'And he asked me to apologize in

advance, but he suggests Chilswood cemetery.'
Polly paused again, but when Rona didn't
speak, she continued.

'It was the only place he could think of where
you'd be private. And he added that the police
and sightseers have all gone now, and you
needn't worry about there being any trace left
of Julia.'

'Right. Thanks, Poll. What time did he say?'

'As near two o'clock as you can manage.'

'Just time for a bite of lunch, then.'

Rona rang off and ran down the two flights of
stairs to the kitchen. At least Finn had contacted
her, though his choice of rendezvous left much
to be desired. Still, as he'd said, after the hordes
of police, scenes of crime officers and sightseers, it must be thoroughly purged of Julia's
poor ghost.

Hurriedly she opened a tin of sardines and
made some toast. Why, she wondered as she sat
down to eat, was he so anxious they shouldn't
be seen together? Because of Ginnie? Or because of some development on the fire? Whatever the reason, he'd be able to give her a first-
hand update, and some idea of whether or not
her services with the papers were still required.

Lunch finished, she clipped on Gus's lead and
walked with him round to the garage in Charlton Road. There was warmth now in the sun,
and after a cold spring, blossom was at last appearing. Rona felt a sudden wave of optimism.
Perhaps, after all, the damage at the factory

would turn out not to be as extensive as was feared. Though Genesis was undeniably lost, if the rest could be salvaged, that, at least, would be a bonus.

It was ten minutes to two when she turned into the lane leading to the church. There was no car park and the country road was narrow, but the state of the grass verge suggested it was the custom to park on it, so she did likewise. No other car was in sight; Finn might have left his at the factory, as he had before, and walked over the fields.

'You'd better stay here,' she told Gus, who opened one eye in acknowledgement. She left the window ajar for him, locked the car, and set off up the path that led, between the weathered old stones, to the Curzon plot.

Despite herself, she felt a tremor as she went through the green archway into the enclosed space. But unlike on her previous visit, the sun, still almost overhead, shone directly into the clearing, making it considerably less threatening.

No sign of Finn; she decided to sit on the bench and wait for him. But as she started towards it, in that sunlit space the nightmare was suddenly, horrifyingly reborn. She stopped abruptly, watching, mesmerized, as, from the shadows behind the bench, a figure rose up and, even as the strangled scream clogged her throat, revealed itself as the figure of a man. No, of a boy.

Eyes wide, fists clenched, and poised for flight, Rona stared at him across the fifteen feet or so that separated them, and some of her panic abated as recognition came. It was the de Salis boy – what was his name?

'It's Aidan, isn't it?' she said, above the hammering of her heart. And then, ridiculously, 'Shouldn't you be at school?'

'It's a private one,' he said. 'We don't go back till tomorrow.'

'But you live in Woodbourne, don't you? What are you doing here?' Another ghoulish sightseer?

'I came to meet you,' he said, and walked round the bench to face her.

'How could you—?'

Fear, cold and insistent, drenched her again. It seemed that this spotty youth, on the last day of his school holidays, was suddenly, incredibly, a threat to her.

She licked dry lips. 'I don't know what you mean,' she said, hating the shrillness in her voice, 'but Finlay Curzon will be here any minute, and he—'

She stopped again, as a smile spread over the boy's face, and the hideous truth came to her a split second before he confirmed it.

'He won't, you know,' he said. 'It was me that sent the message.'

Rona stared at him. 'Why?' The word was barely above a whisper.

'Well, I couldn't text, could I, 'cos I don't

335

have your mobile number. And if I'd rung you at home, you'd have known I wasn't Finlay bloody Curzon. I thought it was cool, phoning the mag.'

'I meant, why did you want to see me?'

He opened his mouth to reply, then she saw him stiffen as his eyes moved past her, and in the same instant a voice demanded angrily, 'Aidan! What the *hell* do you think you're doing?'

Rona spun round, to see Nigel de Salis advancing towards them across the grass. A stirring of air behind her warned that the boy had moved, and the next instant she was simultaneously aware of his breath on her neck and the sharp prick of metal.

'Don't come any nearer, Dad,' he said, 'or she's for it.'

Nick Curzon slid on to the bench seat opposite his brother. Oliver, dreading the conversation ahead of him, thought he looked tired and ill.

'Sorry I'm late,' he said. 'I got bogged down by a phone call.'

'Have you eaten?' Oliver asked.

'No; are they still serving lunch?'

'They serve food all day here. What would you like?'

'Nothing too heavy. Antipasto or something.'

Oliver raised a hand and called the waiter over, ordering food for them both and a bottle of Chianti.

'So,' Nick said, 'why did you want to see me? Have they found out what caused the fire?'

'Not that I've heard.' Oliver twirled the salt shaker in his fingers. 'Nick, there's no easy way to say this.'

'Now you *have* got me worried.'

'So you should be.' Oliver looked up, reluctantly meeting his brother's eyes. 'You were seen here in Chilswood, on the afternoon of the murder.'

Nick went on staring at him, and a little tick jumped at the corner of his eye. 'Impossible,' he said.

'No.'

'Who says they saw me?'

'Someone who wouldn't lie. God, Nick, don't you realize how serious this is? You stated categorically, to the police and the rest of us, that you went straight home from Aylesbury. Now it turns out you were here – and what's more, at the crucial time of five o'clock. What the hell's going on?'

Nick was silent for a moment. 'Are you going to shop me?'

Oliver said steadily, 'Yes, if you killed Julia.'

'Oliver!'

'Well, why else would you keep quiet about it? You were taking one hell of a risk, thinking no one would see you. You're pretty well known around here.'

'I didn't *know* I was taking a risk, for God's sake! Ordinarily, no one would have thought

337

twice about seeing me. God, where's that wine?'

As if summoned, a waiter appeared with the bottle.

'Never mind the ceremony, just pour it,' Nick ordered, and the waiter, with an offended glare, did so. He took a long drink, then sat back again.

'So?' Oliver said. 'I'm waiting for an explanation.'

'I was with someone. All right?'

'Who?'

'A woman.'

'Surprise, surprise! Well, what's the problem? Surely Saskia will give you an alibi?'

'It wasn't Saskia.'

'Whoever it was, then.'

Nick shook his head. 'That's why I kept quiet. It couldn't come out that we'd been together.' He hesitated. 'She's married,' he said.

'God, you are the limit!' Oliver exploded. 'You're telling me you were cavorting with some married woman while your ex-wife was being murdered?'

Nick flinched. 'I wasn't to know that, was I?'

'Who is she? You can at least tell me.'

Nick shook his head. 'Actually, I can't. Her husband's big in local government; there's no way this can come out.'

Oliver sat back disgustedly. 'So to protect some fling, you lay yourself open to suspicion, putting the fear of God into your family?'

'Ah! So it was someone in the family who saw me?'

'You can thank God it was, or whatever you want or don't want to come out, you'd have had no option.'

'I appreciate that.' Nick sighed and drank some wine. 'When the appointment fell through, a free couple of hours seemed too good a chance to miss. But there's something we need to get straight, Oliver; this is no fling. Saskia's just a screen.'

'Does she know that?'

'Of course not, but she's nothing to complain about. There's nothing heavy between us; we just have a good time.'

'You're incorrigible,' Oliver said heavily.

'No doubt. But I'm not a murderer.'

The waiter returned with two plates of antipasto and laid them on the table. The brothers sat in silence, accepted a generous sprinkle of black pepper, and waited till he'd moved away.

Then Nick said, 'Whoever it was has been a long time coming forward.'

'They hadn't realized the significance. It only struck home when I happened to say you'd not been anywhere near here that afternoon.'

'How many people know?'

'Three, including myself.'

'I'd be grateful if you could keep it that way. Hell's teeth, Oliver, you didn't really suspect me, did you?'

'Let's just say I had some uneasy moments.'

At the sight of his brother's stricken face, he relented. 'No, you oaf, of course I didn't, but I did wonder what the hell you'd been up to.'

'And now you know.'

'Yes,' Oliver agreed, spearing an olive. 'Now I know.'

'I said, what the hell are you doing?'

The boy's breathing was rapid in Rona's ear. He's frightened, she thought; he might be panicked into doing something stupid.

Instead, to her relief, he tried to brazen it out. 'Never mind me, Dad,' he retorted. 'What are *you* doing here?'

De Salis advanced a few paces, but when Aidan tensed warily, he halted, his eyes suddenly suspicious. 'What's that in your hand?' he demanded.

'Just answer the question, Dad.' The tremor in the boy's voice belied the bravado. 'Why are you here?'

There was a pause, while de Salis tried without success to make out what his son was holding. 'I heard you on the phone at lunchtime,' he said eventually. 'I'd called in to collect my bank book, and caught the tail end, something about the cemetery. And you were speaking in an odd voice, which added to my curiosity. So I parked the car round the corner, then waited till you came out and followed you on foot.'

'You *spied* on me?' Aidan broke in furiously, but his father went on speaking.

'When you got on the Chilswood bus, I dashed back for the car, but as luck would have it, a tractor broke down in front of me, which is why you beat me to it. Now, are you going to tell me what this all about?'

'She knows too much,' Aidan replied, prodding Rona in the ribs – mercifully with his free hand. 'She's solved murders before; it said so in the paper, and she's been watching us. She followed us to Netherby's, and Mum said she'd been to the shop, too, sniffing around.'

Nigel frowned, glancing at Rona's rigid face. 'Well, if she solves this one, so much the better.'

Aidan gave a hoarse laugh. 'That's a matter of opinion.'

'Why? Everyone knows Nick Curzon killed her; they just can't prove it.'

'But why would he?' Rona broke in, curiosity overcoming her fear. 'They were divorced; she didn't matter to him any more.'

Nigel said stiffly, 'I really don't see it's any of your business.'

'Answer the lady, Dad,' Aidan said softly.

His father hesitated, and with a flourish, the boy brought the knife into full view, holding it at Rona's throat. Oh God, she moaned inwardly, why did I leave Gus in the car? But hard on the thought came the knowledge that if he'd gone for the boy – as he undoubtedly would – the knife would have struck home.

The seriousness of the situation appeared

341

to strike Nigel for the first time. He looked completely dumbfounded, but almost immediately recovered himself. 'Put that away at once!' he ordered. 'It's not a toy – you could do serious damage.'

There was an agonizing pause, then a lifetime's obedience to the authority in that voice prevailed. Aidan lowered the knife and Rona released her breath.

'Go on, then,' he said truculently. '*I* deserve an explanation, even if she doesn't. Why do you think he killed her?'

Nigel's eyes remained on the knife, now harmlessly pointing at the ground. 'Because of what I asked her to do,' he said in a low voice. 'The bastards must have found out.'

'*What* did you ask her?'

'In the first instance, to get to know Miss Parish; one of the reps heard on the grapevine that she was going to be shown the new line.'

'The new line?' Aidan repeated in bewilderment. 'What's that got to do with anything?'

'Word is, it'll make their fortune; we've a right to our share.'

Aidan gave an uncertain laugh. 'How do you work that out? Going off with one of their wives isn't likely to make them generous.'

'It's not a question of generosity, they owe us.' Nigel de Salis paused, then drew in his breath. 'Well, you were going to hear one day, so it might as well be now. George Curzon was your great-great-grandfather.'

342

There was a long silence. Then Aidan said incredulously, 'You're saying we're *related* to them? The Curzons?'

'Yes. Marie de Salis was among a group of immigrant workers employed by the factory. George had a roving eye, she became his mistress and had a child by him. When his wife died, he married her.'

'There's no proof of that,' Rona interrupted, before she could stop herself.

Nigel's eyes swivelled to her. 'What do you know about it?'

'I know she was given a generous, once-and-for-all settlement.'

'Do you, indeed? Well, that's correct as far as it goes. She bought a stall in Chilswood market, got her hands on some seconds from the factory, and started what eventually became De Salis China and Crystal. As soon as he was old enough, her son Georgie helped on the stall. Then, when old Mrs Curzon died, George married her, though he kept it from his family.'

'You've no proof,' Rona repeated.

'Only because the relevant pages in the register were removed. Doesn't that strike you as suspicious?'

'Perhaps she took them, because no record existed.'

He shook his head dismissively. 'After old George died, she went to one of his sons, told him the story, and asked for his help. He refused to believe her – or pretended to – and sent

343

her packing.'

He moved impatiently. 'But this is past history. To get back to Julia, I'm saying the Curzons had her silenced because they realized what she was up to.'

From the corner of her eye, Rona could see the knife still pointing downwards, and risked another question. 'Why was it so important to know in advance? Why not wait for the announcement, and then make your claim? In all the euphoria, you might have stood a better chance.'

Nigel gave a harsh laugh. 'No way. The only money I'd ever get out of it was by pre-empting thcm and selling the secret to the press, for what they call "an undisclosed sum". And given the chance, that's what I'd have done. I owe it to Marie.'

Rona said softly, 'Did you start the fire?'

He held her gaze. 'No, though I would have if I could. I tried once, but I couldn't get near enough, and the blasted thing didn't catch.' His voice was bitter. 'So I was reduced to writing anonymous letters, telling them I knew what they'd done. I hope they at least had sleepless nights.'

He gave a harsh laugh. 'Being involved in ceramics, I suppose I'm a modern-day "Rogue in Porcelain". Blood will out, after all.'

Aidan spoke for the first time in a while, and the nearness of his voice made Rona jump.

'If she hadn't died, you'd have gone off with

her again.'

Nigel turned to him. 'Of course I wouldn't. What makes you think that?'

'Because you'd been meeting her. Before she came here.'

Nigel looked taken aback. 'Where did you get that idea?'

'One Sunday when you were gardening, you left your mobile in the kitchen, and it beeped.'

His father tensed. 'You didn't—?'

'Mum was at the garden centre, and I thought she might be wanting to check something. So I read it. But it was from *her*!' There was a wealth of hurt and betrayal in the young voice, and Rona flinched.

Nigel de Salis stood immobile, waiting for his son to continue.

'It said she'd managed to convince her firm Marsborough would be a good place to canvass. Which meant she'd be coming up regularly for a while, and it would save you going to London.'

'Oh, God,' Nigel said flatly. 'All the same, Aidan, you must believe I never intended—'

'And when you came back last time,' the boy went on inexorably, 'I heard Mum say if you ever went off again, she'd kill herself.'

Nigel looked stricken. 'But she didn't mean it, son!'

'Oh, she meant it. You didn't see how she was last time. All right, so she put on a brave face at the shop, but not at home. She couldn't have gone through it again.'

Rona felt a sudden, creeping coldness, emphasized by the dawning realization on Nigel's face.

He said urgently, 'Aidan—'

'I couldn't let you do that to her, Dad.'

'Aidan, stop! Don't say any more! We'll go home and talk this through calmly. There's no need for Miss Parish—'

'I knew her number must be on your mobile, though it took a while to find, because it was listed as JT. That foxed me for a while, till I heard she was calling herself Teale.'

'For God's sake—'

'So when you were in the shower that morning, I sent her a text from your mobile, asking her to meet you here, and to erase the message as soon as she'd read it.'

Before Rona could reassess the position, her eye was caught by a movement in the entrance. In the same instant several uniformed figures materialized, one of them with a dog on a leash. She heard Aidan gasp as he raised the knife again – possibly in self-defence – and Nigel, seeing their frozen faces, spun round as the foremost policeman said evenly,

'Now, we don't want any accidents, do we? Look at me, lad!' This as Aidan glanced frantically from side to side, seeking a means of escape. Then, more firmly, *'Look at me!'*

An officer stepped forward and took Nigel's arm. 'Will you come with me, please, sir?'

346

Nigel struggled against his grip. 'But my son—'

'The situation's in our hands now, sir. We'll deal with it.'

To Rona's surprise, some of the tension left Aidan as his father was led, still protesting, out of the enclosure.

'Now,' said the first man calmly, 'I'm going to ask you to drop the knife on the ground and kick it away from you. Will you do that for me?'

Aidan didn't move, and his knife hand, now shaking violently, was only inches from Rona's arm. Briefly, she contemplated knocking the weapon from his hand, but he might, in a panic, turn it on her. Then, once again, this normally law-abiding young man responded to authority; with a frightened little whimper he dropped the knife, kicked it aside, and covered his face with his hands.

Rona, feeling her knees buckle, was incapable of moving, but everything now happened at once. The police moved forward, and a woman officer helped her out of the clearing to where Nigel de Salis waited with his escort, his face a travesty and his body shaken by harsh, guilt-ridden sobs.

So once again she found herself at Chilswood police station.

'I might have known you'd be there,' Barrett said, eying her dispassionately. Then, noting

347

her pallor, he added abruptly, 'You OK?'

She nodded, and he relaxed again.

'Not as clever as you thought, are you, falling for the same ploy as your friend Julia? Lucky you didn't end up the same way. I suppose you're going to tell me you knew it was the boy all along?'

Rona shook her head tiredly. 'No; though I thought it might have been his mother.'

'She'd a cast-iron alibi.'

'I didn't know that.'

'There are a lot of things you don't know, Ms Parish. Might be better if you left matters to those who do.'

'How did you find out we were there?'

'A 999 call. Woman visiting her husband's grave passed the entrance to the plot, and saw the boy with the knife.'

'He wouldn't have used it,' Rona said.

'He did before.'

'Not once we'd started talking, and with his father there.'

'Then how do you imagine it would have ended? With handshakes all round?'

Rona smiled, shaking her head. 'I'm not saying I'm not grateful, Inspector. I was extremely relieved when the police arrived. What I don't understand, though, is how Aidan even knew about that enclosure.'

'I can tell you that; his father took him there himself, a few years back.'

'Why on earth...?'

Barrett paused, obviously wondering whether to satisfy her curiosity. Then, with a dismissive shrug, he complied. 'De Salis has some hare-brained idea he's related to them. He took the boy to the pottery first, then said he should see the graves of the people responsible for their livelihood. In fact, as he admitted in his statement, he wanted to show him his supposed forebears. Couldn't have guessed how it would rebound on him.'

Rona nodded thoughtfully, and, since the inspector was being unusually forthcoming, ventured another question. 'Could I ask you something else?'

'You can ask. No saying I'll answer.'

'Has the cause of the fire been established?'

He nodded. 'The report came through this morning. Electrical fault. No sign of arson, despite all the rumours.'

'How bad was the damage?'

'Despite appearances, it was mainly confined to the wing containing the new line. The whole place will need a massive clean-up, but then it should be business as usual.'

The phone on his desk rang and he spoke briefly into the receiver.

'Your husband's in the foyer, Ms Parish. And he says to tell you he's got the dog. You'll be required to sign your statement when it's been typed, but that should be all we need from you.'

Rona rose to her feet. 'Thank you, Inspector.'

He nodded briskly. 'Just mind you keep out of our way in future.'

'I'll try,' she said meekly, and went to meet Max.